# THE BEST OF Archie® COMICS

## BOOK FOUR

# THE BEST OF Archie® COMICS
## BOOK FOUR

Published by Archie Comic Publications, Inc.
325 Fayette Avenue, Mamaroneck, New York 10543-2318.
www.ArchieComics.com


Printed in U.S.A. First Printing.

ISBN: 978-1-61988-942-2

## *Welcome to*
## *THE BEST OF ARCHIE COMICS Book Four*

The fourth volume of the most well-loved and memorable Archie stories is here! The BEST OF ARCHIE series continues to be a massive hit and, as long as we have dedicated fans like you, we'll keep unearthing more of the best and brightest Archie has to offer. We are consistently humbled and amazed by all of the story choices nominated by Archie writers, artists, editors, contributors and even fans.

Selecting which stories to include from over seventy years and thousands upon thousands of pages is no easy task. When we turn to people to not only pick their favorites but also include special anecdotes about why they love these stories, it is clear how huge of an impact Archie has had on the lives of many. What also makes these books so remarkable is the source material we pull from. In some cases it is from high-quality line art and color files. In other cases, because some of these classic hand-picked stories have not been printed in many years and the original art is no longer available, we've worked from scans of the original printed comics. Some of the stories have even been scanned from vintage proofs and combined with modern recoloring—both the original comics and the proofs can date all the way back over sixty years!

Thanks for making BEST OF ARCHIE such a success. We hope you enjoy yet another installment of this fun-filled trip through Riverdale!

*The stories, characters and incidents in this collection are entirely fictional. This book contains some material that was originally created in a less racially and socially sensitive time in our society and reflects attitudes that may be interpreted as offensive today. The stories are reprinted here without alteration for historical reference.*

## *Stories:*

Bob Montana, Ed Goggin, Frank Doyle, Dick Malmgren, Rod Ollerenshaw, Mark Waid, Bob Bolling, Kathleen Webb, Barbara Slate, C.J. Henderson, Craig Boldman, Bill Golliher, Angelo DeCesare, Dan Parent and Tom DeFalco

## *Art:*

Bob Montana, Janice Valleau (Ginger), Harry Sahle, Bill Vigoda, Samm Schwartz, Dan DeCarlo, Rudy Lapick, Vincent DeCarlo, Harry Lucey, Barry Grossman, Terry Szenics, Marty Epp, Sal Contrera, Bill Yoshida, Jim DeCarlo, Stan Goldberg, Jon D'Agostino, Mike Esposito, Rex Lindsey, Chris Allan, Doug Crane, Bob Smith, Rich Koslowski, Dan DeCarlo Jr., Henry Scarpelli, Dan Parent, Vickie Williams, Jim Amash, Teresa Davidson, Jeff Shultz, Jack Morelli, Fernando Ruiz, John Workman, Gisele and Digikore Studios

# THE BEST OF Archie COMICS BOOK FOUR

# The 1940s

## Archie
## *Pep* #46, 1942
## by Bob Montana

*This story features the first appearance of Veronica! Her arrival in Riverdale is the subject of a later story, "Prom Pranks," which was featured in* ***The Best of Archie Comics Book One,*** *but this is the story that introduced her to readers. The rest is history!*

## Archie
## *Jackpot* #5, 1942
## by Bob Montana

*Here Archie's life is complicated forever after by the introduction of two of his eternal adversaries—both Reggie Mantle and Mr. Weatherbee enter the scene in this story!*

## Archie
## *Archie* #10, 1943
## by Ed Goggin and Janice Valleau (Ginger)

The best, worst, classic automobile in comic book history. Two gorgeous girls that equally dig dudes with cross-hatching in their hair. Chocolate spelled with both a "k" and the rarely used apostrophe. That incredibly unique "teeny, weeny, magic beanie." Big Ethel. Little Archie. A teacher with the name "Flutesnoot." Impossible, never-ending stacks of hamburgers, moments away from disappearing into a bottomless, carb-resistant gut. If these amazingly original things are not what sums up the Best of Archie, then I can't wait to find out what does.

**Neil Kleid**
*Writer & artist*
***Brownsville, Kings & Canvas***

# Archie

by Montana

GOSH !! WHO CARES ABOUT THE STAMP ACT WHEN **VERONICA'S** MAKING HISTORY RIGHT HERE IN SCHOOL.

HISTORY

EGYPT HAD ITS CLEOPATRA!-- HOLLYWOOD, ITS HEDY LAMARR!----AND NOW RIVERDALE HAS VERONICA LODGE, WHO HAS JUST MOVED INTO TOWN----- AND TAKEN IT---AS FAR AS THE BOYS OF RIVERDALE HIGH SCHOOL ARE CONCERNED, ANYWAY!

R

KEEP OFF THE GRASS

LATIN

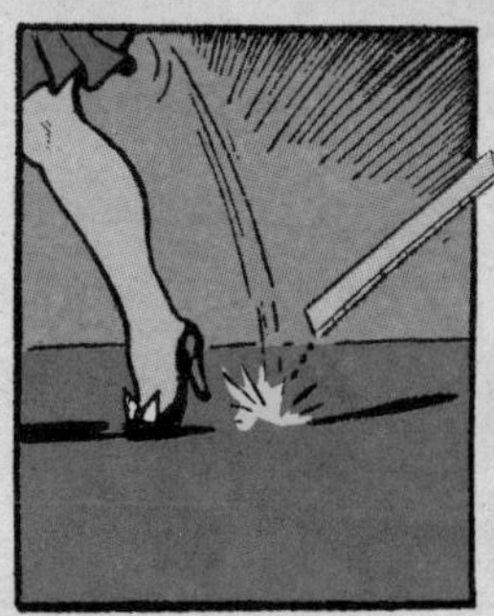

OH, HOW CLUMSY OF ME. THANK YOU,---AH---
JUST CALL ME ARCHIE! COULD I---ER-- MAYBE--- I OUGHT TO CARRY IT HOME FOR YOU!

I DON'T USUALLY WALK HOME, BUT I WRECKED MY CAR AND DAD HAS THE TOWN CAR AND SIS USES OUR STATION WAGON AN--
YEAH! SAY, I'LL BET YOU'RE PRETTY BUSY EVENINGS, HUH!
MY, HOW UTTERLY EXTRAVA-GANT!!

BOY, OH BOY! I DID IT! JUGHEAD! I'VE GOT A DATE NEXT WEEK! WITH VER-ONICA LODGE!
KINDA FLYIN' HIGH, AREN'T YOU, EAGLE? HER OLD MAN IS "MONEY BAGS" LODGE OF BEACON HILL!

WHY, SHE'S A SUB-DEB!! WHAT'RE YOU GONNA USE FOR MONEY--- BUTTONS?
SHE IS!!! "(GULP)" HEY, HOW ABOUT THAT FIF-TEEN CENTS YOU OWE ME!!

BUT POP!!! ALL I AM ASKING FOR, IS $10 ON MY AL-LOWANCE!
TEN DOLLARS! YOU'VE DRAWN INTO 1943 AL-READY!! EARN IT LIKE I DID AT YOUR AGE! GET A JOB!! WHAT ARE YOU, LAZY---- DON'T ANSWER THAT QUESTION!

LET'S SEE--- WANTED BUS BOY, APPLY IN PER-SON AT THE "EL CROCA-DEARO"--- BOY!! A SWELL PLACE LIKE THAT OUGHTA PAY ABOUT THIRTY BUCKS!!
WANT ADS

YOU'LL DO! THE JOB PAYS $12 A WEEK
IS THAT ALL!

OF COURSE, WE SUPPLY THE TUX!!
TUX! DID YOU SAY TUX? I'LL TAKE IT!

THEN CAME 6 DAYS OF DIRTY DISHES-------

HOT DOG " THAT'S WHAT I NEED --- FOLDIN' MONEY!

I HOPE THE BOSS DOESN'T MISS THIS TUX TONIGHT!

MISS LODGE WILL BE RIGHT DOWN, SIR! WILL YOU STEP INTO THE LIBRARY PLEASE?
SOME JOINT!

WELL, WHERE WOULD YOU LIKE TO GO VERONICA?
I'D JUST LOVE TO GO TO MY FAVORITE PLACE!

THE EL CROCADEARO
WHAT! OH GOSH--Y-YOU WOULDN'T LIKE IT THERE!
CAN'T WE GO SOMEWHERE ELSE?
DON'T BE SILLY, EVERY ONE WHO'S ANYONE GOES THERE!

DID YOU BRING YOUR CAR OR ARE WE TAKING A TAXI?
TAXI?
YES SIR!
I MEAN - TAXI!
SQUREECH

ARCHIE DON'T YOU THINK THE EL CROCADEARO SERVES DELICIOUS AVOCADO CRAB-MEAT?
UH-HUH
14 50
TICK
TICK
TICK

PENNY REEMS AND ORCH
WOW! $4.70!
KEEP THE NICKEL BUD.
GEE, THANKS MR. BENNY!

WELL, WELL !!! HELLO ARCHIE!
OH GOSH! AH-- HELLO. VERONICA GO AHEAD I'LL JOIN YOU IN A MINUTE!
DEAR ME, ARCHIE IS SO IN-FLU-ENTIAL!
3

WHAT'S THE IDEA GOIN' HOME WITH THAT TUX ! THE OTHER BUS-BOY NEEDS IT. NOW TAKE IT OFF !!
AW GEE, BOSS ! I HAVEN'T GOT ANY OTHER CLOTHES !! AND I'VE GOT MY GIRL HERE !

SOMEBODY'S GOT TO TAKE THESE DISHES OUT !! NOW YOU CAN EITHER TAKE THAT TUX OFF OR WORK.
I'LL WORK WAIT'LL I EX-PLAIN !

COME ON, VERONICA. LET'S DANCE.

OH ARCHIE, YOU DANCE DIVINELY.
JIGGERS, THE BOSS !! I GOTTA DO SOME-THIN'

MEET PENNY REEMS, VERONICA HERE'S THAT DANCE I PROMISED YOU, PENN!
WISH I COULD REMEM-BER WHERE I MET THAT CHARACTER

PHEW ! THEY DIDN'T SEE ME ! TWO MORE LOADS AND I CAN REST !

(PUFF) JUST GOT BACK IN TIME !
RIGHT HERE, WAITER ! WE'RE READY TO TO ORDER.

DID YOU SAY AVO-CADO CRAB-MEAT, VERONICA !
OH MY GOSH ! THAT'S $5 A PLATE AN I HAVE ONLY $ 7.25 LEFT OF MY $12 SALARY !

I'D BETTER GIVE THE ORDER TO PIERRE, THE CHEF, MYSELF SO IT WILL BE JUST RIGHT !
GOODNESS ARCHIE ! DO YOU KNOW THE CHEF TOO ?

WHAT A SPOT ! --- ENTER-TAINING A SUB-DEB, AN' BEIN' A BUS-BOY AT THE SAME TIME !
4

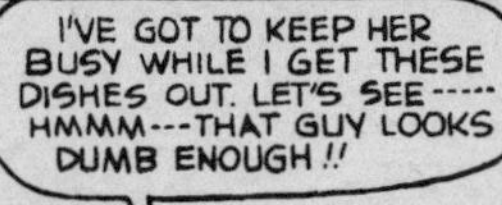
I'VE GOT TO KEEP HER BUSY WHILE I GET THESE DISHES OUT. LET'S SEE----- HMMM---THAT GUY LOOKS DUMB ENOUGH!!

PSST! VERONICA LODGE IS OVER HERE AND SHE'S JUST DYING TO MEET YOU!
HUH! WHO ME?

ARCHIE WHERE-EVER HAVE YOU BEEN?
I WANT YOU TO MEET AN OLD PAL--MR.--AH---MR.
DEBILLS-BURY.

SURE, SURE! YOU TWO GO AHEAD AND DANCE-- I'LL SEE YOU LATER!!
GOSH SHE'S PURTY.

PHEW ONE MORE!
HEY SQUIRT! TAKE THE SILVER-WARE OFF OF YOUR TRAY THIS TIME!!

ARCHIE ANDREWS! WHAT ARE YOU DOING WITH THAT TRAY?

OH, I'M--AH--JUST SEEIN' IF I CAN LIFT IT-----IT'S A BET!!
WELL, OF COURSE IF YOU'D RATH-ER MAKE SILLY BETS THAN BE WITH ME--- WHY-----

I'LL PUT IT DOWN RIGHT NOW! WAIT, RIGHT THERE!
ARCHIE LOOKOUT!

IT LOOKS LIKE **ARCHIE** HAS HIS FILL OF SUB-DEBS. BUT WE'VE GOT A HUNCH VERONICA'S NOT THROUGH WITH **ARCHIE**! DON'T MISS THE NEXT HOWLING ADVENTURE OF **ARCHIE IN PEP AND JACK-POT COMICS.**

Archie
by Montana
CLASS DAY! GOSH IT'S FUN. TO-NIGHT I JOIN THE PHILOMATHIAN AND SATURDAY IS THE BOAT RIDE!

ARCHIE ANDREWS MAY BE "UP THE CREEK" BUT TONIGHT HE GETS THE PADDLE... THE OCCASION IS HIS INITIATION INTO RIVER-DALE HIGH'S PHILOMATHIAN CLUB!
THIS ISN'T GOING TO **HURT**, IS IT, FELLAS?
OH, NO!
WOO!
WHACK!
FOR PETE'S SAKE! HAVEN'T YOU INITIATED ME **YET?**
NOPE! THERE'S **ONE** MORE! COME ON, GANG, LET'S GO!

ALL RIGHT, MEN, THIS IS THE PLACE.. BRING HIM UP ON THE PORCH!
HOLD OUT YOUR HAND! NOW TAKE THIS AND DON'T TOUCH IT... AND HAND IT TO THE NEXT PERSON WHO SPEAKS TO YOU!
OKAY, I CAN GO ALONG WITH A GAG!
DID YOU RING THE BELL, SCOTTY?
YEAH! SHHHH..
WELL?
HERE!
WHAT IS IT? A TELEGRAM? I CAN'T SEE!
SNAP
VICTOR
MOUSE TRAP
YEOW
OOH! GOOD GOSH! IT'S MR. WEATHERBEE, THE PRINCIPAL!
OH NO YOU DON'T! COME IN HERE WHERE I CAN SEE WHO YOU ARE!
AH-HA! ARCHIE ANDREWS! I MIGHT HAVE KNOWN! WELL, YOUNG MAN, I'LL TAKE CARE OF YOU TOMORROW MORNING... IN MY OFFICE BEFORE SCHOOL!
WELL, ANYWAY, YOU'RE A PHIL-OMATHIAN NOW!
YEAH! WHAT GOOD WILL THAT DO AFTER TOMORROW? I MAY NOT EVEN BE A STU-DENT!

NEXT MORNING.
I WONDER WHAT WEATHER-BEE WILL DO TO ME...I'M BEGINNING TO WONDER IF BEING A PHILOMATHIAN IS WORTH ALL THIS!
R.H.S.
61 W35
OH, LOOK, REGGIE, THERE'S ARCHIE IN HIS CAR... HELLO, ARCHIE!
TSK! TSK! THE CITY SHOULD KEEP THE ROADS CLEANER!
?
HUMPH! VERONICA WITH THAT SNOOTY REGGIE MANTLE SHOWING OFF IN HIS ROAD STER. THE BIG FATHEAD ALMOST DROVE ME OFF THE ROAD!
WELL, WELL, CAUGHT UP WITH THEM ALREADY! I WONDER WHAT... HA-HA-OH BOY! HE'S GOT A FLAT TIRE!
WHAT'S THE MATTER, VERONICA-DID THAT PIKER FINALLY TREAT YOU TO A "BLOW-OUT"?
OH, ARCHIE! POOR REGGIE HAS A FLAT-TIRE AND I JUST KNOW WE'LL BE LATE FOR SCHOOL!
WELL, HOW ABOUT SWITCHIN' OVER TO OLD RELIABLE?
OH, THANK YOU, ARCHIE! YOU DON'T MIND-DO YOU, REGGIE?
YOU KNOW, I'M GLAD REGGIE GOT A FLAT TIRE!
WHY, ARCHIE, HOW CAN YOU SAY THAT?
BECAUSE NOW I CAN ASK ...ER...THAT IS...WILL YOU GO ON THE BOAT TRIP WITH ME SATURDAY?
W-E-E-L-L-L- REGGIE ASKED ME FIRST...
AW, YOU DON'T WANT TO GO WITH THAT TIN HORN PLAY BOY.. DO YOU?
EEP'EM FLYING
WELL, THANKS FOR GETTING ME TO SCHOOL ON TIME, AND.... YOU CAN CALL FOR ME ON SATURDAY MORNING!
I CAN ? GEE, THANKS, VERONICA... G'BYE, NOW!
KEEP'EM FLYING

GOSH, I WAS SO WRAPPED UP IN VERONICA SAYING "YES" I NEARLY FORGOT MY DATE WITH THE PRINCIPAL!
BUY DEFENSE STAMPS
OFFICE

HARUMP! WELL, MR. ANDREWS, I SUPPOSE YOU THINK THAT WAS A VERY FUNNY STUNT YOU PULLED LAST NIGHT... WILL YOU TELL ME WHATEVER MADE YOU DO SUCH A THING ?

I'M SORRY, SIR, I CAN'T TELL YOU.
HMMM! VERY WELL! I KNOW JUST HOW TO PUNISH YOU! YOU MAY NOT GO ON THE BOAT RIDE SATURDAY!

I FEEL TERRIBLE, MISS TOKAR, I CAN'T EVEN WRITE WITH THIS CON-FOUNDED FINGER!
YOU NEED A REST, MR. WEATH-ERBEE, AND I KNOW JUST THE THING!

WHAT ARE YOU LOOKING SO GLUM ABOUT? I THOUGHT YOU AL-WAYS LIKED GYM-CLASS!
AW, I JUST CAME FROM THE OFFICE AND "THE BEE" SAYS I CAN'T GO ON THE BOAT-RIDE!..JUST WHEN I GOT VER-ONICA TO SAY "YES" TOO!

I WOULDN'T LET THAT STOP ME! WHY DON'T YOU GO ANYWAY?
WHAT?

SURE, WHO'S GONNA KNOW THE DIFFERENCE! WEATHERBEE NEVER WENT ON A BOAT RIDE IN HIS LIFE.. HE HATES BOATS!
SAY, YOU GOT SOME-THING THERE, JUG!

SATURDAY MORNING AND THE GOOD SHIP "PETER STUYVESANT" SETTLES INTO THE HUDSON AS RIVERDALE HIGH CLAMBERS ABOARD FOR A HAPPY TRIP TO BEAR MOUNTAIN..
LINE
DAY

IT WAS AWFUL NICE OF YOU TO MAKE THIS BIG LUNCH, VERONICA!

GOODNESS! IT LOOKS LIKE EVERYONE IN SCHOOL IS GO-ING ON THE TRIP!

SHALL WE GO ON BOARD, ARCHIE ?

YEAH, SURE, YOU GO AHEAD ON WHILE I GET THE TICKETS!

TWO ROUND TRIPS TO BEAR MOUNTAIN, PLEA.. **OHMIGOSH!** AM I SEEING THINGS OR IS THAT **WEATHERBEE!**

TICKETS

WOW ! IT **IS** WEATHERBEE!

COME ON, VERONICA.. LET'S GO ON THE TOP DECK.. QUICK!

DARN THAT JUGHEAD-GAVE ME A BUM STEER!

?

DJOOOOO

ALL ABOARD!

ISN'T THIS SWELL UP HERE ? DOESN'T THAT AIR MAKE YOU FEEL GOOD?
YES, BUT IT ALSO MAKES ME FEEL HUNGRY !
NOW DON'T YOU WORRY, VERONICA. I'M NOT GOING TO LET YOU GO HUNGRY... JUST SIT RIGHT HERE AND I'LL BE BACK IN A MINUTE WITH THE BEST LUNCH YOU EVER HAD!
STAND UP AN' CHEER! CHEER LONG AND LOUD FOR DEAR OLD RIVERDALE
SO MISS NORTON SAYS "HOW WOULD YOU PUNCTUATE THIS SENTENCE.. "DORA, THE PRETTY BLONDE IS GOING DOWN THE STREET".. I SAYS "I'D MAKE A DASH AFTER DORA"!
PEP
YEAH ! DIG ME, SEYMOUR !
HA! CAUGHT YA, ARCHIE ANDREWS!
FOR PETE'S SAKE, STREAKY, QUIT YELLIN' MY NAME-- I----
I'LL YELL ALL I WANT! LISSEN- ARCHIE- WHAT'S THE IDEA SWIPIN' MY GAL'S LUNCH !
ARCHIE ?? DID I HEAR SOMEONE YELL.. "ARCHIE"?
OOO°°° OH! NOW YOU'VE DONE IT... LISSEN, STREAKY, DON'T GIVE ME AWAY-I'M DUCKING!
WAS THAT YOU HOLLERING "ARCHIE", STREAKY ?
ME ? WHY NO! THAT MUSTA BEEN A SEAGULL, MR. WEATHERBEE! I DON'T THINK ARCHIE CAME ON THE TRIP!

BEAR MOUNTAIN........
AND THE HAPPY STUDENTS START THE LONG CLIMB UP
HEY, IGGY, LET'S TAKE THE BUS!
NAW! IT COST A DIME!

HERE'S A SWELL PLACE TO EAT OUR LUNCH, ARCHIE! RIGHT ON TOP OF THIS ROCK!
SWELL, JUGHEAD! GIVE ME YOUR HAND, VERONICA!

BOY, IF OLD WEATHERBEE COULD ONLY SEE ME NOW!

OH, BE CAREFUL, ARCHIE! YOU'RE SPILLING THE HONEY!
OH, GEE! SO I AM!

WHAT IN SAM HILL !

GOOD GRIEF! RIGHT ON WEATHER-BEE'S TOUPEE!
? ? ?

KEEP OUT

NOW I'M SURE ARCHIE'S ON THIS TRIP (PUF.PUF). AND I'LL GET THAT DAD-RATTLED IMP IF IT'S THE LAST (PUF) THING I DO!
KEEP OUT

ALL RIGHT, ARCHIE, I KNOW YOU'RE IN THERE-- COME OUT!

COME ON, ANDREWS! I HERE YOU MOVING AROUND IN THERE... COME ON OUT!

SLUP

BOY! AM I GLAD I DIDN'T GO IN THAT CAVE!
YEEOW! HELP! HELP!

CRACK
JEEPERS! THE LIMB IS BREAKING!
OOOOOOOH! GET'IM OFF! GET'IM OFF!

?

MY BOY, HOW CAN I EVER THANK YOU. I NEVER SAW ANYTHING SO BRAVE, LEAPING UNARMED ON THAT FEROCIOUS ANIMAL. YOU SAVED MY LIFE!
AW GEE! ...IT WAS NUTHIN', MR. WEATHERBEE ....REALLY! NUTHIN AT ALL!

LISSEN, KID! YOU STAY OUT OF THE BEAR CAVES, SEE? THEM BEARS IS VERY TAME AND YOU'LL SCARE'EM SO THEY'LL BE SICK FOR A WEEK!
SHHHH! NOT SO LOUD, PLEASE!
THREE CHEERS FOR ARCHIE
Montana

YA KNOW, VERONICA! IT WAS A PRETTY SWELL TRIP... EVEN IF I DID LOSE THE LUNCH!
YES, ARCHIE, ----- -------- BUT I AM HUNGRY!

WHAT WOULD YOU THINK IF **ARCHIE** WERE TO BECOME PRESIDENT OF RIVERDALE HIGH? WELL DON'T TRY TO IMAGINE! JUST BUY **PEP COMICS** AND SEE FOR YOURSELVES!

WITH HIS **FANGS** WHAT DOES HE NEED US FOR?
SEE, FELLAS, LIKE THIS! CHOMP! CHOMP!
GINGER—
STORY BY GOGGIN

BOY! WITH THESE BEAVERS I CAN GO INTO THE FUR BUSINESS!
I HOPE DAD IS IN GOOD HUMOR SO'S I CAN TALK HIM INTO LETTING ME KEEP THEM!
TOOO

I'LL PUT 'EM IN THE CELLAR FOR NOW-THEN I'LL TALK TO HIM!
I'M REALLY THE ONE WHO MADE A COUNTRY CLUB OUT OF THAT HAY FIELD!

OH OH THIS DOESN'T SOUND TOO GOOD--
WE ONLY HAD $1,000 TO PLANT THAT ROW OF POPLARS AT HOLE SEVEN AND NOW THEY ONLY WANT TO GIVE ME $500 TO BUILD A LOG DAM AT HOLE ELEVEN

WHAT DO THEY WANT ME TO DO? CHEW THOSE TREES DOWN!

IDEA

NOW'S THE TIME FOR YOU BEAVERS TO SHOW YOUR WORTH! LET'S GO--

WHAT'S THE IDEA OF TAKIN' THOSE BEAVERS TO THE COUNTRY CLUB?
DAD WANTS A LOG DAM BUILT AT THE CLUB-SO WE'LL DO IT!!
2

BUT WHY BUILD A DAM OF ALL THINGS ?
TO MAKE A LAKE OVER AT HOLE SEVEN, STUPID !
RIVERDALE COUNTRY CLUB

HM--WAS IT HOLE SEVEN OR ELEVEN??
IT WAS SEVEN!

HOW CAN WE BUILD A DAM? WE HAVE NO LOGS!
WHY WE'LL USE THESE TREES HERE OF COURSE!!
7

IF YOU THINK I'M GONNA CUT DOWN THESE TREES YOU'RE CRAZY!
DON'T GET EXCITED-- **THESE BEAVERS** ARE!
7

C'MON NOW- DO YOUR STUFF! CHOP DOWN THESE TREES-- YOU CAN DO IT!
?

SEE-- THIS IS WHAT YOU DO-- YOU BEAVERS KNOW HOW
WONDER IF HE HAS A UNION CARD?

SEE, JUG, IF WE BUILD THE DAM **HERE** A LAKE WILL FORM UP THERE!
CHOMP CHOMP

LATER
GOSH-HOW MUCH LONGER WILL THIS TAKE?
JUST A FEW MORE AND WE'RE THROUGH!
WAIT'LL DAD SEES THE JOB WE DID WON'T HE BE SURPRISED?
NEXT MORNING
ARCHIE, WILL YOU DRIVE ME TO THE STATION TO MEET THE PRESIDENT OF THE COUNTRY CLUB?
YEAH-OKAY POP-YAWN-I'LL BE RIGHT DOWN!
UH, SAY, DAD D'YOU KNOW THAT THE BEAVER PELT BUSINESS RUNS INTO MILLIONS?
SO WHAT!! I HOPE THAT TRAIN IS ON TIME-HERE IT COMES NOW!
HELLO, CRAIG OLD MAN, WELCOME HOME!
THANKS, FRED, HOW'S EVERYTHING AT THE CLUB?
WAIT'LL YOU SEE IT! I'VE PUT HEDGES ALONG THE DRIVE! FLOWER BEDS IN FRONT AND THE GREENS ARE LIKE VELVET!
GOOD BOY! I KNEW I COULD DEPEND ON YOU!
WAIT'LL THEY SEE MY LITTLE CONTRIBUTION
AND JUST OVER THIS HILL YOU CAN FEAST YOUR EYES ON ONE OF THE FINEST ROWS OF POPLAR TREES IN THE COUNTRY
POPLAR TREES EH?
I WANT TO SEE THE LOOK ON THEIR FACES WHEN THEY GAZE AT THE NEW DAM!
R

WHAT TREES ??

WHY—WHAT'S HAPPENED ?? WHERE'S THE COURSE ??

ANDREWS- YOU'LL PAY FOR THIS! WHAT IN THE WORLD DID YOU DO ?
GULP!

MY TREES!! MY BEAUTIFUL TREES!!

WHAT COULD HAVE HAPPENED TO THEM ??
NOW DON'T TELL ME WE'RE INFESTED WITH BEAVERS OR TERMITES!

BEAVERS ??
OH OH

ARCHIE! COME BACK HERE!
5

I WOULD BUILD THAT DAM ON THE WRONG END OF THE CLUB AND FLOOD THE PLACE!
JUST WAIT'LL I GET MY HANDS ON YOU-- WHOOPS-- KINDA —
SHAKY! YIII!
GLUB
YOU AND YOUR BEAVERS! GET ME OUT OF HERE!!
B-BUT-GOSH POP-I CAN EXPLAIN EVERYTHING HONEST!
Dear Uncle Jake,
I'm sorry I can't keep the beavers so I am sending them back--- Could you send about TEN Poplar trees instead?
Your nephew,
Archie
THE END

## Double Date
### *Archie* #7, 1944
### by Ed Goggin, Harry Sahle and Ginger

*This story establishes one of the most enduring and beloved aspects of Archie's life from here on—the love triangle between Archie, Betty and Veronica. It also introduces a plot device that never gets old, no matter how often it's used—Archie has a date with both girls at the same time! What will he do?!*

## Puppy Love
### *Pep* #62, 1947
### &
## Photo-Finish
### *Archie* #27, 1947
### by Bill Vigoda

Archie's Pals and Gals were my pals and gals, and his standard attitude—"Well, I messed up again, but I know things will turn out okay because fate is kind"—became my attitude. There are worse ones to have during the storms of adolescence, believe me. And, as a slightly overweight high school freshman who was always puffing before the phys ed calisthenics were even half over, Jughead Jones was a beacon of hope. If he could eat that much and stay thin, I figured, maybe someday so could I (that day never came, alas).

**Stephen King**

*Bestselling American author*

*(Excerpted from* ***Archie Americana: Best of the Forties****)*

### ~BONUS PAGE~
### *Jackpot* #4, 1941
### by Bob Montana

*Featuring Archie's first appearance on a comic book cover ever!*

Archie in
THE LYRIC THEATRE Presents THE FALL OF NIAGARA
A COMEDY WITH
SHORTEN & SAHL
NOTHIN' BUT THE BEST FOR A. ANDREWS ESQ., VERONICA!
$4.40 ORCHESTRA SEATS! YOU'RE CERTAINLY SPLURGING TO-NIGHT, ARCHIE!
GGIN CAB CO.
BOY! IF I WERE ONLY TWINS!! JUGHEAD!

*in*

# DOUBLE DATE

HOW ABOUT A SODA OVER AT TATE'S, BETTY!
OKAY ARCH- LET'S GO!
ICE CREAM
TATE'S PARLOR

WHAT TH' ?
WELCOME! WELCOME! YOU TWO LUCKY PEOPLE ARE THE 10,000TH CUSTOMERS TO ENTER THIS PARLOR!

AS A REWARD, I HEREBY PRESENT YOU WITH THE TWO CHOICE SEATS FOR TONIGHT'S PERFORMANCE OF "THE FALL OF NIAGARA" AT THE "LYRIC"...
GOSH! GOLLY! GULP! LET'S GO, BETTY!
LYRIC THEATER

I'M SORRY, ARCHIE BUT, I DON'T THINK I CAN GO... WHY DON'T YOU TAKE JUGHEAD?
OH...ER... THAT'S A GOOD IDEA! I'LL CALL HIM!

JUGHEAD WOULDN'T GO ANYWAY... SO I'LL CALL VERONICA!
HELLO VERONICA? THIS IS MR. A. ANDREWS.. WOULD YOU CARE TO GO TO THE LYRIC T'NIGHT?

WHY, ARCHIE, YOU DARLING! I DO HAVE A DATE WITH REGGIE MANTLE, BUT I'LL BREAK IT! JUST FOR YOU!
3

THAT NIGHT...
ZZ TA TA TA

ARCHIE! THERE'S SOME-ONE HERE TO SEE YOU!
OKAY! MOM, I'LL BE RIGHT DOWN... MUST BE JUGHEAD.

BETTY!

I'VE DECIDED TO GO AFTER ALL. ARCHIE!
BUT WHAT ABOUT ER.. A.. JUGHEAD?

OH.. I SAW JUGHEAD AND HE'S STAYING HOME WITH HIS FATHER!
BUT... BUT... ER.. A...

YOU WOULDN'T THINK OF TAKING SOME OTHER GIRL, WOULD YOU?
WHO? ME?
GULP

HMM - WHAT TO DO? I'VE ALREADY GOT A DATE WITH VERONICA. MAYBE I'D BETTER CALL THE THEATER FOR A COUPLE OF TICKETS!

YOU WAIT THERE, BETTY! I'LL BE RIGHT BACK!

HELLO! LYRIC THEATER? THIS IS MR. ANDREWS! DO YOU HAVE TWO TICKETS FOR TONIGHT'S SHOW?
YEAH... JUST TWO--THEY'RE $4.40--EACH!

WHAT? 4.40? EACH?
YEOW'E!
I'LL TAKE THEM!

GOSH.. $8.80 FOR TWO TICKETS.. THERE'S ONLY $2.19 HERE!

ER..A.. BETTY! COULD YOU A... LOAN ME $6.61 IT'S AN EMERGENCY!
WELL.. IF IT'S AN EMERGENCY, I GUESS IT'S ALL RIGHT!

?
I WON'T BE GONE LONG, BETTY.. RELAX FOR A WHILE...

I DON'T SEE HOW IT'S POSSIBLE FOR A GUY OF MY AGE TO GET INTO THESE ENTANGLEMENTS!

HERE YOU ARE YOUNG MAN, $8.80 AND YOU'RE LUCKY TO GET 'EM
YEAH! SURE A LITTLE MORE OF THIS KIND OF LUCK AND I'LL END UP IN JAIL!

VERONICA'S PROBABLY WAITIN' FOR ME NOW C'MON JEEP! JUSTLE!

HURRY! VERONICA WE HAVEN'T MUCH TIME!
WHAT'S THE RUSH ARCHIE? WE'VE LOADS OF TIME!

WHY ALL THE SPEED ARCH?? I'VE NEVER SEEN YOU LIKE THIS BEFORE...
OH.. YOU WOULDN'T UNDERSTAND GULP! I'M SURE YOU WOULDN'T!

BUT ARCHIE! WHERE ARE YOU GOING? WE JUST GOT HERE!
ER... I'M GOING OUT FOR A HEADACHE..UH.. I MEAN AN' ASPIRIN! I'LL BE RIGHT BACK, VERONICA!

NOW TO GO GET BETTY. WHAT A SPOT! I GOTTA BE IN TWO PLACES AT TH' SAME TIME TONIGHT!
RIC

C'MON, BETTY, LET'S MAKE WITH THE SPEED!
GOSH, ARCHIE, I THOUGHT YOU WERE NEVER COMING BACK!

ER... AH... YOU SURE YOU WOULDN'T RATHER GO TOMORROW NIGHT, BETTY?
OF COURSE I'M SURE! WHAT IN TH' WORLD'S COME OVER YOU, ARCHIE! YOU'RE NERVOUS AS A CAT!

WHERE ARE THESE SEATS LOCATED BUD! NOT IN THE ORCHESTRA, I HOPE!
BROTHER, YOU SURE GOT YOUR HOPE! UPSTAIRS!

YEAH— I KNOW UP!
UP!
UP!

BUT ARCHIE! WHERE ARE YOU GOING?
SIT DOWN!
QUIET!
JUST SIT DOWN AND ENJOY THE SHOW, BETTY.. I..UH .. HAVE A HEADACHE AND WHAT A HEADACHE! BE RIGHT BACK!
TSK, TSK

ZIP
WHEW! AM I GLAD I'M NOT AT A DOUBLE FEATURE MOVIE!!
HELLO, ARCHIE! HEADACHE GONE?
NO! SHE'S UP.. ER.. I MEAN YEAH! SURE! FOR A LITTLE WHILE, ANYWAY!
I'VE BEEN SITTIN' HERE LONG ENOUGH! BETTER GET BACK TO BETTY BEFORE SHE GETS WISE!
EXCUSE ME, VERONICA-I'M AFRAID I'LL HAVE TO LEAVE AGAIN--
WHY, YOU POOR BOY! YOU DO LOOK A LITTLE GREEN AT THAT!
(PUF) YOU'D THINK (PUF) A JOINT WITH AS MANY BALCONIES AS THIS (PUF) WOULD HAVE AN ELEVATOR!
NOW I WISH I HAD HAD SEATS NEAR VERONICA!
HEH, HEH NICE SHOW, BETTY!
HOW WOULD YOU KNOW? YOU HAVEN'T SEEN ANY OF IT!
UH.. 'SCUSE ME! BE RIGHT BACK!
WHAT! AGAIN?
SHH
SHH!
I'M BEGINNING TO FEEL LIKE A MOUNTAIN GOAT PUF
LOOK, BUD! WHERE DO YOU THINK YOU ARE... AT A MARATHON?
8

BUT LISTEN, I'VE JUST GOT TO GET IN THERE!
WISE GUY, EH? WHAT'S THE IDEA RUNNING IN AND OUT, DISTURBING PEOPLE?
GULP, VERONICA!
UNHAND MY ESCORT... HE DOESN'T FEEL WELL!
SHH!
SHH!
WHAT'S THE DISTURBANCE DOWN THERE?
SO! THAT'S WHERE HE GOES! TO THAT MINX, VERONICA!
YOU POOR BOY.. YOU GO LIE DOWN.. I'LL BE ALL RIGHT!
THANKS, VERONICA! YOU DON'T KNOW WHAT THIS MEANS TO ME!
SHE'S GONE MAYBE I CAN SNEAK UPSTAIRS TO BETTY!
9

HELLO BETTY, I'M BACK!
SO I SEE! AND I ALSO SAW THAT ASPIRIN YOU WENT FOR!
..SITTING IN THE ORCHESTRA!
SLAP
AW, SHUT UP! HAVEN'T I GOT TROUBLES ENOUGH?
YOU SHUT UP..OR I'LL THROW YOU OUT OF THIS THEATER!
GOOD GRACIOUS! THAT'S, ARCHIE UP THERE AND WITH BETTY!
AW.. BUT BETTY, BELIEVE ME.. I'M A VICTIM OF CIRCUMSTANCES!
HMPF!
HONEST, BETTY.. I ONLY HAD THE BEST INTENTIONS.
ALL RIGHT THEN! SUPPOSE YOU EXPLAIN THAT "EMERGENCY" YOU BORROWED $6.61 FROM ME FOR!
ULP..OH THAT.. GULP
SEE HERE ARCHIE! JUST BECAUSE YOU TAKE ME TO A SHOW WITH $4.40 SEATS DOESN'T MEAN YOU CAN MAKE ME LOOK LIKE A FOOL
SO! THAT'S THE "EMERGENCY" YOU BORROWED MONEY FROM ME FOR!
10

**DON'T FORGET!** THERE WILL BE A FULL PAGE PORTRAIT OF ***VERONICA LODGE,*** SUITABLE FOR FRAMING IN THE ***NEXT ISSUE*** OF

**ARCHIE COMICS**

Archie IN
PUPPY LOVE
BOY! HE'S A CUTE LITTLE POOCH, AIN'T HE, JUG? WONDER IF HE BELONGS TO ANYBODY?
Bill Vigoda

HE DOES NOW! LOOK!
GULP! THE DOG CATCHER!
JUG! WE CAN'T LET HIM GRAB THE LITTLE GUY! LET'S GO!
HEY! COME BACK WITH THAT MUTT! HE'S GOT NO LICENSE!
WHEW! HE'S OUT OF SIGHT!
AND I'M OUT OF BREATH!
JUG, HE'S THANKING ME! THINK OF THAT!
YEAH! AND NOW THAT YOU GOT HIM, WHAT'RE YOU GONNA DO WITH HIM? THINK OF THAT!
GEE WHIZ! WE CAN'T JUST LET HIM LOOSE IN THE STREETS!
NOW, YOU STAY RIGHT HERE WHILE I TALK TO POP ABOUT KEEPING YOU!
R

UH-- POP, A DOG IS MAN'S BEST FRIEND, ISN'T HE?
I DON'T LIKE THE WAY YOU SAY THAT! WHAT HAVE YOU GOT UP YOUR SLEEVE NOW?

OH-OH-- OUR CANINE FRIEND HAS CAUGHT SIGHT OF AN OLD ENEMY.. LOOK OUT FOR TROUBLE...
GRRR GRRR
DAILY
PERSIAN CAT
WINS FIRST

ARF! ARF!

CRASH

DAD! ARE YOU ALL RIGHT? G-GOSH!
SLOP SLOP

GET THAT FLEA TRAP OUT OF THIS HOUSE AT ONCE!
BUT POP, PLEASE..
WHAT'S GOING ON HERE?

MY, ISN'T HE THE CUTE THING?
YES! CUTE LIKE AN ATOM BOMB!
I CAN KEEP HIM THEN, HUH, MOM?
I DON'T SEE WHY NOT!
BAH!
FIRST THING IS TO BUILD YOU A HOUSE, POOCHY!
OH, ARCHIE, WILL YOU RUN AN ERRAND FOR ME?
SURE, MOM!
GO DOWN TO THE BUTCHER'S, AND PICK UP MY MEAT!
OKAY!
HAVE YOU GOT MY MOTHER'S MEAT READY, MR. SCHMIDT?
YES, ARCHIE!

ACH GOTT! MY PRESHUSS MEADS!
SLOP SLOP

GO AHEAD! YOU MIGHT AS VELL LED 'IM FINISH IT!
HUH?
BOY! HOW'M I GONNA EXPLAIN THIS TO MOM?
ARF! ARF!

I'M POODING IT ON YOUR BILL ANYVAY!

HERE IS THE MEAT, MOM.. ER.. GUESS WHAT HAPPENED AT THE BUTCHER STORE?
WHY.. I CAN'T IMAGINE! WHAT WAS IT, DEAR?
BENDICKS WASHER

MEANWHILE OUTSIDE IN THE YARD, POOCHY HAS AGAIN SPOTTED AN ANCIENT ENEMY.. BUT THIS TIME IN THE FLESH..
BOW! GROWL! BOW! BOW!
PHT.T.T.T. PHT.T.T.T.

ARF! ARF!
BOW! BOW! BOW! BOW!
MEOWWW

YIPE!
ZIP

EEEEK!
BENDICKS WASHER

PLOP

CRASH!

WHAT'S HAPPENED?

SO ONCE AGAIN PEACE AND QUIET SETTLES OVER THE ANDREWS DOMICILE.. BUT NOT FOR LONG! THE WORST IS YET TO COME!

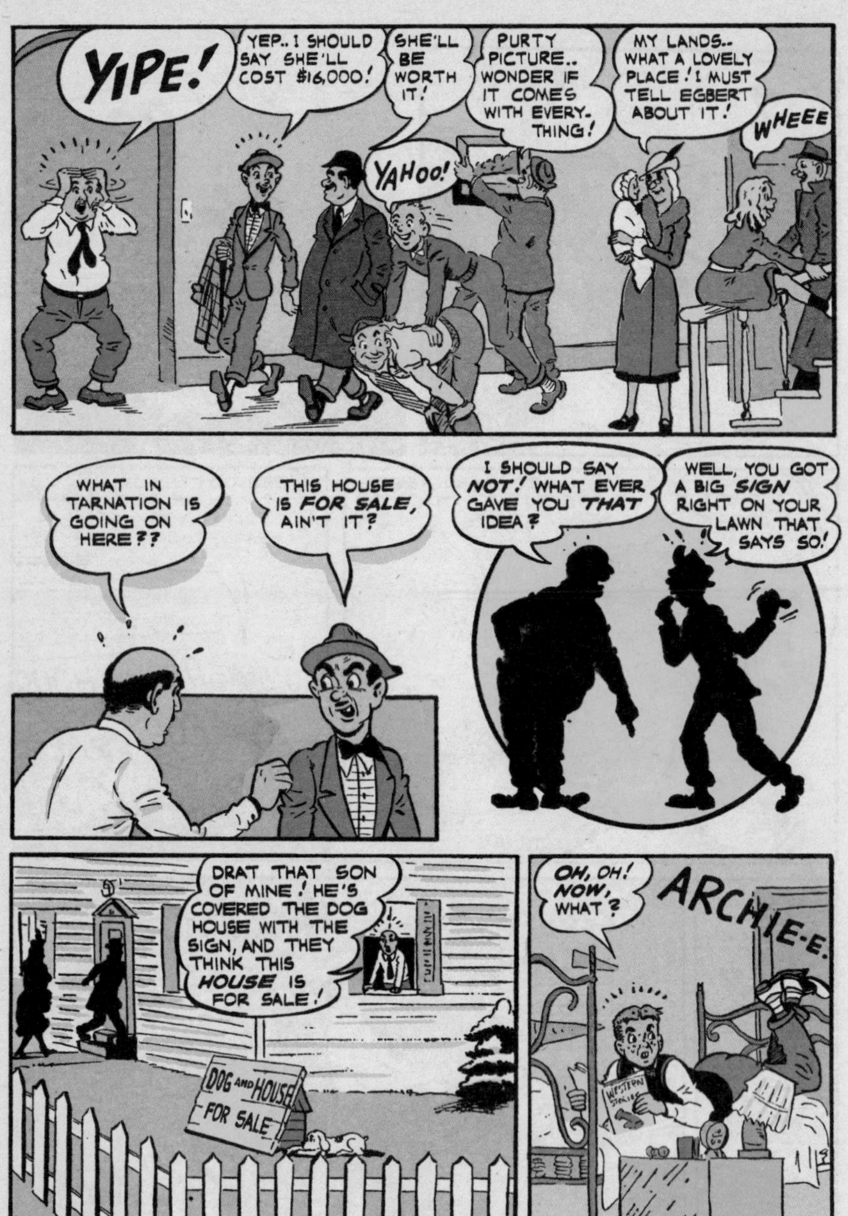
YIPE!
YEP.. I SHOULD SAY SHE'LL COST $16,000!
SHE'LL BE WORTH IT!
YAHOO!
PURTY PICTURE.. WONDER IF IT COMES WITH EVERY-THING!
MY LANDS.. WHAT A LOVELY PLACE! I MUST TELL EGBERT ABOUT IT!
WHEEE
WHAT IN TARNATION IS GOING ON HERE??
THIS HOUSE IS FOR SALE, AIN'T IT?
I SHOULD SAY NOT! WHAT EVER GAVE YOU THAT IDEA?
WELL, YOU GOT A BIG SIGN RIGHT ON YOUR LAWN THAT SAYS SO!
DRAT THAT SON OF MINE! HE'S COVERED THE DOG HOUSE WITH THE SIGN, AND THEY THINK THIS HOUSE IS FOR SALE!
DOG AND HOUSE FOR SALE
OH, OH! NOW, WHAT?
ARCHIE-E-E.
WESTERN STORIES

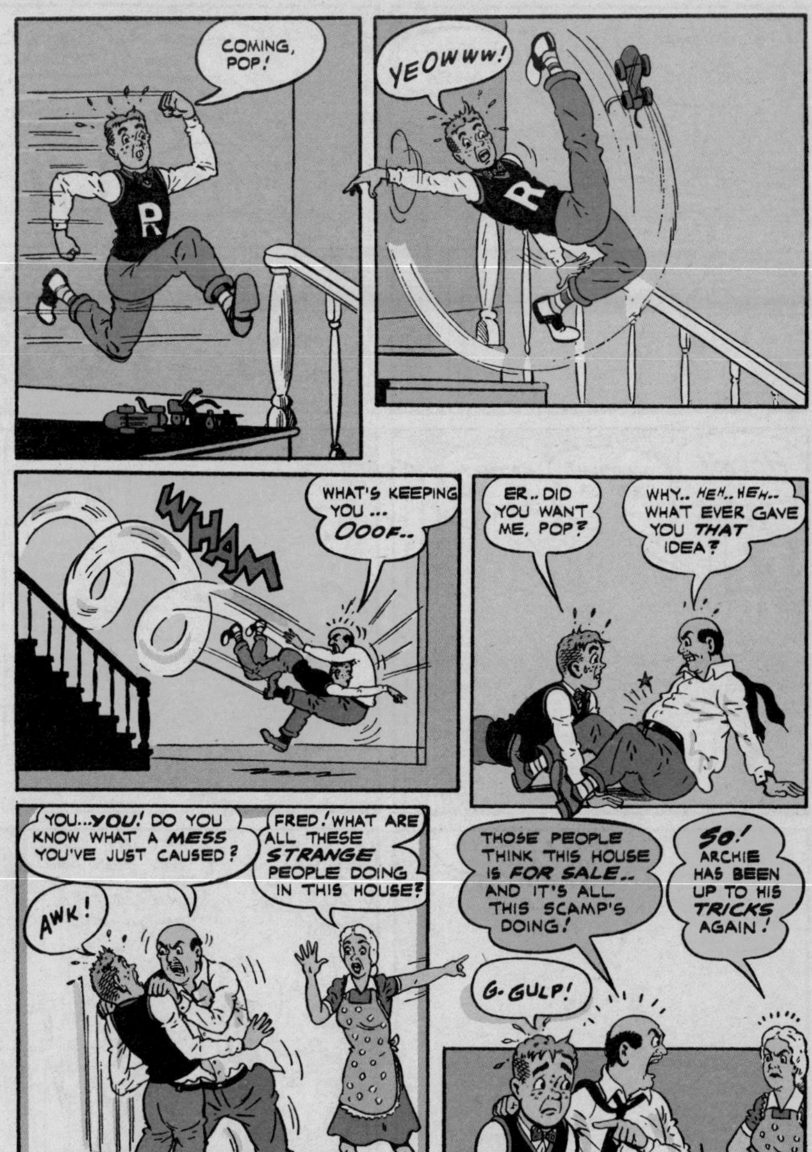
COMING, POP!
YEOWWW!
WHAM
WHAT'S KEEPING YOU ... OOOF..
ER.. DID YOU WANT ME, POP?
WHY.. HEH.. HEH.. WHAT EVER GAVE YOU THAT IDEA?
YOU...YOU! DO YOU KNOW WHAT A MESS YOU'VE JUST CAUSED?
AWK!
FRED! WHAT ARE ALL THESE STRANGE PEOPLE DOING IN THIS HOUSE?
THOSE PEOPLE THINK THIS HOUSE IS FOR SALE.. AND IT'S ALL THIS SCAMP'S DOING!
SO! ARCHIE HAS BEEN UP TO HIS TRICKS AGAIN!
G-GULP!

(SNIFF SNIFF) I SMELL SOMETHING!
EEEeee! THE HASH IS BURNING!
HOUSE ON FIRE!
GET A FIREMAN!
DAISY! COME TO MAMA!
HALP!
FIRE!
HALP!
YEOW! LET US OUT!
STOP! LET ME EXPLAIN!
WELL! THAT'S THE LAST STRAW!
FRED! WHAT ARE YOU GOING TO DO?
GET RID OF THAT SIGN AND THAT DOG HOUSE!

YOU'RE NOT GOING TO MAKE ME ANY MORE TROUBLE! NOT IF I CAN HELP IT!

GLORY BE!
BUS STOP

THERE'S A LAW IN THIS TOWN AGAINST KILLING DOGS, YOU FIEND!
BUT OFFICER, I WASN'T GOING TO KILL THAT DOG!

OH NO! TRYIN' TO TELL ME I'M BLIND, ARE YOU? C'MON, I'M RUNNIN' YOU IN!
BUT.. BUT.. I CAN EXPLAIN!

(GULP) S.. S'LONG, POOCHY.. YOU AND ME... WE'RE BOTH IN THE DOG HOUSE!

IT SHOULDN'T HAPPEN TO A DOG! THAT'S ALL I SAY! IT SHOULDN'T HAPPEN TO A DOG!
EXPENSES
NEW GAS STOVE $ 100
POLICE FINE $ 10
DAMAGES TO BUTCHER $ 5
HOUSE REPAIR $ 50
TOTAL

Archie
IN PHOTO-FINISH
HOT ZIGGIDY DOG! A BEAUTY CONTEST VERONICA!
RIVERDALE NEWS
PRIZE FOR THE PRETTIEST GIRL IN RIVERDALE
SEND IN PHOTOS TO RIVERDALE NEWS
?
HEY, HOW ABOUT ME ENTERING YOU, VERONICA?
YOU REALLY THINK I COULD WIN, ARCHIE?
YOU'RE A CINCH. C'MON, JUG. LETS GO GET YOUR CAMERA.
I'LL MEET YOU AT MY HOUSE, ARCHIE.

WHAT'RE YOU GRIPING ABOUT? YOU GOT MY CAMERA, DIDN'T YOU?
DID YOU HAVE TO DRAG THAT MUTT ALONG?
HERE I AM, ARCHIE. HOW DO I LOOK?
GULP
THIS SHOULD BE A NICE POSE, ARCHIE.
GOT IT
CLICK!
OKAY, RONNIE. I'LL SEND THE NEGATIVE TO THE PAPER. THEN ALL YOU HAVE TO DO IS SIT BACK AND WAIT FOR THE PRAISE.
YOO HOO! ARCHIE
HIYA BETTY.
2

ARCHIE, WILL YOU SNAP MY PICTURE? I'D LIKE TO ENTER THAT CONTEST.
SURE BETTY.

HOW'S THIS?
SWELL! HOLD IT.

CLICK!

BOY, WON'T THEY BE SURPRISED WHEN THEY SEE WHAT THEY LOOK LIKE IN TOMORROWS PAPER.

HEY, EDDIE, GET A LOAD OF THESE TWO PICTURES WE JUST DEVELOPED.

HA HA HAW HO HO
3

AND SO.. THE NEXT DAY
OH BOY! WON'T THE GIRLS BE PROUD TO SEE THEIR PICTURE IN THE PAPER.

PHOTOS SUBMITTED BY ARCHIE ANDREWS
VERONICA LODGE
BETTY COOPER

ARE YOU SURE ARCHIE ISN'T HOME, MRS. ANDREWS?
WHY NO. I HAVEN'T SEEN HIM ALL DAY.
THE END

NO. 4
JACKPOT
10¢
comics
WITH
ALL BRAND NEW STORIES

STEEL STERLING

BLACK HOOD

MR.JUSTICE

SERGEANT BOYLE
DANGER
NEW FEATURE
ARCHIE

# THE BEST OF Archie COMICS BOOK FOUR

# The 1950s

## Rag Mop
### *Jughead* #3, 1950
### by Samm Schwartz
### &
## Policed To Meet You
### *Laugh* #80, 1950
### by Frank Doyle and Samm Schwartz

Archie and his friends brought me out of my shell. They showed me that I could speak to girls. I could be myself. Many would say that they created a monster, but to me they created a door, one that led out of the shell I'd made for myself and into the light.

If you've read Archie's adventures before, then you know what I mean, and I welcome you to this collection. And if this is your first foray into the world of Riverdale High, then I salute you, for the adventure you are about to embark on will last you the rest of your life, as it has mine.

But don't be scared; because with Archie, Jughead, Veronica, Betty and even Reggie beside you all the way, you'll be just fine.

**Tony Lee**
***New York Times*** *bestselling author*

In the end, it's Archie's ability to be simultaneously right now and 1957 that lead us to make grabby hands at the cash register display when we were children, and to be excited to pick up a *Best of Archie* compilation in adulthood.

**Brenna Clarke Gray**
*English faculty member at Douglas College*
*Writer for* ***Book Riot Graphixia***

Archie's Pal

# Jughead

"RAG MOP"

R-A-G-G-M-O-P-P--
RAGMOPPPP!!

UNCLE HERMAN!! PLEASE!!

EGAD! WHAT A BOON TO WOMANKIND IF SOMEONE WERE TO DEVISE A GADGET TO ELIMINATE THE MOPPING OF FLOORS! HMMM-M! IT SEEMS TO ME THAT I PLANNED SUCH A GADGET, SOME TIME BACK-- YES, I'M SURE I DID!
OH--OH!
LET'S TAKE A LOOK IN MY TRUNK UPSTAIRS! THE PLANS MUST STILL BE THERE!
YOU BETTER NOT TRY OUT ANY OF YOUR INVENTIONS IN THIS HOUSE, UNK! POP'S GOT THE MORTGAGE ALMOST PAID!
LET'S SEE--THIS ISN'T IT--NOR THIS--WHAT'S THIS--HMMM--JUST A TICKET FOR A SHORT BEER--THAT'S NOT IT---
MAYBE I OUGHT TO ALERT THE POLICE AND FIRE DEPARTMENTS NOW--
HA! HERE IT IS, M'LAD! A MASTER STROKE OF SHEER INGENUITY!! YOUR MOTHER WILL PROBABLY HAVE ME RUN FOR PRESIDENT!
MY MOTHER WILL PROBABLY RUN YOU OUT OF THE HOUSE!
SEE? IT WORKS LIKE A ROLLER-TOWEL! YOU SIMPLY PRESS A BUTTON, THE MOTOR MOVES THE CONTINUOUS STRIP OF LINOLEUM SO A CLEAN SIDE ROLLS UP WHILE THE DIRTY SIDE IS SPRAYED CLEAN ON THE CELLAR CEILING AND IS READY WHEN YOU PRESS THE BUTTON AGAIN!
CONTINUOUS STRIP OF LINOLEUM
MOTOR
SPRINKLERS
SWITCH
2

FIRST, I'LL CALL UP AND HAVE THE LINOLEUM SENT OVER-- I CAN DETACH THE MOTOR FROM THE OIL BURNER --AND WE CAN USE THE WHEELS FROM THE LAWNMOWER! NOW, WHERE DOES YOUR FATHER KEEP HIS TOOLS?
P-POP AIN'T GONNA LIKE THIS, UNK!

--HAVE TO--(GRUNT!) RIP SOME OF THIS FLOORING UP! HA! CAN'T YOU JUST PICTURE YOUR FATHER'S FACE WHEN HE SEES THIS?
Y-YES! AND IT'S A HORRIBLE PICTURE!!
RIP!

AH, BUT YOUR MOTHER WILL LOVE ME FOR THIS, NEPHEW!
AND WILL ALWAYS REMEMBER YOU WITH KINDNESS, TOO, UNCLE HERMAN!
CLANG!
BANG!
WHAM!
CLANG!

A FEW HOURS LATER
THERE! NOW ALL YOU HAVE TO DO TO GET A CLEAN FLOOR, IS PRESS THE BUTTON ON THE WALL BEHIND YOU!

LIKE THIS?
YI-I!!
R-RR

CONGRATS, UNK! IT WORKS!
OF COURSE IT WORKS!! BUT HERE-AFTER, DON'T WORK IT WHILE I AM STANDING ON IT!!

GOSH, UNK-- I'M AWFULLY SORRY!
AND I'M SORRY I LOST MY TEMPER, JUGHEAD! IT'S ALL MY FAULT FOR GEARING THAT MOTOR UP SO FAST!
I'LL MAKE A FEW ADJUSTMENTS TO SLOW IT DOWN! YOU CAN PRESS THAT EMERGENCY BUTTON FROM TIME TO TIME TO TEST IT OUT!
JUST SAY WHEN, UNK!
MEANWHILE...
OBOY! IT'S GOOD TO BE HOME! I REALLY HAD A HECTIC DAY AT THE OFFICE!
JUGHEAD'S POP!
OKAY, JUGHEAD! TRY IT!
YOWZAH!
MY GRACIOUS!
W-WHAT H-HAPPENED??
I STEPPED INTO THE HOUSE--
--OR DID I--??
4.
YES!! I WAS IN HERE--
--AND THEN THE FLOOR MOVED-- OR--SEEMED TO MOVE-- HA! HA! THAT'S SILLY!!
HOW COULD A FLOOR MOVE?

I MUST HAVE IMAGINED IT! THAT'S IT! MY NERVES ARE SHOT! I'VE BEEN WORKING TOO HARD!
SURE! THIS FLOOR IS SOLID!

JUGGY, M'BOY-- WOULD YOU PRESS THE BUTTON AGAIN? I DON'T KNOW WHETHER I'VE SLOWED THIS DOWN OR SOUPED IT UP!
COMING, UNK!
REGGIE COMICS

I BETTER GO UPSTAIRS AND LIE DOWN! WHEN A MAN STARTS IMAGINING THAT THE FLOOR BENEATH HIM IS MOVING, IT'S--

OH-H-H-H-H-H-H-H!
R-R-R-R-R-R-R-R-R-R
SWOOSH!

5.

AND JUST DOWN THE STREET..
I SAW YOUR HUSBAND PASS BY, BEFORE MRS. JONES-- HE'S NOT LOOKING WELL, IS HE?
THE POOR DEAR HAS BEEN WORKING VERY HARD!

GULP!! JOHN, DEAR!! WHAT'S THE MATTER??
OH-H-H-H! I'M A SICK MAN, MARY! CALL A DOCTOR! CALL AN AMBULANCE! CALL ANYBODY! BUT THEY PROBABLY WON'T GET HERE IN TIME! I'M GOING, FAST!

OH, YOU POOR DEAR! YOU'RE SO OVERWORKED!! COME INTO THE HOUSE AND--
NO, MARY, NO! DON'T GO THROUGH THAT DOOR!! THE KITCHEN FLOOR DOESN'T LIKE ME!! IT'S--TOSSED ME OUT TWICE!!

JOHN!! W-WHAT D-DID YOU S-SAY?? THE FLOOR--??
YOU SEE, MARY? I'M OFF MY TROLLEY! I'M A GONE GOOSE! I'M NUTTIER THAN A FRUIT CAKE!! CALL THE WAGON! PUT ME AWAY IN A SQUIRREL CAGE

HI, MOM! HI, POP! BOY! YOU SHOULD SEE THE SLICK TRICK UNCLE HERMAN DID TO OUR FLOOR!
OUR FLOOR?
OUR KITCHEN FLOOR?

ALL Y'GOTTA DO IS PRESS A LITTLE BUTTON, AND--
--AND THE FLOOR TOSSES PEOPLE OUT?
WOULD YOU DEAR PEOPLE STEP OUT OF MY WAY--?
6

BUT I TELL YOU THE EXPRESS LEFT AN HOUR AGO!
YES--I KNOW--BUT GIVE ME A TICKET ANYWAY, M'GOOD MAN, AND JUST SHOW ME THE TRACK IT LEFT ON!!
TICKETS

Archie
POLICED TO MEET YOU!
TEN GALLONS OF ICE CREAM? SURE! I'LL DELIVER IT AT EIGHT O'CLOCK!

TEN GALLONS! WOW! THAT'S A LOT OF ICE CREAM, POP!
YUP! LOOKS LIKE A BIG PARTY AT THE LODGE'S HOME TONIGHT!

THE LODGE'S? I DIDN'T KNOW THEY WERE THROWING A PARTY!
THAT WAS VERONICA! IT'S HER PARTY!
ROCK N' ROLL SPECIAL 20

VERONICA'S GIVING A PARTY? ... AND DIDN'T INVITE ME?

ARCHIE! YOU DIDN'T FINISH YOUR SODA!
I'VE LOST MY APPETITE, POP!

I JUST CANT BELEIVE VERONICA WOULD THROW A PARTY AND LEAVE ME OUT!
I'LL BET HER FATHER IS BEHIND THIS! HE MUST HAVE FOUND OUT THAT I ALMOST BROKE HIS MANCHU VASE!
--HE LOOKS AT ME AS IF I WERE SOMETHING THE CAT DRAGGED IN!
HI, ARCH!
JUGHEAD, AM I REPULSIVE?
NO MORE THAN USUAL!
YOU LOOK SICK, ARCH! MAYBE YOU HAVE THE 24 HOUR VIRUS!
IT'S WORSE THAN THAT!
36 HOUR VIRUS?
48 HOUR VIRUS?
YOU WOULDN'T UNDERSTAND, JUG.
I FEEL LOW ENOUGH TO JUMP OFF THE BRIDGE!
BEFORE YOU DO, CALL VERONICA! SHE'S BEEN TRYING TO GET YOU!
WHY DIDN'T YOU TELL ME?
I THOUGHT HE WAS SICK!.. HE'S JUST NUTS!

ARCHIEKINS!
(PUFF! PUFF!) HI, LAMBIE!

I'M SO GLAD YOU CAME OVER! MOTHER AND I ARE PLANNING A SURPRISE PARTY FOR DADDY AND WE NEED YOUR HELP!
GOOMBYE!
ARCHIE!

ARCHIE ANDREWS! DON'T YOU WANT MY DADDY TO HAVE A HAPPY BIRTHDAY?
SURE! THAT'S WHY I'M LEAVING!

YOUR FATHER AND I GET ALONG LIKE MATCHES AND GUN POWDER!
BUT I'M ONLY ASKING A LITTLE FAVOR!

I JUST WANT YOU TO MEET DADDY AT THE STATION WITH YOUR CAR AND TAKE AT LEAST AN HOUR TO DRIVE HOME!

AN HOUR? FOR A TEN MINUTE DRIVE? YOUR DAD WOULD SLAUGHTER ME!
HE'LL BE SO HAPPY ABOUT THE PARTY HE'LL FORGIVE YOU!

THIS IS LIKE STICKING MY HEAD IN A LION'S MOUTH WHEN HE HASN'T EATEN FOR WEEKS!

THERE HE IS! .... AND HE LOOKS MAD ALREADY!
CONFOUND IT! WHERE IS JENKINS? I TOLD HIM TO MEET THIS TRAIN!
RIVERDALE

OH, NO!... A HARD DAY AT THE OFFICE AND NOW YOU!!
HI, MR. LODGE!

YOUR CHAUFFEUR ... ER- - I MEAN YOUR CAR BROKE DOWN! BUT MY CAR IS HERE!
THANKS! I'LL TAKE A CAB!

CONFOUND IT! THERE ISN'T A CAB IN SIGHT!
PLEASE, MR. LODGE... LET ME RUN YOU HOME!
TAXI STAND

AGAINST MY BETTER JUDGEMENT, I'M GOING TO ACCEPT YOUR OFFER!
I'LL HAVE YOU HOME IN A JIFFY!

PLEASE, ARCHIE! I JUST WANT TO GET HOME IN PEACE AND QUIET! I'VE HAD A TRYING DAY, AND MY NERVES ARE ON EDGE!
DON'T WORRY! I'VE GOT THIS OLD CRATE PURRING LIKE A KITTEN!

POW!

THIS ISN'T THE WAY HOME!
I THOUGHT A NICE RIDE IN THE COUNTRY WOULD SOOTHE YOUR JANGLED NERVES!

I DON'T WANT A RIDE IN THE COUNTRY! I JUST WANT TO GO HOME!!
Y-YESS'R!

NOW WHAT?
I DUNNO! I CAN'T BE OUT OF GAS! I PUT IN A QUART YESTERDAY!
SPUT!
SPUT!
SPUT!

I GUESS I SHOULD HAVE PUT IN **TWO** QUARTS!

WHAT A GROUCHY GUY AT THAT GAS STATION! MADE ME BUY A WHOLE **GALLON**!

DON'T WORRY, MR. LODGE! SOON AS SHE GETS A LITTLE NUTRIMENT SHE'LL BE RARIN' TO GO!
GASOLIN

OH-OH! THE MOTOR ISN'T TURNING OVER...
ARCHIE, ARE YOU SURE THIS HEAP HAS A MOTOR?

IF YOU COULD JUST PUSH A LITTLE FASTER, I THINK WE CAN GET HER TO KICK OVER!
K210

ZOWIE! I THINK WE DID IT!
POW!

OKAY, MR. LODGE! SHE'S GOING!
HOP IN!

NO, ARCHIE! YOU HOP **OUT**!! I'M TAKING OVER!

MR. LODGE.... ER... AREN'T YOU GOING A LITTLE FAST?
I WANT TO GO FAST, ARCHIE! I'M TRYING TO GET HOME BEFORE I LOSE MY TEMPER!

--AND SINCE WHEN DOES A LITTLE SPEED BOTHER YOU?
OH, I DON'T MIND!

.... BUT I DON'T THINK THAT COP LIKES IT!
RRRRRRR!

DON'T TELL ME! LET ME GUESS! YOU'RE LATE FOR A T.V. SHOW! YOU'RE GONNA BE THE NEXT AMERICAN IDOL!
LOOK, OFFICER, I CAN EXPLAIN! I'M MR. LODGE!

THAT DOESN'T EXPLAIN ANYTHING! LEMME SEE YOUR LICENSE! ....OR IS YOUR BROTHER THE MAYOR?
AS A MATTER OF FACT, HE IS!

HE SHOULD'VE REMINDED YOU TO BRING YOUR LICENSE WHEN YOU DRIVE! FOLLOW ME!
VERONICA IS NEVER GOING TO BELIEVE THIS!

I'M SORRY, MRS. LODGE! SPEEDING AND DRIVING WITHOUT A LICENSE ARE SERIOUS CHARGES! HE'LL HAVE TO STAY UNTIL COURT OPENS!
AND WE PLANNED SUCH A LOVELY PARTY!.. ALL THAT ICE CREAM AND CAKE!
ICE CREAM!
... AND CAKE!

MY COMPLIMENTS TO YOUR COOK, MRS. LODGE!
THANK YOU, SERGEANT!
THE SERGEANT SAID I COULD BRING YOU A PIECE OF CAKE! HAPPY BIRTHDAY, DADDY!!
END

## Say it with Flour
## *Pep* #126, 1958
## By Dan DeCarlo

Growing up, I had the same aversion to Archie comics as all superhero fans did. They were "cartoony." They weren't "serious." They were "for kids." Man, I was a dope. I had a short turn on staff in the Archie editorial department in 1990, and part of the gig was to assemble information for an internal dossier on all the characters, which meant I spent days and days reading every single Archie comic in the library (there were a lot fewer then). I have never been more entertained in my life. Archie and his cast of characters have, over the years, been refined to a razor-edge of comedy and characterization by the dozens of writers and artists who've contributed to his canon. Don't believe me? Read on.

**Mark Waid**

*Eisner Award-winning comic book writer*

## Flip Flopped
## *Betty & Veronica* #38, 1958
## By Frank Doyle, Dan DeCarlo, Rudy Lapick, Vincent DeCarlo

Looking over the art in this story you can easily tell why Dan DeCarlo was given the keys to the kingdom! Beautiful girls, sharp clean lines—excellent DeCarlo at his best! Wait, this story title has multiple meanings! A strange story: first, the girls' cheerleading coach is Coach Kleats (a male coaching them in 1958?) Second, Betty is a flop at the tumbling routines required for the team, and third, Veronica is an expert tumbler. Didn't we know 18 years into the characters that Betty is the athlete, not Veronica? Talk about flip flopped! Still a good story with a funny ending, but a must just because it's so out of character!

**Jack Copley**

*Archie Comics historian*

Jughead
IN
Dan DeCarlo
"SAY IT WITH FLOUR"
RIVERDALE FAIR
BIG BAKING CONTEST
PIES COOKIES
CAKES PASTRIES
OPEN TO ALL RIVERDALE RESIDENTS!
FIRST PRIZE .......... $50.00
LOOK AT THAT, JUG! A BAKING CONTEST!
SO WHAT?

SO WHAT?? WE'VE GOT AS GOOD A CHANCE AS ANYBODY TO WIN THAT 50 DOLLAR PRIZE!
YEAH! ABOUT AS MUCH OF A CHANCE AS AN ALLIGATOR IN A SHOE FACTORY!

JUG, I'LL BET WE COULD WHIP UP A BATCH OF DOUGHNUTS THAT WOULD FRACTURE THE JUDGES!
MAYBE SO!- BUT HOW DO WE GET THEM TO STAND STILL WHILE WE THROW THEM AT THEM?

AW, COME ON, JUGGIE!- WHAT HAVE YOU GOT TO LOSE?
MY APPETITE!

WHY DON'T WE TRY SOMTHING SIMPLE---. LIKE AN UPSIDE-DOWN CAKE?
I CAN'T BAKE THOSE KIND OF THINGS! THE BLOOD KEEPS RUSHING TO MY HEAD!

THAT'S IT-JUST KEEP ON BEATING UNTIL IT GETS GOOD AND STIFF!
MY ARM OR THE BATTER?
COOK BOOK

THERE!-NOW TO POP THEM IN THE OVEN!
HOLD IT, ARCH! WHAT ABOUT THE HOLES?

HMM!! THAT'S RIGHT! ACCORDING TO CUSTOM, DOUGHNUTS ARE SUPPOSED TO HAVE HOLES, AREN'T THEY?

MUST BE AN INFERIOR TYPE OF DOUGH! -IT WON'T EVEN HOLD A SQUARE KNOT!
TRY A SHEEP-SHANK!

MAYBE IF WE GOT AHOLD OF A FEW MOTHS THAT LIKE DOUGHNUTS---
YOU'RE ABOUT AS HELPFUL AS A FLAME-THROWER IN A DYNAMITE FACTORY!

HOLD IT, ARCH!! HERE COMES THE ANSWER TO OUR PROBLEM!
IT'S SKIPPER BARNACLE!!

SO WHAT'S AN OLD SEA CAPTAIN GOT TO DO WITH PUTTING HOLES IN DOUGHNUTS?
YOU'LL SEE IN A MINUTE!

JUGHEAD MUST BE CRACKING UP! I WAS AFRAID THOSE LAST MID-TERMS WERE TOO MUCH FOR HIM!

CLEVER!?
YO-HO-HO! AND A TWO CENT PLAIN!

HOW'S THAT, BOY, HUH?
I ALWAYS SAID YOU WERE A GENIUS, JUG! DUMB, BUT A GENIUS!

BUT LISTEN-THESE AREN'T ENOUGH DOUGHNUTS TO ENTER IN THE CONTEST! WE'VE ONLY GOT FIVE OF THEM!

CORRECTION, PLEASE...FOUR!
SLURP!

SKIPPER BARNACLE APPROACHING OFF THE STARBOARD QUARTERDECK!
OKAY! HERE'S THE NEXT BATCH!

...OH, IT'S A SAILOR'S LIFE FOR ME!

WHU....?!?
SQUASH!

WELL, MARBLE HEAD? WHAT DO YOU THINK OF YOUR BRAINSTORM, NOW?
HOW DID I KNOW WHICH FOOT HE WAS GOING TO STEP ON THEM WITH?

BOY, THIS IS ONE BATTER THAT REALLY STRUCK OUT!
WELL-IT WORKED THE FIRST TIME!

HERE COMES VERONICA!
UH-OH! I CAN'T LET HER SEE WHAT A FLOP WE'VE MADE OF THIS BAKING CONTEST!

ARCHIE ANDREWS! WHAT ON EARTH ARE YOU HIDING BACK THERE?
HIDING?... ME?... NOW HOW DID THOSE THINGS GET THERE, I WONDER?

THEY LOOK LIKE SOME SORT OF SHOE LEATHER!
WELL, THEY'VE BEEN STEPPED ON, IF THAT'S WHAT YOU MEAN!

NOW I UNDERSTAND! YOU BOYS BAKED SOMETHING FOR THE COUNTRY FAIR, AND NOW YOU'RE ASHAMED TO ENTER THEM!
WELL DON'T WORRY- I'LL ENTER THEM FOR YOU!

BUT, RONNIE-YOU DIDN'T LET ME EXPLAIN! THOSE DOUGHNUTS WERE ALL CRUSHED! WE WERE GOING TO THROW THEM AWAY!
DOUGHNUTS?
JUDGES STAND

I'LL TAKE THESE, YOUNG LADY! THE JUDGING IS JUST ABOUT TO START!
B-BUT... BUT..

QUICK!-L-LET'S GET OUT OF HERE BEFORE THEY ARREST US FOR MANUFACTURING HOCKEY PUCKS WITHOUT A LICENSE!

I HATE TO ADMIT IT, YOUNG LADY, BUT THESE ARE THE BEST WAFFLES I'VE TASTED ALL DAY!
WAFFLES?

ARCHIE! I SIMPLY MUST HAVE THAT RECIPE!
THERE ISN'T ANY! I JUST USED MY HEAD!...AND SKIPPER BARNACLE'S FOOT!
BLESS HIS SOLE!
END

Archie's Girls
Betty and Veronica
"FLIP FLOPPED"
BRAVO, BETTY! THAT WOULD MAKE A PEACHY VAUDEVILLE ROUTINE, BUT IT ISN'T EXACTLY WHAT WE EXPECT FROM OUR CHEER LEADERS!
COACH
WHUMP!
I'LL GET IT THIS TIME, COACH!
ALLEZ-OOP!
OOF!
WHAM!
I THINK I KNOW WHAT I DID WRONG, COACH!
SO DO I!
YOU SIGNED UP AS A CHEER LEADER!

HI, ATHLETES! WHAT'S GOING ON IN THE----
GYMNASIUM

EEEP!!
WHUMP
THUMP

OOF!
"AND THAT'S WHAT I CALL BALL IN' THE JACK!"
WHAP!

I SUPPOSE YOU COULD DO BETTER?

WELL, I USED TO BE QUITE AN ACROBATIC DANCER!
THEN WHY AREN'T YOU ON THE CHEERING SQUAD?

AT LEAST I TRY TO CHEER OUR TEAM ON TO VICTORY!
WHERE'S YOUR SCHOOL SPIRIT?

CHEERING SQUADS ARE FOR ENERGETIC CHILDREN LIKE YOU, DEARIE!

I PREFER TO NURSE THE WOUNDED WARRIORS AFTER THE BATTLE!

VERONICA! PLEASE! WILL YOU JOIN OUR CHEERING SQUAD?
WHY NOT?
I THOUGHT THIS STUFF WAS TOO CHILDISH FOR YOU?
WELL, THE TEAM IS SUPPOSED TO BE PLAYING BASKETBALL!
WE CAN'T LET THEM LAUGH THEMSELVES INTO DEFEAT!
HOW'S THIS, COACH?
MAGNIFICENT!
HMPH! SHOW OFF!
VERONICA, YOU WILL LEAD THE SQUAD!
I LEAVE THEM IN YOUR HANDS!
LET'S FACE IT, GIRLS!
WE'RE DEAD!
LINE UP, SQUAD!
IF WE'RE GOING TO PLAY FOLLOW THE LEADER, I QUIT!

ON THE CONTRARY! YOU GIRLS CAN RELAX FROM HERE ON IN!
HERE'S ALL YOU HAVE TO DO!
ONLY THAT?
NOTHING ELSE!
I'LL DO THE HARD WORK!
I DON'T GET IT! SHE'S BEING VERY EASY ON US!
YOU DON'T GET IT?
SHE WANTS EVERY EYE ON HER!
NOBODY WILL EVEN NOTICE US!
GAME TIME:
WHAT A GAME! DID YOU SEE THAT SHOT?
WHAT GAME?
LOOK AT THAT CHEER LEADER!
WOW! IT'S VERONICA!

HMPH! I DON'T THINK ANYONE'S WATCHING THE GAME!
WHAT'S TO WATCH?
THE TEAM'S ARE WATCHING SO MUCH, THERE'S HARDLY ANY SCORE!
RONNIE! WHAT PEP! WOW!!
(PUFF, PUFF!) I'VE G-GOT TO DRESS F-FOR THE DANCE!
LATER:
WHEEE!!
MAN DIG THAT BEAT!
WHAT A SESSION!
SAY! THAT'S ABOUT TEN DANCES YOU'VE HAD WITH ARCHIE!
HOW COME?
AFTER HER PERFORMANCE, I THOUGHT RONNIE WOULD MONOPOLIZE THE STAG LINE!
HEE, HEE! SO DID SHE JUGGIE!
BUT SHE'S JUST TOO POOPED TO POP!
Z Z Z Z Z Z
THE END

# THE BEST OF Archie COMICS BOOK FOUR

# The 1960s

## Sssh!
## *Archie* #120, 1961
### by Frank Doyle and Harry Lucey
### &
## A New Twist
## *Archie* #121, 1961
### by Frank Doyle, Harry Lucey and Terry Szenics

The 1960s were a great time for the Archie company and its fans. The artists and writers who helped build these titles for twenty-some years had matured into the styles that would define them. DeCarlo could draw girls. Schwartz could do zany Jughead material, and Bolling handled all those great Little Archie stories. But it was Harry Lucey who could handle everything from great looking girls to physical comedy to pantomime silliness better than the rest.

**Pat and Tim Kennedy**
*Archie Comics pencillers*

## Foul Bawl
## *Archie Giant Series* #13, 1961
### by Frank Doyle, Dan DeCarlo, Rudy Lapick, Vince DeCarlo and Barry Grossman

Betty, Veronica (and the rest of the Riverdale gang) taught me how to read... Three older sisters in the workforce when I was a wee lad meant paydays brought comics for their baby brother. It started out with them reading the words to me, and me following along in the pictures, but led me to teaching myself to read. I was always a Betty kinda guy... she was the girl next door... athletic, perky... and when I look at my wife, I can't help but think that Betty might have been an early influence for future decisions.

**Howard Mackie**
*Renowned comic book writer and editor*

# Archie in SSsh!

ONE DOZEN

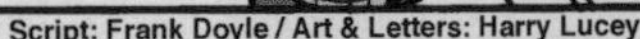
Script: Frank Doyle / Art & Letters: Harry Lucey

R-R-RIP

ONE DOZEN

KERPLUNK!

CRUNCH!!
3.

WOOSH!

4

ANDREW

ANDREWS

HI, ARCH!

HE KNOWS I PREFER THEM SCRAMBLED!
The End

# Archie "A NEW TWIST"

Script: Frank Doyle / Pencils: Harry Lucey / Inks: Terry Szenics

JUST TRYIN' TO SEE WHAT YOU'RE *UP* TO, ARCH!

I'M UP TO HERE WITH THIS STIFF NECK -*THAT'S* WHAT I'M UP TO!

*STIFF NECK?*
YEAH!

I JUST CAN'T STRAIGHTEN IT OUT!

UP ONTO THE WALL, ARCH!

NOW LIE DOWN!
DO YOU THINK YOU CAN *FIX* IT?

NO!...BUT THIS WAY WE CAN AT LEAST TALK FACE-TO-FACE!
2

CHEE! -WHAT A GROUCH!

HEY, ARCH!...ARE YOU STUCK IN THAT POSITION?
YEAH!

IT'S ALL THOSE ROCKS IN YOUR HEAD, PAL!
VERY FUNNY!

THEY MAKE YOU LOPSIDED, AND...
TILT!

HEE! HEE! TOUCHY LIL' DEVIL, ISN'T HE?

ARCHIE, DO YOU KNOW WHAT YOUR TROUBLE IS?
NO, BETTY! DO YOU?

YOU JUST HAVE THE WRONG SLANT ON THINGS!
3

BOY! WHAT FRIENDS I'VE GOT! I'M IN A JAM AND EVERYBODY'S A COMIC!

I'M SORRY, ARCHIE!
I'LL TRY TO HELP YOU!

BEND OVER THE WALL!
EASY, NOW!

STEADY PRESSURE DOES IT!
OWOOOOOOOOO

...AND A SNAP!

B-BETTY! -IT WORKED! LOOK! YOU STRAIGHTENED OUT MY NECK!

BOY! WHAT A RELIEF! IT FEELS GREAT!
4

!

YOUR TURN, DARLING!
HEY!
I'M STUCK!
'BYE, NOW!
?

ARCHIE! WHAT IN THE WORLD??
IT'S MY BACK, RON!

HOLD STILL, ARCHIEKINS! I'LL TRY TO STRAIGHTEN IT!

THIS IS NO GOOD! WE'VE GOT TO KEEP YOUR FEET DOWN! ..PERHAPS IF YOU STOOD AGAINST THE WALL...

YOWWWL!
5

WHEW! I'M AFRAID IT'S NO USE, ARCHIEKINS! WE'D BETTER....

T-W-A-N-G!

HEY! I DID IT! I'M ALL STRAIGHT AGAIN!

I DIDN'T HEAR ANY "TWANG" WHEN I APPEARED!
ULP! N-N-NOW WAIT!
6

NEVER UNDERESTIMATE THE POWER OF A WOMAN!
The End
6

# Betty and Veronica in "FOUL BAWL"

WAH! MY ARCHIEKINS! HE'S LEAVING ME!!

NOW, NOW, HONEY!

RONNIE! IT'S ONLY FOR TWO DAYS!

IVERDALE

Script: **Frank Doyle** Pencils: **Dan DeCarlo** Inks: **Rudy Lapick** Letters: **Vince DeCarlo** Colors: **Barry Grossman**

I'M DESTITUTE WITH GRIEF!
YOU MEAN DESOLATE?
RIVE
(SOB) T-THAT T-TOO!
YOUR NOSE IS SHINY!
(SNIFF) I M-MUST KEEP UP APPEARANCES! ARCHIE WOULD WANT IT THAT WAY!

HERE I AM, RONNIE! RIGHT ON TIME!
?

OH! -ER-AH..FINE, BERT! I'LL-ER-BE RIGHT WITH YOU!

RONNIE LODGE! YOU HAVE A DATE WITH THAT BOY!
W-ELL, I DID SORT OF...

...B-BUT IT'S JUST TO GET MY MIND OFF THE TRAGEDY OF LOSING DEAR ARCHIE! T-TO KEEP ME FROM BREAKING DOWN!
2

I HOPE YOU DON'T THINK I'M DOING THIS J-JUST TO **ENJOY** MYSELF!
HEAVENS TO BETSY, **NO!**

TENNIS, GOLF, BOATING, SWIMMING? YOU NAME IT, BEAUTIFUL!

TSK! POOR KID! SHE'S **SO** BROKEN UP!

IT'S NICE THAT SHE HAD THE FORESIGHT TO PROVIDE A SHOULDER TO **WEEP** ON!

BETTY!

***ARCHIE!!***
THE TRAIN BROKE DOWN ABOUT A MILE UP THE TRACK!

I DECIDED TO WALK BACK! I WAS SO WORRIED ABOUT POOR RONNIE!
WHO? ..OH! YES! RONNIE!
3

SHE WAS IN SUCH A DESPERATE STATE, I THOUGHT I'D TRY TO CALM HER DOWN!
OH, YES! DESPERATE!
NOW

I FIGURE I'LL CATCH THE LATE AFTERNOON TRAIN!

BY THE WAY! WHERE **IS** SHE?
WHO?

RONNIE, OF COURSE!
OH! **HER!**

ER- I DON'T KNOW! S-SHE MIGHT HAVE GONE TO THE BEACH TO DROWN HER SORROWS!

EEYIPE! D-DROWN?
NO! I DIDN'T MEAN....

IN HER DEPRESSED STATE SHE'S LIABLE TO DO SOMETHING FOOLISH!
THAT'S A MATTER OF OPINION!
4

I J-JUST H-HOPE WE'RE NOT TOO LATE!

Y-YOU GO THAT WAY, AND I'LL GO THIS WAY! WHISTLE IF YOU SEE HER!
THAT'S THE ONLY THING I EVER PUCKER UP FOR!

(GULP) I'LL ASK T-THE LIFEGUARD!
LIFE GUARD

ER-GUARD! H-HAVE YOU S-SAVED ANY BRUNETTES LATELY?
LIFE GUARD

NAH! I DON'T SAVE THEM! THEY SPOIL TOO QUICKLY!
YAK! YAK!
YUK!

MEANWHILE:
THERE'S TEARFUL TESSIE NOW! LOOK AT THE MOURNING CLOTHES, WILL YOU?
5

DON'T TAKE IT SO HARD, DEAR! ARCHIE HAS RETURNED! HE'S LOOKING FOR YOU!

YOICKS! HERE? ON THE BEACH?
NO! HE'S LOOKING THROUGH THE LOCKERS AT THE TRAIN STATION!

ER-BERT! WOULD YOU DO ME A FAVOR? I'D LIKE SOME ICE CREAM!

I'LL BE BACK IN A FLASH, LOVER!
NO!

DON'T GO TO THAT FIRST STAND! GO TO THE SECOND ONE!

B-BUT THAT'S TWO MILES UP THE BEACH!!
BUT THEIR PISTACHIO IS SO MUCH BETTER!

(SIGH)-YOUR WISH IS MY COMMAND!
OH, BROTHER!
6

YOUR TEARS HAVE DRIED, DEARIE! SHALL I GET YOU AN **ONION?**
BETTY! YOU WOUND ME! **DEEPLY!**

WAIT! I'LL FIND YOU A SHOULDER TO CRY ON!
HOW ABOUT THAT LIFEGUARD?
LIFE GUARD

WELL, I'LL BE DARNED!

ARCHIE ANDREWS!!
BERT COOK! WHAT ARE **YOU** DOING HERE?

HA! WAIT TILL YOU SEE! I'M HERE WITH THE MOST BEAUTIFUL GIRL IN THE WORLD!
NO KIDDING?

YOU MUST HAVE FOUND **MY** GIRLFRIEND!
HA, HA! FUNNY, MAN! **FUNNY!**
7

COME ON ALONG AND MEET HER! YOU'LL FORGET **YOUR** GIRL!
IF WE FIND **MINE**, YOU'LL FORGET **YOURS**!
MAN! IT MUST BE A YEAR SINCE I SAW YOU! WHAT HAVE YOU BEEN DOING?
GOING WITH THE WORLD'S MOST GORGEOUS GAL!
LOOK! NOW YOU'VE GOT SOMETHING TO **CRY** ABOUT!
ULP!
ARCH! **THAT**, IS A **GIRL**!
YOU CAN SAY **THAT** AGAIN, BERT!
SWEETS FOR THE SWEET!
T-THANK Y-YOU!
SAY! THAT WAS REAL NICE OF YOU, BERT!
SUCH BEAUTY DESERVES FAR MORE!
8

MAN! DID YOU EVER SEE ANYTHING SO PRETTY?
NEVER!

YOU KNOW, ARCH! ALL MY LIFE I'VE LOOKED FOR A GIRL LIKE THAT!

BERT, I KNOW JUST HOW YOU FEEL! IT'S TOO BAD WE CAN'T ALL BE LUCKY!

THANKS, ARCH! I KNOW HOW DISAPPOINTED YOU MUST BE!
AFTER ALL, BERT! YOU'RE MY FRIEND!

RON! DO YOU REALIZE WHAT'S GOING ON?
ARCHIE THINKS I'M A STRANGER TO BERT!

YES! AND BERT THINKS YOU'RE A STRANGER TO ARCHIE!
9

WELL, NOW THAT I KNOW EVERYTHING IS ALL RIGHT, I'VE GOT TO GO!

I'VE GOT TO CATCH THE AFTERNOON TRAIN!
I'LL WALK YOU TO YOUR CAR!

WHEW!
_TOO CLOSE FOR COMFORT!
PLOP!

RONNIE! YOU DON'T KNOW HOW LUCKY YOU ARE!
I CERTAINLY HOPE THIS TEACHES YOU A LESSON!

NEXT TIME MAYBE YOU WON'T BE SO ANXIOUS TO PLAY THE FIELD AND...AND...

-RONNIE?
LIFE GUARD
10
The End

## Two Little Words
### *Archie Annual* #13, 1961-62
### by Frank Doyle, Harry Lucey and Terry Szenics

Frank and Harry always had a special magic together. Their Archie stories always seemed funnier, wilder and, sometimes, more emotional and heart-breaking than all the rest. Whenever Frank and Harry teamed together, they created a special sense of wonder that burst upon the page—a comic book reality powerful enough to grab you by the throat and hurl you from panel to panel until you found yourself gasping from laughter as you slammed into the last page. That takes a special kind of magic, my friend.

**Tom DeFalco**
*Renowned comic book writer and editor*

## Lawbreaker
### *The Adventures of Little Archie* #22, 1962
### by Bob Bolling, Victor Gorelick and Barry Grossman

*A typically funny, whimsical and vividly imaginative Little Archie story from the 1960s.*

## Mr. Inferno
### *Betty & Veronica* #75, 1962
### by Frank Doyle and Dan DeCarlo

One of the most talked-about Archie Comics stories ever: Betty & Veronica sell their souls to the devil! This one has taken on such legendary status that many don't even believe it exists. Well, here it is! But don't worry... it's all in good fun. After all, you know no devil is ever going to get the upper cloven hoof on Archie's favorite gal pals!

**Paul Castiglia**
*Writer & archivist*
*Archie Comics*

# Archie in "TWO LITTLE WORDS!"

ARCHIE!

VERONICA!

ARCHIE!

VERONICA!

ARCHIE!

V-VERONICA!
2.

ARCHIE!
R-RIP!

VERONICA!

ARCHIE!

VERONICA?
VERONICA!

VERONICA!

VERONICA??
VERONICA!

ARCHIE!
3.

VERONICA?

ARCHIE

VERONICA?

ARCHIE?

VERONICA?

ARCHIE---?

VERONICA!
4.

VERONICA---?

ARCHIE!

VERONICA!

ARCHIE!

VERONICA!

ARCHIE!
VERONICA!

ARCHIE!
VERONICA!
The End

# Little Archie

## "LAWBREAKER"

Bolling / Gorelick / Grossman

TEN MINUTES IN JAIL FOR YOU!
I DON'T THINK I LIKE THIS GAME!

LET ME OUT IN TEN MINUTES, OR ELSE—
OR ELSE YOU'LL STAY IN LONGER! HEH! HEH!
POLICE

WHAT'S WRONG, OFFICER?
COME HERE AND TELL ME ALL ABOUT IT, BLUE EYES!
CUT IT, RONNIE, I'M IN UNIFORM!

YOU LADIES WENT THROUGH A GREEN LIGHT!
SO WHAT !?!
2

GREEN IS A LOT PRETTIER THAN RED... THAT'S WHY YOU SHOULD HAVE STOPPED TO LOOK AT IT... THAT'S **MY LAW!** AND FOR BREAKING IT YOU GET TEN MINUTES IN JAIL!
*HMMM,* THAT'S FIVE MINUTES APIECE!

YOU MEAN WHAT WE DID WAS AWFUL UNLAWFUL?
YEAH AND ILLEGAL, TOO!
I ALWAYS THOUGHT AN *ILLEGAL* WAS A SICK BIRD!

LET ME OUT... MY TIME'S UP!
HEY, IT'S MY TURN TO BE COP!
POLICE

POLICE

3

JUGHEAD! YOU'RE UNDER ARREST FOR FLYING WITHOUT A LICENSE!
WHAT A CRAZY LAW!
POLICE

THAT'S MY LAW, I MADE IT UP!
I'LL BE GLAD WHEN THIS GAME IS OVER!

JUG, MEET THE JUG!
IT SURE IS A FULL ONE!

LET US OUT!
TIME'S UP!!
MY TURN TO BE COP!

NOW I'D LIKE TO SHOW YOU ALL A FEW MAGIC TRICKS!
GROAN!
CAN YOU DISAPPEAR ?

NOW WATCH WHAT HAPPENS WHEN I DROP A COIN INTO MY HAT!
4

JAIL

HA! HA! HA!
A WUNNERFUL TRICK!
A REAL HIT!
AMBROSE!!

I'LL CATCH HIM!
NEVER! HE'S GOT THE FASTEST CART ON THE WEST SIDE!

AMBROSE'S CART IS BIGGER AND HEAVIER THAN YOUR'S!
HERE HE COMES AGAIN!

HA!
HA!
HA!
JAIL

HMMMM... YEAH, WHAT I NEED IS SOMETHING BIG 'N' HEAVY...
5

UH OH! LITTLE ARCHIE'S GOT THAT FUNNY LOOK IN HIS EYE'S AGAIN!

WHAT'S THAT POUNDING!?
LET US OUT!
GAME'S OVER!
JAIL

GAME'S OVER! GAME'S OVER!
LITTLE ARCHIE LAW NUMBER 703, SAYS THE GAME ISN'T OVER!

JAIL
THUD-!

GAME'S OVER!

GAME'S OVER!
6

HA! I'M GAINING!!

"KILLER" CURVE AHEAD!! EVERYONE LEAN TO THE RIGHT!

GAME'S OVER! GAME'S OVER!

GAMES
OVER!

AMBROSE! STOP IN THE NAME OF THE LAW!

7

DID YOU EVER NOTICE HOW CROWDS OF PEOPLE SUDDENLY SHOW UP WHENEVER THERE'S AN ACCIDENT ?
-ER- THE GAME'S OVER, KIDS... HEH, HEH!

HI, GANG, WHAT'S THIS ALL ABOUT!
AW, WE'VE BEEN AFTER LITTLE ARCHIE 'CAUSE HE'S BEEN MAKING UP HIS OWN LAWS!

BUT I DON'T THINK WE'LL GET HIM!
SURE YOU WILL! THERE'S ONE LAW LITTLE ARCHIE NEVER HEARD OF!

GEE, DILTON, YOU'RE ALL BRAIN.,, WHAT IS IT!
THE LAW OF GRAVITY WHICH SAYS-

WHAT GOES UP MUST COME DOWN!
END

Archie's Girls

# Betty and Veronica in "Mr. Inferno"

ARCHIE! I COULD LISTEN TO YOU ALL DAY!

I COULD TALK TO YOU ALL DAY, BETTY!

-SOMEDAY WHEN RONNIE IS OUT OF TOWN!

HMPH! I FEEL LIKE A STAND-IN FOR A STAR WHO NEVER GETS SICK!
1

THERE'S **NOTHING** I WOULDN'T DO TO GET THAT RED-HEADED RASCAL!

POP

THAT'S **MY** CUE!

**NOTHING** YOU WOULDN'T DO?
W-WHO ARE YOU?

JUST CALL ME, ER-MR. INFERNO!
I JUST DROPPED UP...ER-**IN**, TO GRANT YOUR WISH!

Y-YOU CAN GET ARCHIE FOR ME?
FOR A PRICE, WHICH YOU WILL PAY AT A LATER DATE!

PRICE-SHMICE! YOU'VE GOT YOURSELF A DEAL, MISTER!
I HOPE YOU LIKE **WARM** CLIMATES, BETTY!
SNAP
2

"WARM CLIMATES?"
SOME DAY I WILL EXPECT YOU TO VISIT ME IN MY HOME IN... WHAT WE MIGHT CALL THE SOUTH!

WHY NOT? I DON'T DIG SNOWTIME!
TEAM UP WITH ME, GIRL, AND YOU'LL NEVER BE COLD AGAIN!

GREAT! I LIKE HOT PLACES!

OH, THIS ONE IS ALMOST TOO WILLING!

NOW LET'S GET TO YOUR END OF THE DEAL!

LEAVE THAT TO ME! AND DON'T BOTHER TO INTRODUCE ME TO ARCHIE!

YOU SEE, I CAN ONLY BE SEEN BY THE PEOPLE I HELP!
?
3

B-BUT HOW...?
DON'T WORRY! JUST WALK UP TO HIM!
HI, ARCHIE!
B-O-I-N-G!
D-UH! BETTY! YOU'RE **LOVELY**!
SMOOCH!
DARLING! HOLD ME CLOSE! I'M **MAD** ABOUT YOU?
ER-WHAT ABOUT VERONICA?
VERONICA **WHO?**
YOU SAY THE SWEETEST THINGS, YOU LITTLE DEVIL!
**PLEASE!** YOU **INSULT** ME!
4

ARCHIE! YOU MUST TELL RONNIE ABOUT US!
WHATEVER YOU SAY, DEAR!

BREAK IT TO HER GENTLY!
YES, SWEETHEART!

IT'S NO USE, VERONICA! I'M MAD ABOUT BETTY!

I'M GETTING PRETTY MAD ABOUT HER MYSELF! WHERE IS SHE?

UH, OH! HERE SHE COMES!

OOPS! I'VE-ER-G-GOT TO GO! YOU CAN HANDLE HER ALONE!
WHY ARE YOU SO NERVOUS?

-YOU CAN ONLY BE SEEN BY THE PEOPLE YOU HELP!
ER-AH... YES, B-BUT...!
5

(GASP)-MR. INFERNO! SO YOU'RE BEHIND ALL THIS!!
Y-YOU SEE HIM?

YOU SEE HIM, TOO?
HE WAS HELPING ME MAKE MY WISHES COME TRUE!

WHY THAT DOUBLE DEALING LITTLE DEVIL!!

HOW DO YOU THINK I WAS ALWAYS SO SUCCESSFUL WITH ARCHIE?

H-HE MADE THE SAME PACT WITH BOTH OF US!!

N-NOW GIRLS! RELAX! I'LL FIX EVERYTHING! LET'S TALK THIS OVER!!

..ULP!! THE DEAL IS OFF! TEMPERS LIKE THAT ARE EVEN TO MUCH FOR MY PLACE!
WHOOSH
The End

## Daily Newspaper Strips,
## April 20-25, 1964
## &
## Sunday Newspaper Strip
## May 10, 1964
## by Bob Montana

*The week's worth of daily strips and a Sunday strip presented here are great examples of Archie's success in a variety of media in the 1960s.*

## Dance Crazy
## *Archie* #162, 1966
## by Frank Doyle, Harry Lucey and Marty Epp

Words and pictures—they are the very essence of comics! When they are the right words and pictures, they draw us into fictional worlds and make us fall in love with two-dimensional line drawings as if they were real people. Some writers can type great words. Some artists can depict fantastic pictures. Pair a certain writer and a specific artist together and you have magic. You have Frank Doyle and Harry Lucey.

**Tom DeFalco**
*Renowned comic book writer and editor*

## The Unkindest Cut
## *Betty & Veronica* #141, 1967
## by Frank Doyle, Dan DeCarlo, Rudy Lapick and Vincent DeCarlo

I love this story! When Veronica chops Betty's hem a little crooked, she walks home leaning, making everyone check for the wind. Simple and so much fun!

**Jack Copley**
*Archie Comics historian*

HA HA HA!
© 1964, Archie Comic Publications, Inc.

HEE HEE! YOU BIT, TOO!

HAW-HAW!
Distributed by King Features Syndicate.

BOB MONTANA 4-20

SOMEONE UPSTAIRS IS EATING PEANUTS AND THROWING THE SHELLS DOWN ON MY WINDOW BOXES!

HMMM! LET'S SEE? THAT WOULD BE FLUTESNOOT'S ROOM!
© 1964, Archie Comic Publications, Inc.

WHOEVER IS EATING PEANUTS UP THERE I WANT SENT DOWN TO MY OFFICE IMMEDIATELY!
Distributed by King Features Syndicate.

BOB MONTANA 4-21
OFFICE

THERE'S THE SCHOOL BOARD! DOES THE COACH KNOW IT?
ARCHIE IS SUPPOSED TO TIP HIM OFF!
OFFIC

THEY'RE HEADING OUT TO THE ATHLETIC FIELD NOW!
DID ARCHIE GET WORD TO THE COACH?

HE'S UP ON THE ROOF!
ON THE ROOF?

BOB MONTANA 4-22

MISS PINWHISTLE HAS WON THE PERFECT-ATTENDANCE AWARD FOR THE SECOND YEAR!
SHE EVEN COMES WHEN THERE IS NO SCHOOL! ...CAN'T HEAR THE SIGNAL!

AND IN HONOR OF WINNING AGAIN THIS YEAR...I WANT TO GIVE YOU THESE LILIES!
WHAT? WHO GIVES ME THE WILLIES?

NO, NO! LILIES! ONE FOR EACH YEAR!
BOB MONTANA 4-23
© 1964, Archie Comic Publications, Inc.

Distributed by King Features Syndicate.
NO! NOT ONE FOR EACH EAR.....
NEVER MIND!

THERE'S A HORSE OUTSIDE!
THAT'S NOTHING TO GET EXCITED ABOUT, MISS GRUNDY! A HORSE IS A FAIRLY COMMON ANIMAL!
© 1964, Archie Comic Publications, Inc.

BUT HE'S JUST STANDING THERE!
WHAT DO YOU WANT ME TO DO, TELL HIM TO SIT DOWN?
Distributed by King Features Syndicate.

HE BANE GOT LOOSE FROM DER RIDING SCHOOL!
BEFORE YOU TAKE HIM BACK, I WANT YOU TO DO SOMETHING!

BOB MONTANA 4-24

ARCHIE, YOUR FATHER CALLED! HE SAID, "WHAT-EVER YOU DO.... **DON'T** DRIVE YOUR CAR INTO THE DRIVEWAY TONIGHT"!
COURSE NOT! I DON'T *HAVE* MY CAR!

IT BROKE DOWN IN JUGHEAD'S YARD.....SO I BORROWED HIS BICYCLE!
© 1964, Archie Comic Publications, Inc.

MORNING
YES! I TOLD ARCHIE NOT TO DRIVE HIS CAR IN!??
YOU SHOULD HAVE TOLD HIM **WHY**!

BOB MONTANA 4-25
?!
RED DUNN PAVING
Distributed by King Features Syndicate.

Archie
by
BOB MONTANA

ARCHIE! COME SIT BY THE FIRE!
WATCH THIS! I PUT A MARSHMALLOW ON THE DRUM.....

BOOM!

WHO'S POUNDING ON MY AFRICAN THREE-MILE DRUM?

DADDY, WE'RE JUST TOASTING MARSHMALLOWS IN YOUR DEN!
I'M EXPECTING THE GREAT AFRICAN "WHITE HUNTER", CLAUDE SHOLDERS, ANY MINUTE!

GOSH! MR. LODGE, ARE YOU GOING ON ANOTHER SAFARI?
YES! AND I SPARED NO EXPENSE TO HIRE "KENYA CLAUDE" TO GUIDE ME!

DID YOU HEAR HOW HE STALKS A WOUNDED WATER BUFFALO IN THE BUSH?

AND DID YOU READ HOW HE STANDS FAST IN THE FACE OF A CHARGING RHINO?

AND DID YOU KNOW HE......
YIPE! MY MARSHMALLOW CAUGHT FIRE AND FELL OFF!
THE BEAR RUG!!

OPEN THE DOOR!

5-10

DID YOU SEE HOW HE WENT UP THAT TREE?

# Archie

## DANCE CRAZY

YOU CAN STOP NOW, ARCHIE! THE DANCE IS OVER!

I THINK YOU'D BETTER DRIVE HOME, RONNIE!
OKAY!

HERE WE ARE!
WOULD YOU MIND DRIVING YOURSELF HOME, RON? I STILL CAN'T STOP!

I HOPE I'LL BE ABLE TO SLEEP!

RIVERDALE

NEXT DAY
ARCHIE! DIDN'T THAT STOP YET?

NO, AND I DIDN'T GET A WINK OF SLEEP LAST NIGHT EITHER!

WHAT'S THE MATTER WITH TWINKLE TOES?
HE CAN'T STOP DANCING!

WE'VE GOT TO DO SOMETHING!
I'VE HEARD OF CASES LIKE THIS! SOME-TIMES A GOOD SOCK BRINGS THEM OUT OF IT!

WELL DON'T JUST STAND THERE ..TRY IT!

OKAY! HERE GOES!
3

EEP!
ZIP

SWISH!

SWOOSH!

I THOUGHT YOU WERE GOING TO HIT HIM?
I'M TRYING!

..BUT HE ..WON'T.. HOLD...
WOOSH!

STILL!
4

I GIVE UP! CRAZY LEGS IS YOUR PROBLEM!

I CAN'T STOP! IT MUST BE A DEEP-ROOTED NERVE SPASM OR SOMETHING!

RONNIE! HELP ME!
I WISH I COULD!

ARCHIE!! STOP DANCING IN THE HALLS!

HEY!... I STOPPED!

WHEN MR. WEATHERBEE YELLS AT ME, EVEN MY DEEP-ROOTED NERVE SPASMS CAN'T DEFY HIM!
The End

# Betty and Veronica in "The UNKINDEST CUT"

DO YOU REALLY, RONNIE? DO YOU REALLY LIKE MY NEW OUTFIT?
VERY MUCH, BETTY! THE COLOR IS NICE, IT'S WELL CUT, ...IF ONLY...

NONSENSE! JUST HOLD STILL! I'LL HAVE YOU BACK IN STYLE IN A JIFFY!

LET'S NOT BE HASTY, RON!

NOW HOLD STILL! THIS TAKES A STEADY HAND AND A KEEN EYE!

CAREFUL! **PLEASE BE** CAREFUL!!

SNIP! SNIP! SNIP!

THERE! YOU CAN STOP WORRYING! IT LOOKS **GREAT!**

IT DOES?

HEY! IT DOES!! RON! YOU DID A GREAT JOB...

NO! NOT ON YOUR LIFE! I SHOULD HAVE KNOWN BETTER! THIS IS A JOB FOR A TAILOR!

WELL, YOU'RE GOING TO LOOK STRANGE IF YOU GO OUT IN THE STREET LIKE THAT!
I'LL HIDE IT!

IF I LEAN BACK ENOUGH THE HEM WILL BE PARALLEL WITH THE GROUND AND NO ONE WILL NOTICE THAT IT'S CROOKED!
MY, MY! THERE MUST BE QUITE A GALE BLOWING UP!

?

NO WIND! NO WIND AT ALL!
3

BETTY! BETTY! WAIT!

WHY ARE YOU LEANING?
LEANING? WHO'S LEANING?

DO YOU SEE WHAT I SEE?
HOW COME MY HAT DOESN'T BLOW OFF?

MAYBE BECAUSE THERE'S **NO** WIND!
MAYBE WE OUGHT TO TELL **THEM**!

ER- IT MAY SEEM LIKE A SILLY QUESTION...
...BUT WHY ARE YOU TWO **LEANING**?
WHAT? **US**, LEAN?
?
NO PA||||G
4

HEY! THIS IS CRAZY AS WELL AS UNCOMFORTABLE! NOW LET'S ALL STRAIGHTEN UP!

COME ON, BETTY! UP YOU GO!

THERE'S YOUR PROBLEM! SHE WAS TRYING TO HIDE A CROOKED HEM!

SHUCKS! IS THAT ALL?
WHY DIDN'T YOU TELL US, BETTY! WE CAN CUT THAT STRAIGHT FOR YOU!

NO! NO! YOU LEAVE ME ALONE!
SOMEBODY GET ME A PAIR OF SCISSORS!

NO! NOT A CHANCE! THIS HEM HAS BEEN HACKED AT ENOUGH!
5

WELL, FOR GOODNESS SAKES!

WHO WOULD HAVE THOUGHT IT?

VERONICA! WHAT IN THE EVER LOVIN' BLUE-EYED WORLD DID YOU DO?
DON'T ASK ME TO EXPLAIN IT, DADDY!

I KNOW IT LOOKS SILLY! THAT'S WHY I DELIBERATELY HACKED UP BETTY'S HEM!

...BUT YOU SHOULD SEE THE REACTION IT GET'S FROM THE BOYS!
The End
6

# THE BEST OF Archie COMICS BOOK FOUR

# THE 1970s

## Protest

### *Laugh* #276, 1970

### by Frank Doyle and Samm Schwartz

&

## Summer Prayer for Peace

### *Life with Archie* #93, 1971

### by Dick Malmgren, Dan DeCarlo, Rudy Lapick, Sal Contrera and Bill Yoshida

*Two very different stories relating to similar and timely topics: the Vietnam War and the general political unrest of the late 1960s and early 1970s. The first story is a light-hearted, satirical comedy, while the second is a surprisingly serious, level-headed (and extremely rare) political statement that ends with The Archies performing their real-life hit "Summer Prayer for Peace."*

## Mister Jughead

### *Jughead* #191, 1971

### Frank Doyle, Samm Schwartz and Barry Grossman

The girls are horrified as they witness Jughead taking money from kids! They send Archie and Reggie to see for themselves. The story is very clever and Samm's storytelling in this issue shines. I want to give my money to Mr. Jughead too!

**Jack Copley**
*Archie Comics historian*

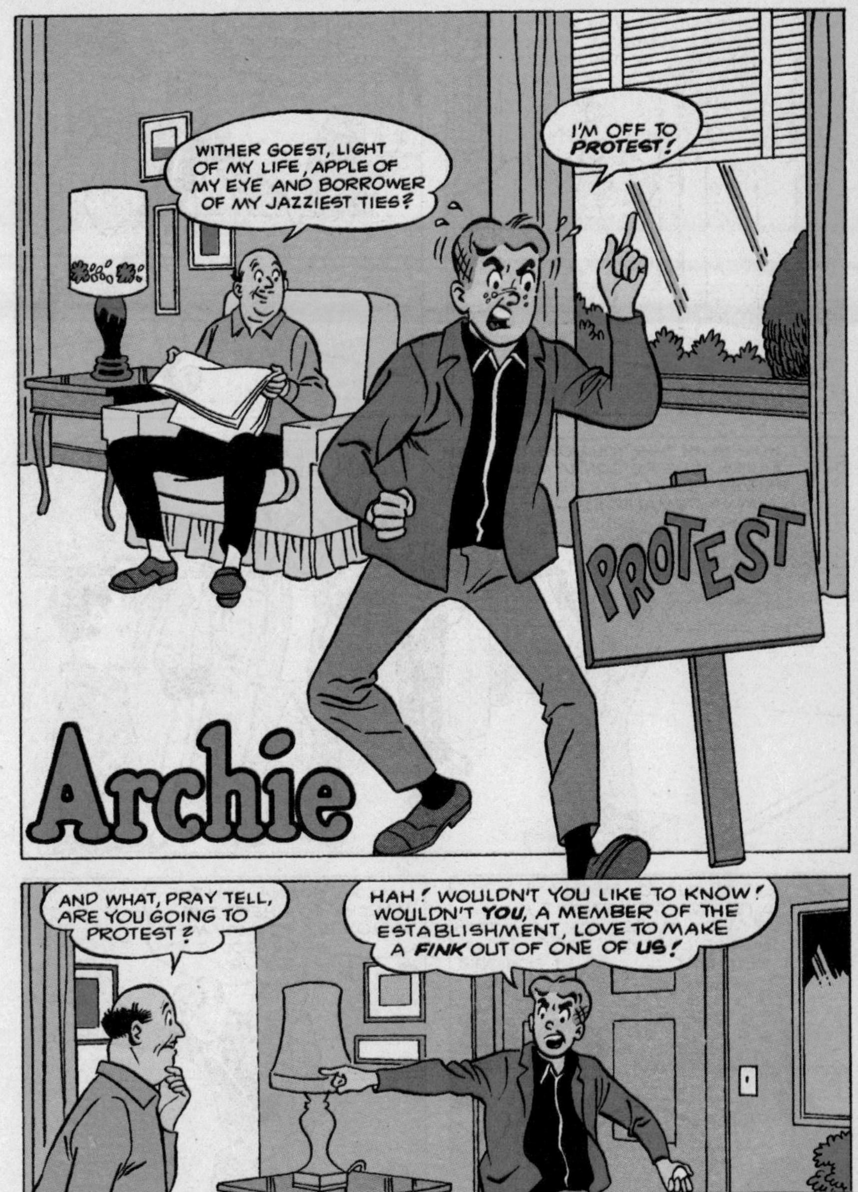
WITHER GOEST, LIGHT OF MY LIFE, APPLE OF MY EYE AND BORROWER OF MY JAZZIEST TIES?
I'M OFF TO PROTEST!
PROTEST
Archie
AND WHAT, PRAY TELL, ARE YOU GOING TO PROTEST?
HAH! WOULDN'T YOU LIKE TO KNOW! WOULDN'T YOU, A MEMBER OF THE ESTABLISHMENT, LOVE TO MAKE A FINK OUT OF ONE OF US!

HOW ABOUT THAT?
SUDDENLY I'M AN ENEMY
OF THE PEOPLE!
SLAM!

WHAT I'LL DO IS
I'LL ROUND UP
THE GROUP!

NOW HEAR THIS, YOU DOWNTRODDEN MASSES! WE'RE GONNA MAKE OURSELVES HEARD! WE'RE GONNA DEMAND A VOICE!
HEAR, HEAR!

DON'T LET 'EM PUT YOU DOWN! THEY'LL TELL YOU I'M A RABBLE ROUSER! WELL MAYBE IT'S TIME RABBLE LIKE YOU GOT ROUSED!
IS HE ON OUR SIDE?

WE'RE GONNA JOIN THE MARCH! GO WHERE THE ACTION IS! FOLLOW ME! WE'RE GOING TO A SIT-IN!
2

ER.-I THINK I HEAR MY MOTHER CALLING ME FOR LUNCH!
I HAVE A FITTING AT ONE!
DENTAL APPOINTMENT!
COUNT ME OUT!

HOLD IT! NOBODY GOES ANYPLACE! WE'RE GONNA HAVE A SIT-IN!
WHERE?

I CAN'T THINK OF EVERYTHING! I CAME UP WITH THE IDEA! SOMEBODY ELSE THINK OF WHERE!

HEY! WAIT A SEC! WHY DIDN'T I THINK OF IT BEFORE? THE HIGH SCHOOL!

WE'LL TAKE OVER ONE OF THE BUILDINGS!
WE'VE GOT ONLY ONE BUILDING!
3

OKAY! OKAY! SO WE'LL TAKE OVER THE ONE WE'VE GOT!
NOT ME!

I GET ENOUGH OF THAT PLACE ALL YEAR! YECHHH!
ME TOO! I'D RATHER STAGE A SIT-OUT NEXT TERM!

GET WITH IT, YOU GUYS! YOU'RE NOTHING THESE DAYS TILL YOU DISSENT!

YOU FOLKS WANT TO SIT-IN? HOW ABOUT MY PLACE? PROTEST.. PICKET.. INVITE YOUR FRIENDS!
POP'S

SO LONG AS YOU KEEP BUYING YOU CAN SIT-IN AS LONG AS YOU LIKE!
POP'S
4

THAT SOUNDS FAIR ENOUGH!
WHY NOT?
BAH! YOU DON'T HAVE YOUR HEART IN IT!

HEY! ALAN! PAT! WILL YOU TWO HELP ME TO PROTEST?

GEE, I'D LIKE TO, ARCH, BUT..
BUT WHAT?

WELL, I BEAT OUT REG FOR HIGH SCORING HONORS ON THE BASKETBALL TEAM...
SO?

SO WHEN YOU BEAT "THE GREATEST" WHO CAN REALLY COMPLAIN?
TRUE! TRUE! OF COURSE I WAS OFF MY FEED THIS SEASON!
HOW ABOUT YOU, PAT? JUST A LITTLE SIT-IN?
5

OH, I COULDN'T! FOLKS WHO SIT-IN TEND TO SPREAD OUT! IF I SPREAD OUT I'LL BLOW THE BALLET CAREER! PLEASE INCLUDE ME OUT!
IT'S UNCONSTITUTION-AL! I DEMAND MY RIGHTS!
WHAT RIGHTS, ARCH?
WHAT RIGHTS?
THE WHOLE COUNTRY IS PROTESTING! ALL EXCEPT RIVERDALE! HERE EVERY-BODY IS CONTENT!
WE'RE BEING LEFT BEHIND! I'M GOING TO DEMAND OUR EQUAL SHARE OF MISERY AND DISCONTENT! THEY CAN'T DO THIS TO US!
I THINK WE OUGHT TO STAGE A SIT-ON!
ON ARCH?
JUST TILL HE UNWINDS!
END

# THE Archies "SUMMER PRAYER FOR PEACE"

THE STORY YOU ARE ABOUT TO READ, IS A STORY WITH A MESSAGE FOR EVERYONE! IT IS ABOUT THE FEELINGS AND BELIEFS OF MANY YOUNG MEN WHO ARE BEING DRAFTED INTO THE ARMED SERVICES OF OUR COUNTRY TODAY, BUT IN THIS PARTICULAR CASE IT HAPPENS TO BE ARCHIE AND HIS BUDDIES ---

U.S. ARMY INDUCTION CENTER

OKAY, FELLOWS, CONGRATULATIONS! YOU'VE PASSED YOUR WRITTEN AND PHYSICAL EXAMS AND THAT MEANS YOU'RE IN THE ARMY NOW! SO GO HOME AND PACK YOUR TOOTH-BRUSH AND BELONGINGS AND REPORT BACK HERE IN 48 HOURS!

SGT. BEAN RECRUITING

WELL, HOW DOES IT FEEL TO BE A SOLDIER FOR OUR COUNTRY, FELLAS ?
I DON'T REALLY KNOW, ARCH! ANYWAY WE DON'T HAVE A HECK OF A LOT TO SAY ABOUT IT ONE WAY OR THE OTHER!
416-436

WHAT CONCERNS ME THE MOST IS HOW IS THE ARMY CHOW AND WILL I GET ENOUGH FOR MY YOUNG GROWING BODY ?

HEE! HEE! I'M SURE YOU WILL, JUG! AFTER ALL, THEY SAY AN ARMY TRAVELS ON ITS STOMACH!

I HOPE IT'S NOT BECAUSE THEY ARE TOO WEAK FROM HUNGER TO WALK ON THEIR FEET!
HEY, ARCHIE, WHAT ARE YOU CATS DOING COMING OUT OF THE ARMY INDUCTION CENTER ?
UNITED STATES ARMY INDUCTION CENTER
2

OH! HI, CLYDE! I GUESS YOU MIGHT SAY THAT WE'RE ABOUT TO GIVE A COMMAND PERFORMANCE FOR OUR COUNTRY! WE'VE BEEN DRAFTED!
THAT'S FREAKY, MAN!

WHAT'S GOING TO HAPPEN TO THE ARCHIES' PEACE RALLY YOU WERE GOING TO GET TOGETHER?

WE'LL HAVE TO HOLD IT IN THE PARK SUNDAY AFTERNOON, CLYDE, BECAUSE WE GOT OUR ORDERS TO REPORT BACK MONDAY MORNING TO BE SHIPPED TO A PROCESSING CENTER!
DO YOU CATS WANT TO GO?

OF COURSE WE DON'T WANT TO GO! WHO IN HIS RIGHT MIND WOULD WANT TO GO AND MAYBE GET KILLED?

THEN GET WITH IT, CATS! PROTEST! REFUSE TO GO! BURN YOUR DRAFT CARD!
3

BURN OUR DRAFT CARDS? WHAT WOULD THAT PROVE?
IT WOULD SHOW OUR GOVERNMENT THAT WE NO LONGER WANT TO BE USED AS PAWNS IN A CHESS GAME FOR A SENSELESS WAR BY A FEW FORCEFUL POLITICIANS!

I MEAN, LET'S FACE IT, YOU DON'T SEE THE POLITICIANS RISKING THEIR LIVES ON A BATTLEFIELD! SO WHY SHOULD YOU?

AND YOU HAVE AS MUCH RIGHT TO STAY ALIVE AS THEY DO!
IT JUST SO HAPPENS THAT WE, THE PEOPLE ELECTED THEM AND GAVE THEM THE POWER! NEXT TIME WE WON'T!

I THINK I CAN SPEAK FOR MY BUDDIES, EVEN THOUGH WE ARE AS MUCH OPPOSED TO THE WAR AS ANYBODY ELSE --- WE DON'T INTEND TO COP OUT! THAT'S WRONG!
RIGHT!
4

ARCHIE IS RIGHT! THE ONLY WAY TO MAKE A BETTER SOCIETY FOR EVERYBODY IS BY TEAM WORK! NOT EACH MAN FOR HIMSELF!

BOY, YOU CATS ARE A PACK OF WEIRDOS! YOU SOUND JUST LIKE MOM'S APPLE PIE ESTABLISHMENT WHERE BOYS WERE BRAINWASHED INTO BELIEVING *OUR COUNTRY RIGHT OR WRONG*!

THAT'S A LOT OF BUNK, AND YOU KNOW IT, CLYDE! WE DON'T BELIEVE OUR COUNTRY *RIGHT* OR *WRONG*!

BUT WE DO KNOW THAT TWO *WRONGS* DON'T MAKE A *RIGHT*!
?
5

WHAT DO YOU MEAN BY THAT ?
I MEAN THAT VIOLENT WILD PROTESTING AND SENSELESS RIOTING NEVER REALLY ACCOMPLISHED ANYTHING BUT CONTEMPT AND FEAR !
I'LL GO ALONG WITH THAT !

IT'S LIKE TRYING TO PUT OUT A FIRE WITH GASOLINE, IT ONLY MAKES THE FIRE UNCONTROLLABLE !

AND IF WE DON'T HAVE ANY RESPECT FOR THE LAWS OF OUR COUNTRY, WE WILL HAVE NOTHING BUT CHAOS AND CONFUSION !

SURE, BUT, LOOK AT WHAT THE LEADERS ARE DOING TO OUR COUNTRY ! WHY, WE STILL HAVE WARS, BIGOTRY, AND NOW WE HAVE TO WORRY ABOUT MAN-MADE POLLUTION ! MAN, LET'S TELL IT LIKE IT IS, THIS IS WHY WE PROTEST !
6

WE MAKE THE ESTABLISHMENT AWARE OF THE FACT THAT WE WANT CHANGE, AND WE WANT IT NOW! NOT TOMORROW!

YEAH, CLYDE, YOU DO IT BY MAKING OUR VOICE HEARD-- BUT WITHOUT VIOLENCE!

ANYBODY CAN CRITICIZE AND BE DESTRUCTIVE! BUT IT TAKES SOUND REASONING AND FORESIGHT TO BE CONSTRUCTIVE!
LET'S GET OFF THIS RAP, FELLOWS! IT'S GETTING A LITTLE HEAVY!

WE'LL SEE YOU AT THE RALLY SUNDAY, CLYDE! STAY LOOSE!

I THINK I KNOW THE SONG WE'RE GOING TO LAY ON THEM AT OUR PEACE RALLY, FELLAS!
7

SUNDAY IN THE PARK--

I'D LIKE TO THANK ALL MY BROTHERS AND SISTERS FOR COMING TO OUR PEACE RALLY, AND WE WOULD LIKE TO PLAY A SPECIAL SONG WE HAVE WRITTEN FOR THE OCCASION! IT'S CALLED *SUMMER PRAYER FOR PEACE*, BUT BEFORE WE START I'D LIKE TO TELL IT AS IT IS!

THE Archies

PEACE NOW

LUV

LOVE

LOVE PEACE

I'M SPEAKING FOR THE ARCHIES, AND IT HAS TO DO WITH OUR COUNTRY, THE UNITED STATES OF AMERICA, THE LAND OF FREEDOM!
LOVE PEACE
THE TIME IS NOW!
LOVE

AND WITH THIS FREEDOM, WE HAVE THE RIGHT TO QUESTION AND PROTEST IF WE WISH TO!
8

WE HAVE MANY GROWING PROBLEMS IN OUR COUNTRY, WITH PROTESTING AGAINST EDUCATION, BIGOTRY, POLLUTION AND WE ARE EVEN ENGAGED IN A SENSELESS WAR IN WHICH THE ARCHIES HAVE BEEN DRAFTED TO DO OUR PART!
PEACE
LOVE
NOT WAR
LUV
LOVE

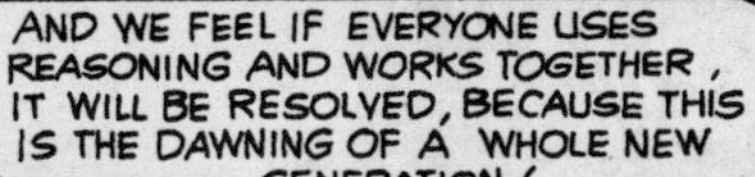
AND WE FEEL IF EVERYONE USES REASONING AND WORKS TOGETHER, IT WILL BE RESOLVED, BECAUSE THIS IS THE DAWNING OF A WHOLE NEW GENERATION!

WE DON'T THINK VIOLENCE OR PREJUDICE OF ANY KIND IS RIGHT, BUT WE DO KNOW ONE THING THAT IS VERY IMPORTANT TO ALL OF US!
PEACE
LUV

THIS IS OUR COUNTRY AND IT'S THE GREATEST! IT'S THE ONLY ONE OF ITS KIND IN THE WHOLE WORLD, SO LET'S NOT DESTROY IT!
PEACE
PEACE
LOVE
LOVE
9

THREE BILLION PEOPLE TOGETHER FOREVER
THREE BILLION PEOPLE SING A SUMMER PRAYER FOR PEACE
OH LOOK - LOOK AROUND YOU, SEE WHAT YOU HAVE DONE
WHERE'S THE WORLD THAT GOT INTENDED
WITH LOVE FOR EVERYONE
SING, SING OF FREEDOM
SING A SONG OF JOY
ALL TOGETHER MAKING BETTER
WHAT SOME WOULD DESTROY
HOW WILL IT END? HOW WILL IT END? HOW WILL IT END?
AMEN AMEN A --- MEN!
THE Archies
PEACE NOT WAR!
LOVE
PRAY FOR PEACE
READERS- REMEMBER THIS! THE ARCHIES ARE STILL A YEAR AWAY FROM BEING DRAFTED, BUT THIS IS THE WAY IT WOULD HAVE HAPPENED, THIS IS NOT REALLY THE END, BUT A MEANS TO AN END!
The End

# "Mister Jughead"

HERE'S MY QUARTER, MISTER JUGHEAD!

I'M SORRY, MISTER JUGHEAD! ALL I CAN GIVE YOU TODAY IS FIFTEEN CENTS!

NEVER MIND THE EXCUSES! YOU HAVE UNTIL FIVE O'CLOCK TO COUGH UP THE OTHER DIME!

HORROR! HORROR! HORROR!
YOU TWO LOOK AS THOUGH YOU'VE SEEN A GHOST! WHAT'S WRONG?
T-TELL THEM, BETTY!

I CAN'T! I JUST CAN'T SAY IT! IT'S TOO AWFUL!
OKAY! IF YOU CAN'T SAY IT, YOU CAN'T!
WE'RE NOT GOING TO FORCE IT OUT OF YOU!

IT'S JUGHEAD! HE'S TURNED INTO A FIEND! HE PREYS UPON LITTLE HELPLESS CHILDREN AND TAKES THEIR MONEY!
WE SAW HIM WITH OUR OWN EYES! HE WAS PUTTING THE MUSCLE ON THE LITTLE TYKES!
ONCE THEY OPEN UP IT REALLY DOES POUR OUT!
2

I KNEW THEY WOULDN'T BELIEVE US! THEY DON'T BELIEVE US! LOOK AT THEM! DO YOU THINK THEY BELIEVE US?
DO YOU OR DON'T YOU BELIEVE US?
I DON'T BELIEVE YOU!
BELIEVE ME, I'D LOVE TO BELIEVE SOMETHING ROTTEN ABOUT JUG— BUT THIS IS UNBELIEVABLE!

HOW DARE YOU? DO I EVER LIE TO YOU?

FREQUENTLY!
I'LL BUY THAT!

WHY DON'T YOU STICK TO THE SUBJECT? WE'RE TALKING ABOUT JUGHEAD AND HIS EVIL WAYS!

OKAY! OKAY! COOL IT! WE'LL GO WATCH JUGHEAD AND SEE FOR OURSELVES!
3

HERE'S MY QUARTER, MISTER JUGHEAD! SORRY I'M LATE!
OKAY! NEXT TIME BE EARLY!
I DON'T BELIEVE IT! IT LOOKS LIKE THE GIRLS WERE RIGHT!
WAIT! HERE COMES ANOTHER KID!
YOU WERE TEN CENTS SHORT LAST TIME!
I GOT IT, MR. JUGHEAD! SEE? THIRTY FIVE CENTS!
OKAY! SAME PLACE, SAME TIME NEXT WEEK! BE HERE!
YES, SIR! I'LL BE HERE, MR. JUGHEAD!
HE MAY BE YOUR GOOD BUDDY, BUT I'M IN FAVOR OF TAKING HIM APART PIECE BY PIECE!
FOR ONCE I AGREE WITH YOU!
MAN! ANYBODY WHO WOULD SINK SO LOW THAT---
HEY! HAVE YOU SEEN MR. JUGHEAD? I DIDN'T MISS HIM, DID I?
4

WE'RE GOING TO SEE "MISTER" JUGHEAD ANY MINUTE NOW, KID!
OH, GOOD! MAYBE YOU CAN HELP ME!
WOULD YOU GIVE HIM THIS QUARTER AND TELL HIM IT'S FROM JOEY?
FORGET IT, KID!
KEEP YOUR MONEY! THERE WILL BE NO MORE PAYMENTS TO "MISTER" JUGHEAD!
WHAM!
WAH!
HEY! WHAT'S WRONG, JOEY?
MISTER JUGHEAD! THEY TOLD ME I CAN'T GIVE YOU ANYMORE MONEY!
YOU GUYS OUGHT TO BE ASHAMED OF YOURSELVES!
FOR TRYING TO STOP YOU FROM STEALING THE KIDS' MONEY?
YOU'RE FOOLS! THEY WOULDN'T CRY IF I ROBBED THEM OF MONEY! MONEY ISN'T IMPORTANT TO KIDS THAT AGE!
THEN WHA..?
5

YOU GUYS ROBBED HIM OF A CHANCE TO DO SOMETHING FOR SOMEONE! YOU CHEATED HIM OF A CHANCE TO SHOW HIS LOVE!

HUH?
WHAT LOVE?
WE'RE COLLECTING FOR A TV SET FOR THE OLD FOLKS AT THE BAKER STREET NURSING HOME!

IT'S OKAY, JOEY! I'LL TAKE YOUR QUARTER! DON'T FORGET NEXT WEEK!
GEE, THANKS, MISTER JUGHEAD!

WELL, WERE WE RIGHT? WASN'T HE TAKING MONEY FROM THE KIDS?
MONEY? BAH! WHAT'S MONEY?

WHEN IT COMES TO REAL VALUES, YOU GO TALK TO MISTER JUGHEAD! HE KNOWS WHERE IT'S AT!
IF WE ASKED HIM REAL NICE, I WONDER IF HE'D TAKE OUR MONEY?
END

## The Big Think
## *Betty & Veronica* #208, 1973
## by Frank Doyle, Dan DeCarlo, Jim DeCarlo, Bill Yoshida

Worried about Dilton's stress, the girls decide he needs to meditate. Like everything about the mind, it comes way easy for our brainy pal! DeCarlo's work here shines. The fourth panel on page four make me laugh just to think about it! Great 1970s clothing styles, too!

## Quiet On the Set
## *Archie Annual* #26, 1975
## by Frank Doyle, Harry Lucey, Barry Grossman and Bill Yoshida

After watching TV and seeing the old movie *The Silent Years,* rolling with delight, Archie and Jugead imagine how their lives would have been in that era. Great classic Lucey slapstick! We get over four pages of wordless fun!

**Jack Copley**
*Archie Comics historian*

## The Book Mark
## *Jughead* #292, 1979
## by Frank Doyle, Samm Schwartz and Barry Grossman

In terms of my career in comics, I think Archie comics taught me an early lesson on the value of clearly establishing personalities for the reader to relate to, and probably influenced me in ways I'm not even totally aware of.

**B. Clay Moore**
*Writer,* ***Hawaiian Dick, Adventures of Superman, Vampire Diaries***

# Betty and Veronica in The BIG THINK

DILTON, WE'VE BEEN WATCHING YOU LATELY! WE'RE WORRIED!
YOU'VE BEEN VERY UPSET AND TENSE FOR THE PAST WEEK!

YEAH! I GET THAT WAY EVERY NOW AND THEN! I'M KINDA HIGH STRUNG, I GUESS!
TOO MANY THINGS ON MY MIND!

MEDITATE! THAT'S WHAT HE SHOULD DO! MEDITATE!
YOU SHOULD MEDITATE, DILTON!
ON WHAT?
1

WE GO TO YOGA CLASSES! WE'RE LEARNING TO ACQUIRE PEACE AND TRANQUILLITY THROUGH CONCENTRATION AND MEDITATION!

IS IT VERY HARD TO LEARN?
IT DOES TAKE A LITTLE TIME!

WE'VE ONLY BEEN AT IT FOR A MONTH, BUT I THINK WE'RE MAKING SOME PROGRESS!

WELL HOW DO YOU BEGIN? I'D LIKE TO GIVE IT A WHIRL!

CLOSE YOUR EYES! RELAX! THINK! CONCENTRATE ON BEING LOOSE--- TOTALLY RELAXED! YOU'RE A FORMLESS MASS OF GELATIN!

NOTHING MUST INTERFERE WITH THE THOUGHT OF TOTAL RELAXA---
PLOP!
2

WHAT HAPPENED?
HE FELL DOWN!

DILTON! PLEASE, DILTON! WHAT'S WRONG?
SLAP SLAP

HEY! WHY DID YOU WAKE ME? I WAS DOING REAL GREAT!
YOU FAINTED!

I DID? THAT'S STRANGE!
LET ME TRY THAT MEDITATION AGAIN! CLOSE THE EYES--- CONCENTRATE---

?
PLOP!
3

DILTON! DILTON! WAKE UP!
SHAKE! SHAKE! SHAKE!

ER-- MAYBE YOU'D BETTER NOT TRY IT!
WHY NOT? I'M JUST GETTING THE HANG OF IT!

WHAT'S GOING ON?

WE'VE BEEN TRYING TO TEACH DILTON PEACE AND TRANQUILLITY THROUGH CONCENTRATION!
DILTON! WAKE UP!

HI, GUYS! I ---

ZZZZZ ZZZ

WE'D BETTER TAKE HIM HOME, JUG!
WH-WHAT'S WRONG WITH HIM?
Z Z Z Z Z Z Z

YOU KNOW DILTON! HE'S GOT ALMOST TOTAL CONTROL OF HIS MIND! HE THINKS SLEEP AND BINGO---HE'S OUT!
SNAP

HE'S NOT LIKE THE REST OF US! WHEN HIS HEAD GIVES AN ORDER HIS BODY OBEYS!

IN THE FUTURE I WISH YOU GIRLS WOULDN'T FOOL WITH SOMETHING YOU KNOW NOTHING ABOUT!
WHAT'S THAT?

BRAINS!!
LET'S TAKE HIM HOME!
Z Z Z Z Z Z Z
5
The End

# Archie in "QUIET ON THE SET"

HEE, HEEE! HA, HOO! WHOEEE!

THAT WAS *FUNNEEE!*

WHAT WAS SO HILARIOUS, BOYS?

HEY! DID YOU EVER THINK WHAT IT WOULD BE LIKE IF LIFE WAS REALLY LIKE THAT?
CLICK!
THE HAMMING IT UP WITH THE EYES? THE JERKY MOVEMENTS? --- THE CHASE SCENES?
---IN THE SCHOOL HALLS? CAN YOU IMAGINE?
2

FETERIA
3

5

HEY! HOW DID WE GET SO WET?
MAYBE WE HAVE TOO MUCH IMAGINATION!
THE END

# Jughead THE BOOK MARK

HOW'S A GUY SUPPOSED TO ENJOY A GOOD BOOK WITH PEOPLE KICKING SAND IN HIS FACE?
YOU WANT TO READ?...GO TO THE LIBRARY!


Script: Frank Doyle / Art & Letters: Samm Schwartz / Colors: Barry Grossman

BEACHES ARE FOR FUN AND FROLIC!
IT'S LIKE THE MAN SAYS..."FUN AND FROLIC!"
"FUN AND FROLIC"? IT SOUNDS LIKE A LAW FIRM!

ANYWAY, I'M TAKING MYSELF AND MY BOOK AWAY FROM THIS WILD AND CRAZY CROWD!

YOU ARE ANTI-SOCIAL!
HOW **WELL** YOU UNDERSTAND ME!

OH, FOR PETE'S SAKE! THEY'RE ALL OVER THE PLACE!

THE TROUBLE WITH OUR POPULATION IS THAT IT'S FULL OF **PEOPLE**!
2

BY GUM! THAT'S IT! THE PERFECT HAVEN FOR A HERMIT!
YOU NEED OUR HELP TO GET AWAY FROM IT ALL?
FOLLOW ME!
HIM! I SEE! IT IS INACCESSIBLE!
AND YOU CAN'T GET TO IT, EITHER!
WAIT HERE! I'VE GOT A TOW ROPE IN THE CAR!
YOU GUYS ARE GOING TO LOWER ME DOWN TO THAT LEDGE!
YOU SURE YOU WANT THAT?
I WANT TO BE ABLE TO READ MY BOOK UNDISTURBED!
SAMM F. DOYLE
3

LET'S GO! GET THIS LOOP OVER YOUR HEAD AND PUT YOUR ARMS THROUGH IT!
HOLD THIS A MINUTE, CHUCK!

I HOPE YOU GUYS ARE STRONG ENOUGH FOR THIS!
YOU'RE NOT THAT HEAVY!

BUT LISTEN, I DON'T WANT TO LOSE THIS ROPE!
COOL IT!

WHEN I'M ON THE LEDGE, I'LL TAKE IT OFF AND YOU CAN HAUL IT UP!

THAT'LL LEAVE YOU STRANDED!
THAT'S EXACTLY WHAT I WANT!
4

FOR A GUY WHO EATS AS MUCH AS HE, HE'S AWFULLY LIGHT!

THAT'S IT, GUYS! I'VE LANDED!

TAKE IT AWAY!

HOW LONG DO YOU WANT US TO LEAVE YOU THERE?
I DON'T KNOW! I LIKE IT HERE! I MAY SET UP HOUSEKEEPING!
5

YOU'RE NUTS, JUG! BE SENSIBLE! WE'RE YOUR ONLY WAY OFF THAT LEDGE!

COME BACK FOR ME WHEN YOU'RE READY TO GO HOME!
OKAY! THAT'LL BE THREE OR FOUR HOURS!

HAPPY READING, OL' BUDDY!
THANKS, GUYS!

THAT MUST BE A GOOD BOOK! I'LL HAVE TO BORROW IT WHEN HE'S FINISHED!

SIGH! HOW COME EVERYTIME YOU GET A PERFECT PLAN..THERE'S ALWAYS **SOME** LITTLE THING!...
END

# THE BEST OF Archie COMICS BOOK FOUR

# THE 1980s

WOW! I WONDER WHO GAVE BETTY AND VERONICA THOSE FANTASTIC HAIRDOS?

IT'S A SHAME WE GOT CAUGHT IN THE RAIN, RONNIE!

Dan DeCarlo

## Women's Work
### *Laugh* #355, 1980
### by Dick Malmgren, Stan Goldberg, Jon D'Agostino, Bill Yoshida and Barry Grossman

For many North American teenagers, they are our first introduction to the world of comics. Sitting at the supermarket checkout, right next to the candy aisle, they sit with their bright, often garish colors. We reach for them as we reach for the tantalizingly packaged sweets. Sometimes, tired parents relent, and we get to take them home: our first comics, our Archie Comics.

**Brenna Clarke Gray**
*Writer & educator*

## Book Marked
### *Jughead* #298, 1980
### by Samm Schwartz
### &
## Input and Outlay
### *Archie and Me* #140, 1983
### by Frank Doyle, Dan DeCarlo, Jimmy DeCarlo, Bill Yoshida and Barry Grossman

As my business world expanded, I found out very quickly that I'd never lost my love for Archie and his friends. They remained—and remain—very dear to me. Many people have written eloquently about their timelessness or the different reasons for their continued appeal. It would be difficult to sing their praises in a way you haven't heard before, but surely the consistent combination of lively art, entertaining stories, solid values and adaptability have enabled their appeal to transcend the trends and fads of each successive era.

**Steve Geppi**
*Founder, Diamond Comic Distributors*
*(Excerpted from* ***Archie Americana: Best of the Eighties****)*

THAT WILKIN BOY
in
WOMEN'S WORK

NOW BE SENSIBLE, BINGO! WE'VE BEEN OVER THIS THING MANY TIMES BEFORE!

DON'T BE SUCH A CHAUVINIST!

YOU CAN'T EXPECT A GUY TO *LIKE* IT, SAMANTHA!

IT'S GOING TO HAPPEN, ISN'T IT? I MEAN, IT ALWAYS HAPPENS!
YEAH!

SO LET ME DO MY THING, AND YOU DO YOUR THING! OKAY?
ARGH!

Script: Dick Malmgren / Pencils: Stan Goldberg / Inks: Jon D'Agostino / Letters: Bill Yoshida / Colors: Barry Grossman

WE AGREED THAT IT'S PRACTICAL AND SENSIBLE.! WE AGREED.!
W-ELL, OKAY.!

MAN.! WILL YOU LOOK AT WHAT'S POURED INTO THAT BIKINI ?

ER- THAT WASN'T EXACTLY THE PROPER THING TO SAY.!
NOW AIN'T THAT A SHAME ?
TAP!

UH-BINGO.!
WHAT IS IT, SAMANTHA ?

WHAT DO YOU WEIGH, BIG MOUTH ?
AH.! I LIKE YOU WHEN YOU'RE ANGRY.!

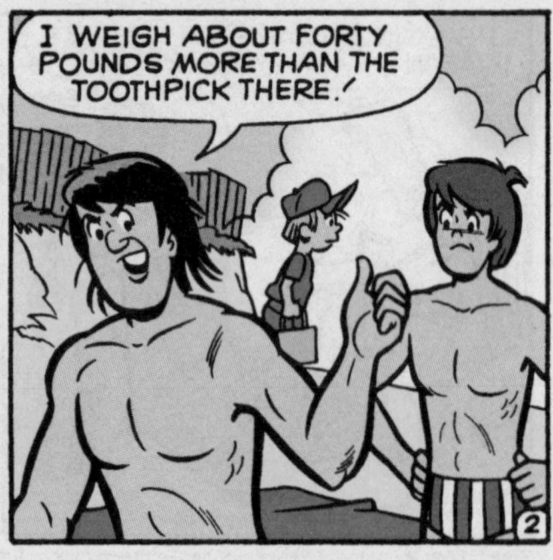
I WEIGH ABOUT FORTY POUNDS MORE THAN THE TOOTHPICK THERE.!
2

WELL, BINGO ?
SIGH! I GUESS YOU'RE RIGHT! HE'S YOURS!

NOW THAT'S SMART, KID! YOU'RE GIVING HER TO ME, HUH ?

SWOOSH!

SLAM!

I HATE TO BE HAVING ALL THE FUN!
IT'S ONLY FAIR, I GUESS! WE DID AGREE!

HEY, BABY! LOOK WHAT YOU JUST FOUND! ME!
3

HMM! LOOKS LIKE ONE OF YOURS AGAIN, SAMANTHA!

LOOK WHAT YOU'VE JUST FOUND, FELLOW! ME!

POW!

THAT LITTLE CREEP DID THAT TO YOU?
NO! I SAW IT ALL!
SHE DID IT!

YOU'RE KIDDIN'! SHE'S ONLY A GIRL!!
MAN! THERE'S NOTHIN' "ONLY" ABOUT THAT GIRL!

SHE'S DEADLY!
AN' THE GUY DIDN'T DO NOTHIN'?
4

HAH! WHAT KINDA MAN ARE YOU ANYWAY? HIDIN' BEHIND YER GIRL'S BIKINI?
AIN'T YOU ASHAMED?

NOW THAT'S JUST PLAIN SILLY!
WE HAVE AN AGREEMENT!

SAMANTHA HANDLES THE GUYS SHE THINKS I'D BE BULLYING...

...LIKE HANDLING YOU CREAM PUFFS!

THEN WHEN THE REAL TOUGH GUYS SHOW UP--I TAKE OVER!
GULP! I -ER- GOTTA GIT HOME!
SOMEBODY CALL ME?
S-SEE YOU GUYS!
End

MISS MARPLE! I'VE GOT TO GIVE A TALK IN CLASS! WHERE DO I GO TO FIND SOME JUNK ON THE ANCIENT SUMERIANS?

# Jughead
## BOOK MARKED

SHH..

SORRY 'BOUT THAT, MISS MARPLE!
50-820

QUIET!

NOW, NOW, JANET! GET A GRIP ON YOURSELF!

MAN! WHY SHOULD ANYONE WANT TO WRITE SO MUCH ABOUT PEOPLE WHO AREN'T AROUND ANYMORE?
THUNK!
2

THIS LOOKS TOO DULL!
PRINT'S TOO SMALL!
SO'S THIS!
HE WAS SENT HERE TO TORMENT ME! I JUST KNOW IT!
WHAM
BANG
WHAP

WILL YOU PLEASE BE QUIET?
I HAVEN'T SAID A WORD, MISS MARPLE!

STOP THROWING THOSE BOOKS DOWN SO NOISILY! DIG?
DIG!

BOY! SHE'S REALLY ON MY BACK TODAY!

CRASH
3

HE'S **STILL** THUMPING BOOKS ABOUT!

I BETTER MAKE TRACKS... BUT FAST!

WHILE SHE GOES DOWN **THAT** AISLE, I'LL...

4

RIVERDALE PUBLIC LIBRARY
MAYBE I'LL GIVE MY TALK ON, "LIBRARIANS AND THE ABUSE OF POWER!"
END

# Archie and Me in "Input and Outlay"

GOLLEE, MR. WEATHERBEE! YOU GOT A COMPUTER!!
YES, ARCHIE! I HAVE TO KEEP UP WITH THE TIMES!

Script: FRANK DOYLE Pencils: DAN DeCARLO Inks: JIMMY DeCARLO Lettering: BILL YOSHIDA Colors: BARRY GROSSMAN

YOU'RE KIDDING ME!
NO! I CAN TEACH YOU!

I KNOW HOW TO PROGRAM AND ALL THAT STUFF!
YOU DO? BUT THAT'S WONDERFUL!

I WANT TO PROGRAM ALL THE SCHOOL RECORDS--HOW EACH STUDENT DOES, DAY BY DAY!
EASY!

THEN WE CAN GET RID OF ALL OUR FILES, AND SAVE OODLES OF SPACE!
WE CAN DO IT WEEK TO WEEK, AND YEAR BY YEAR!

WE CAN ANSWER QUESTIONS - SUCH AS, WHETHER IT WOULD BE CHEAPER TO CLOSE THE CAFETERIA, OR EXPEL JUGHEAD!

AND, IF YOU'RE A PROGRAMMER, WE CAN SAVE MONEY BY NOT HIRING A PROFESSIONAL TO DO IT!
OF COURSE! I CAN SAVE THE SCHOOL A BUNDLE!

I'LL JUST HAVE TO CHECK OUT YOUR COMPUTER, BECAUSE IT'S NOT THE SAME AS THE ONE I LEARNED ON!
2

HOW LONG WILL IT TAKE YOU?
I DON'T KNOW, SIR! I'LL HAVE TO PLAY WITH IT FOR A WHILE!

FINE, ARCHIE! I'LL GO AND LEAVE YOU ALONE WITH IT!

MMM! BRAND-NEW! BLANK! NOTHING ON IT! WOW! IT'S ALL MINE!

I'LL JUST CHECK TO SEE HOW THE LITTLE DARLIN' WORKS! I'LL START BY FEEDING IT A LITTLE PERSONAL INPUT!

A LITTLE OF THIS, A LITTLE OF THAT! JUST ENOUGH TO GET THE FEEL OF IT!
KLIK KLIK KLIK KLIK

THE THING I LIKE BEST IN THIS WORLD IS GETTING SOMETHING FOR NOTHING!- AND HAVING ARCHIE PROGRAM OUR COMPUTER IS EXACTLY THAT!

OKAY, CHIEF! WHY DO YOU LOOK LIKE THE CAT WHO SWALLOWED THE CANARY?
AH, MISS GRUNDY! WAIT UNTIL YOU HEAR!
3

ARCHIE IS GOING TO PROGRAM OUR NEW COMPUTER!
GOOD GRIEF! FOR A MINUTE I THOUGHT YOU SAID, "ARCHIE"!
WHY NOT? I'LL SINK TO ANY DEPTH TO SAVE MONEY!
I'M NOT TOO PROUD TO LEARN FROM MY STUDENTS!
OR BRIGHT ENOUGH TO LEARN FROM BITTER EXPERIENCE!
IF I WANTED TO PLAY GAMES, RIDE A CYCLE, LEARN HANG-GLIDING - WHERE WOULD I GO?
TO KIDS?
OF COURSE! NEVER BE ASHAMED TO ADMIT YOUR SOURCE OF KNOWLEDGE!
EVEN IF IT'S ARCHIE?
EVEN IF IT'S ARCHIE!
PRINC
4

NEXT WEEK:
WELL, HOW'S MY NEW COMPUTER, ARCHIE?
JUST FINE, SIR!

---THEN YOU DO THIS, AND THEN THIS--- THEN THIS, AND THIS---
RIGHT! RIGHT! I THINK I'VE GOT IT!

THANK YOU VERY MUCH, ARCHIE!
MY PLEASURE, SIR!

WELL, WELL! MY VERY OWN COMPUTER AND I DIDN'T HAVE TO PAY SOME EXPERT TO TEACH ME HOW TO USE IT!

WATCHING THE SOAPS AGAIN, CHIEF?
VERY FUNNY, GRUNDY!

SERIOUSLY THOUGH, HOW DID ARCHIE DO, PROGRAMMING YOUR COMPUTER?
OH, MARVELOUSLY!

(SIGH) HE'S FILLED THIS WONDERFUL ELECTRONIC BRAIN WITH THINGS I'VE ALWAYS WANTED TO KNOW!
5

FOR EXAMPLE-- ANY GIVEN WEEK, ARCHIE HAS A 37.5% CHANCE OF DATING VERONICA ON A FRIDAY!
TSK! IMAGINE THAT!

-AS OPPOSED TO ONLY 17.7% CHANCE ON SATURDAY!
A VERITABLE GOLD MINE OF IMPORTANT FACTS!

I CAN ALSO GIVE YOU THE STATISTICS ON 18 OTHER LOVELY GIRLS WHO MIGHT BE AVAILABLE TO ARCHIE!

THE WONDERS OF MODERN SCIENCE! SEVERAL THOUSAND DOLLARS, TO LEARN ALL YOU EVER WANTED TO KNOW ABOUT ARCHIE'S LOVE LIFE!

I HATE TO SAY THIS, BUT I ALREADY KNEW MORE THAN I EVER WANTED TO KNOW ABOUT THAT SUBJECT!
SIGH!
AMEN TO THAT, MISS G.! AMEN TO THAT!
PRINCIPAL
?
The End

## Crowning Glory
## *Jughead* #330, 1983
### by Frank Doyle, Samm Schwartz and Barry Grossman

*Frank Doyle and Samm Schwartz are truly rare talents in that they never seemed to lose their creative spark in the slightest—just as razor-sharp and truly funny here as they had been more than 20 years earlier.*

## Living Legend in Logger's Pond
## *Archie Giant Series* #583, 1988
### Bob Bolling, Mike Esposito, Bill Yoshida and Barry Grossman

Any Bob Bolling Little Archie tale deserves to be in a *Best of Archie* book! In just five pages Little Archie and Jughead get in very real peril, survive and are thankful for their rescue! Did the Perilous Pike of Logger's Pond save his would-be captors' lives? The story leaves us wondering if that would truly be possible.

**Jack Copley**
*Archie Comics historian*

## Karma Comedy
## *Jughead* #11, 1989
### by Rod Ollerenshaw, Rex Lindsey, Jon D'Agostino, Bill Yoshida and Barry Grossman

*Archie* is one of the first comics I enjoyed in my youth. Archie and crew (especially Jughead) moulded my psyche during those formative years, which in turn may explain quite a bit. He's like the brother I never had... but the friends I eventually would.

**Ramón K. Pérez**
*Award-winning cartoonist,*
***Jim Henson's Tale Of Sand***

Jughead
CROWNING GLORY
JINGLE JINGLE
YOU SAY SOMETHING, BETTY?
NOT A WORD!
NO PEEKING
BE A SWEETIE- WIPE OUT GRAFFITI
I'D HAVE SWORN YOU SAID, "JINGLE JINGLE!"
WHY WOULD I SAY THAT?
I DON'T KNOW! MAYBE TO MAKE CONVERSATION!
I'D HOPE I COULD DO BETTER THAN THAT!
LIKE "NICE WEATHER, DON'T YOU THINK?" OR "HOW'S YOUR MOTHER?" IF I JUST WANTED TO MAKE SMALL TALK!

THERE! I JUST HEARD IT AGAIN! IT'S COMING FROM BEHIND THE FENCE!
ANYTHING UNUSUAL BACK THERE?
JUST A COUPLE OF BALD GUYS WITH FLOWING, STRIPED ROBES AND BELLS AROUND THEIR WAISTS!
THAT SOUNDS PRETTY UNUSUAL TO ME!
I'VE SEEN STRANGER THINGS!
ONCE I SAW MY UNCLE HARRY EAT A WHOLE JAR OF PEANUT BUTTER!
LOTS OF PEOPLE HAVE DONE THAT!
WITHOUT OPENING THE JAR? POOR GUY COULDN'T TALK FOR A WEEK!
WHAT WERE THOSE TWO MEN DOING BEHIND THE FENCE?
NOT MUCH! THEY WERE BOTH KIND OF CROUCHED DOWN LOOKING UP AT ME!
2

OH YEAH! ONE OF THEM HAD A BIG SACK, LIKE THE KIND YOU PUT POTATOES IN!
IT SEEMS TO ME THE MEN IN STRIPED ROBES, CROUCHING BEHIND A FENCE, ARE A BIT MORE BIZARRE THAN YOUR UNCLE!
?
JUGGIE? NOW WHERE DID HE GO?
THERE'S NOBODY BACK HERE! WHO'S HE TRYING TO KID?
BALD MEN IN STRIPED ROBES WITH BELLS! WHAT A JOKER THAT BOY IS!
MAKE SURE HE'S TIED SECURELY!
MAY I ASK WHERE YOU GUYS ARE TAKING ME?
QUIET, THIEF!
3

THIEF? WELL, LA-DEE-DA! AREN'T WE THE NAME-CALLERS? CHROME DOMES! BELL-WEARERS! KIDNAPPERS!

AND DIDN'T ANYONE EVER TELL YOU THAT STRIPES MAKE YOU LOOK **SKINNY**!?
WE HAD TO GET A WISE GUY!

YOU'D BE IRRITABLE TOO IF SOMEBODY PUT A SACK OVER **YOUR** HEAD AND SHOVED YOU INTO A VAN!
LOVE

CAN'T YOU STICK A SOCK INTO HIS MOUTH, OR SOMETHING?
YOU KNOW WHAT THE BIGA SHEESH SAYS! "SPEECH IS THE LIFE FORCE OF THE MIND...

...AND CAN BE STOPPED NO MORE THAN THE BREATH OF THE BODY!"
HEY! THAT'S QUITE A MOUTHFUL OF LIFE FORCE! WHO **IS** THIS BIG CHEESE, ANYWAY?
LOVE

THAT'S BIGA SHEESH, YOU USURPER!
I'M NOT A **SURFER**!

I SAID "USURPER!" THAT'S ONE WHO TAKES THE PLACE OF ONE WHOSE PLACE IS IRREPLACEABLE!
HELLO? I THINK WE HAVE A BAD CONNECTION!
4

WE'RE HERE! GET HIM INSIDE!
GLADLY! I WANT TO GET HIM OUT OF MY HAIR!
YOU GREW HAIR?
HEY! NICE PLACE YOU GOT HERE! A LITTLE GAUDY, BUT I CAN TELL YOU'RE A FLAMBOYANT LITTLE GROUP!
THIS IS THE USURPER?
YES, YOUR CHEESI.. I MEAN, SHEESHINESS! HE WEARS THE CROWN!
B.S.
I WANT IT! GIVE ME THE CROWN!
HEY!
THE LAW OF OUR SECT PROHIBITS VIOLENCE! BUT, BOY, ARE YOU GONNA GET IT IN THE AFTERLIFE!
AND IF I DON'T GET MY HAT BACK, YOU'RE GONNA GET IT IN THIS LIFE!
WITH THE WEARING OF THIS CROWN THE LAWS OF THE GREAT GOD, HAROLD, ARE RESTORED!
HAROLD?
HEY! THIS AIN'T MY CROWN!
5

THIS IS SIZE 7 1/4! I TAKE A SIZE 6 3/4 CROWN! YOU GUYS GOOFED!
HERE, KID! TAKE YOUR STUPID-LOOKING CROWN AND GET LOST! SHEE-EESH!
JUGGIE! WHERE HAVE YOU BEEN?
I'VE BEEN OFF BY MYSELF, THINKING...
I'M A FAIRLY TOLERANT, EASY-GOING PERSON, AREN'T I, BETTY?
I WOULD SAY SO!
WELL, I'VE DECIDED I JUST CAN'T HAVE ANY RESPECT FOR A GROUP OF GUYS THAT WORSHIPS A GOD NAMED HAROLD!
EASY-GOING?... YES! TOLERANT? YES! EASY TO TOLERATE? NO!
END

THE PERILOUS PIKE... SOME CALL HIM A LIVING LEGEND AND SWEAR HE CAN'T BE CAUGHT...
...THEY SAY THERE'S ALWAYS A BENT HOOK LODGED IN HIS POWERFUL JAW AND WHEN IT RUSTS OUT...HE LOOKS FOR ANOTHER JUST TO STAY MEAN... THAT'S THE PERILOUS PIKE OF LOGGER'S POND---
Little Jughead
(PUFF!) (PANT!) WHEEZE! I CAN'T KEEP THIS UP, LITTLE ARCHIE!
COOL IT, JUGGIE! FROM HERE ON IT'S ALL DOWN-HILL TO LOGGER'S POND!
"LIVING LEGEND IN LOGGER'S POND"
LOOK AT THE POND!
COVERED WITH FOG!
NAW! IT'S JUST THE MORNING MIST... IT'LL LIFT REAL SOON... ...BESIDES, YOU GOTTA GET HERE REAL EARLY TO CATCH THE PERILOUS PIKE!

I FIGURE THIS TIME I'VE GOT A REAL GOOD CHANCE TO CATCH THE PERILOUS PIKE... I'M GONNA USE A RUBY-EYED WARBLE PLUG WITH SEQUINS AND A BUILT-IN RATTLE ON A SEVENTY-FIVE POUND TEST LINE!

I'M STICKIN' WITH WORMS 'N' STRING!

SOON...

"MORNING MIST"!! THIS IS *FOG*, LITTLE ARCHIE!

SHH! YOU'RE SCARIN' THE FISH!

JUG, PUSH US CLOSER TO THOSE LILY PADS SO'S I CAN CAST NEXT TO 'EM!

JUG! DO YOU HEAR WHAT I HEAR!?!
D-DOES IT KINDA SOUND L-LIKE-
FOSSIL FALLS?
ROAR!

3

WE'RE MOVIN' FASTER 'N' FASTER TOWARDS THE FALLS!
IF WE GO OVER, WE COULD GET KI---
HUH ?
ZZZZZZZ
A STRIKE!
A BIG ONE!... HAFTA SET THE DRAG!
WHAT A TIME TO THINK ABOUT FISHIN'!
JUG! MAYBE, JUST MAYBE--
LITTLE ARCHIE, WE'RE SLOWIN' DOWN--- TURNIN' AROUND, AN'-AN'-
GOIN' BACK... AGAINST THE CURRENT!
HELP! GRAB ME, JUG!!
I-I CAN'T HOLD ON MUCH LONGER!
YOU'VE GOT TO! WHATEVER'S OUT THERE IS PULLIN' US TO SAFETY!
WE'RE GOIN' INTO THOSE ROCKS!
WONDER HOW SHALLOW IT IS THERE?
NEE-DEEP!
4

I THINK WE'RE STUCK!
BUT GOOD!
KRUNCH!

LOOK! THE PERILOUS PIKE!
SNAP!
SNAPPED MY SEVENTY-FIVE POUND TEST LINE LIKE IT WAS THREAD!

THIS WAY! I CAN SEE SHORE!
THAT RAFT'S NOT WORTH SAVIN'!

Script: Rod Ollerenshaw / Pencils: Rex Lindsey / Inks: Jon D'Agostino / Letters: Bill Yoshida / Colors: Barry Grossman

ONE DAY JUGHEAD WAS WALKING DOWN THE STREET!
WHAT A BEAUTIFUL DAY!
STOP
BOOM!
HEY! MY HAT!
WHOOSH!
OH, NO! GONE FOREVER! CHOKE
SLURP!
AND THEN... HEH, HEH
WELL, I STILL HAVE YOU, PAL!
GRRRRR
YOW! WHAT'S GOTTEN INTO YOU, HOT DOG?
RUFF!
2

MAN! WHAT'S HIS PROBLEM?
GGRRRRR
WHEW SANCTUARY!
POP'S CHOC'LIT SHOP
AH, JUGHEAD! WHAT'LL IT BE? A HAMBURGER? STEAK? CHOPS...
YEAH, BUT I'M A LITTLE BROKE RIGHT NOW!
PUFF
NO, PROBLEM! YOUR CREDIT IS GOOD HERE!
SOMETHING'S FINALLY GOING GOOD TODAY!
HERE, THE HOUSE SPECIAL...BROCCOLI FLORETS!
DIG-IN!
OH! YUK...
PPTUIII!
IS SOMETHING WRONG?
THIS TASTES AWFUL!
OH, REALLY...?
3

WHADDYA WANT FOR NOTHING?...
BOOT!
GET OUTTA HERE, YA BUM! AND DON'T COME BACK... EVER!
POP'S SECRET ANTI-JUG POTION
HOT PEPPERS
EVER...?

AND HOW ABOUT...
WHAT A SIGHT FOR SORE EYES! MY BEST PAL...
ARCHIE!

GUESS AGAIN, NEEDLENOSE! I'M REGGIE'S BEST PAL!
EEP!

HE LOOKS A LITTLE DOWN ON HIS LUCK, DOESN'T HE, BUDDY?
THAT HE DOES, CHUM!
GASP!

MAIL FOR JUGHEAD JONES!
THANKS!
F-FMEH
THEY'RE "GOODBYE JUGHEAD" LETTERS FROM DEBBIE, JOANI AND ETHEL!
AND THEY'RE FORM LETTERS, TOO! I'VE BEEN DUMPED IN TRIPLICATE!
WELL, AT LEAST IT STOPPED RAINING!
KA-BOOM!
GOOD GRIEF!
5

THAT'LL SHOW THAT RAT!
IS AN IDIOT
HUH? WHAT'S GOING ON HERE?
NO. 2
ERASE! ERASE! ERAS
YOU'RE NOT THE ONLY ONE WHO CAN INFLUENCE THE CREATIVE TALENT AROUND HERE! I'M SENDING THE ARTIST ON A LITTLE VACATION!
...AND HERE'S MY VERSION OF THE STORY'S ENDING!
10¢ A THROW
GO APE! HIT THE BOOB AND WIN A BOOBY PRIZE!
CIRCUS
ADIOS!
ROTTEN TOMATO
ROTTEN TOMATO
THE END
6

# THE BEST OF Archie® COMICS BOOK FOUR

# The 1990s

## Moose!
## *Pals 'n' Gals* #222, 1991
## by Mark Waid, Chris Allan, Bill Yoshida and Barry Grossman

This is one of the funniest stories of the '90s in my opinion... AND it is written by someone who went on to be one of the most renowned comic book writers of the past two decades: Mark Waid! It also features humorous, animated art from Chris Allan, who became the most popular of Archie's *Teenage Mutant Ninja Turtles* artists.

**Paul Castiglia**
*Writer and archivist,*
*Archie Comics*

## *Betty & Veronica: Summer Fun* #1, 1994
## By Dan Parent and Henry Scarpelli

*This cover features another new take on the classic triangle.*

## For One Brief Moment
## *Betty* #43, 1996
## by C.J. Henderson, Doug Crane, Mike Esposito, Bill Yoshida and Barry Grossman

It's the event of the century as Betty falls in love with... *gasp*... Riverdale's bad boy, Reggie Mantle! Yes, it's the story you thought you'd never see. It all starts when Reggie saves Betty's life. Soon, they're dating every weekend! Of course, an event like this is enough to cause repercussions throughout Riverdale High! Now, Archie can date Veronica without competition from Reggie and Veronica doesn't have to worry about Betty chasing Archie anymore. Everyone's happy, right? WRONG! Archie and Veronica are having a hard time dealing with this shake-up in the routine. What will happen? Will Reggie and Betty stay steady? Will Reggie become a rat once more? What tricks do Archie and Veronica have up their sleeves? Move over, Melrose Place—this one's got it all!

**Paul Castiglia**

Story and Art: Mark Waid and Chris Allan, Letters: Bill Yoshida, Colors: Barry Grossman

OH, NO! REMEMBER WHAT HAPPENED LAST TIME MOOSE GOT ANGRY!
IT TOOK A FIRE HOSE TO COOL HIM OFF!
NOW, DON'T PANIC! IT MIGHT NOT BE SO... WHAT'S THAT FLYING THIS WAY?
IT LOOKS ALMOST... HUMAN!
POP'S
MIDGE ...FREE!
JUG?
WHAP!
JUG? BUDDY? SPEAK TO ME!
MOOSE... COMING ... RAMPAGE...
... MAIN STREET ...FLAMES...
OH, NO...
...THINGS... BROKEN...
OKAY... STAY CALM! RIVERDALE'S STILL SAFE IF WE CAN GET MIDGE AND MOOSE BACK TOGETHER...
...BEFORE REGGIE MOVES IN ON MIDGE...REGGIE? REGGIE?!
2

LATER, DOWNTOWN...

AAAAAAAHHHHRRRR!

SO... MY LOQUACIOUS-- UMMM-- COMPATRIOT--

...IT IS I... DILTON DOILEY, GENIUS BOY... HERE TO CON--

-- UMM-- CONCILIATE YOUR DISPOSITION AND ASSUAGE YOUR SEETHING RAGE!

DILTON... FRIEND?

OF COURSE I'M DILTON! CAN'TCHA TELL BY ALL THE BIG WORDS, YOU...

...OOPS!

3

NOT DILTON!
♪

OH, MY!
JUST IN THE NICK OF TIME!
AH, MIDGE... MY SWEET SPRING FLOWER OF LOVE...
OH, REGGIE!

READY?
SET!
MAYBE JUST ONE LITTLE KISS...
THAT'S THE SPIRIT!

GO!
SHOOP

ONWARD! TO MOOSE– AND SALVATION!
REGGIE!
♥
4

AND SO...
YIPES! THAT MUST HAVE BEEN ONE HECKUVA FIGHT YOU TWO HAD, MIDGE!
IT'S UP TO YOU, GIRL... ONLY YOU CAN SAVE RIVERDALE NOW! TALK TO THE BOY!

NOPE!
WHAT!?

MIDGE-- WE'RE ALL GOING TO BE GRAPE JELLY IN ABOUT TWO SECONDS! NOW MAKE UP WITH MOOSE!
I REFUSE! HE DOESN'T CARE ABOUT ME!

MIDGE-- IF HE DIDN'T CARE... WOULD HE DO THIS?!
HYDRANTS... BILLBOARDS ...CARNAGE...
WELL... I...

OH, MOOSE, YOU BIG LUG... YOU'D REND AN INNOCENT MAN LIMB FROM LIMB... JUST FOR ME?
DUH... I... HUH?
MASON
SKIP IT, LOVER-BOY! JUST BRING THOSE MARVELOUS MOOSELIPS TO MAMA!
DUH-H... MIDGE, BABY--YER THE GREATEST!
OH, MAN! NICE WORK, BETS! WHAT A RELIEF--EVERYONE'S FINALLY OUT OF DANGER!
HEY, MIDGE! HOW ABOUT THAT KISS?
YOU WERE SAYING?
END

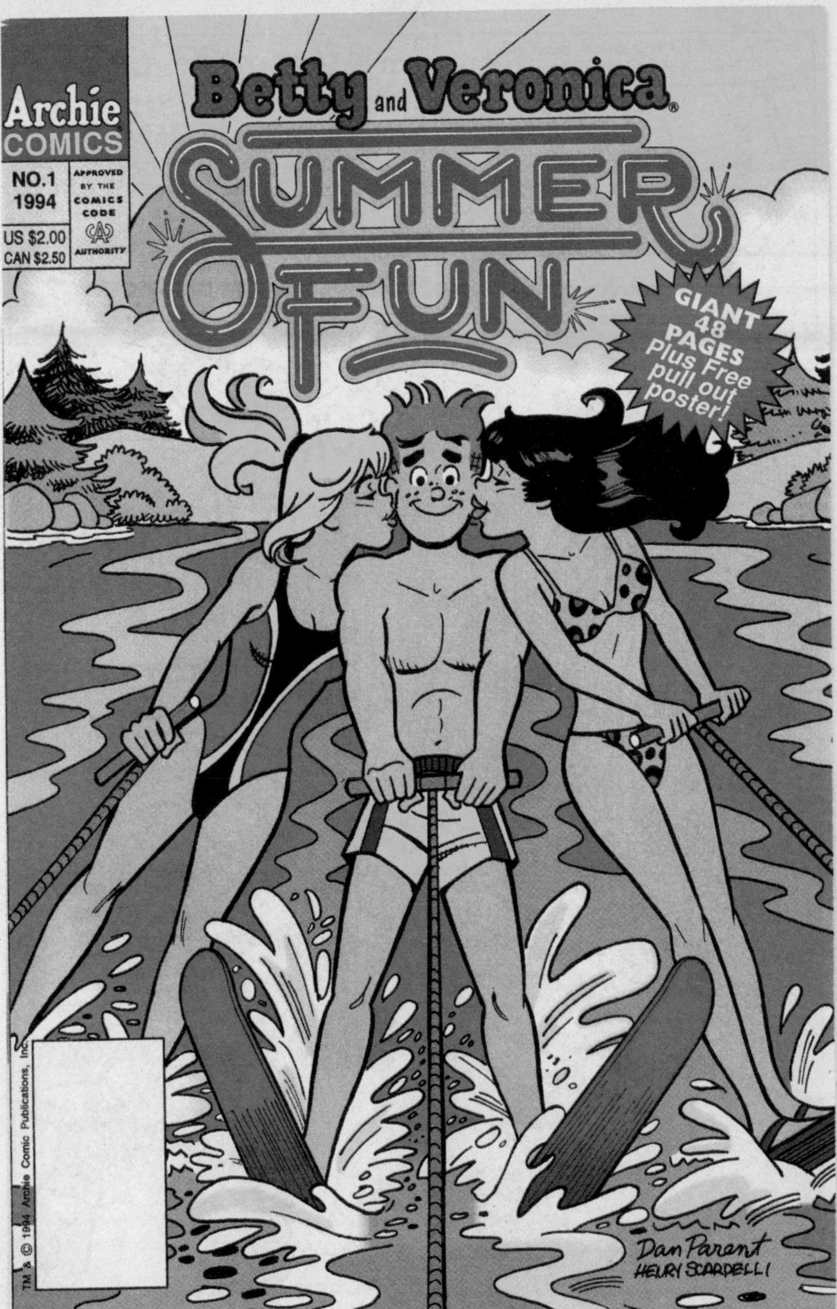
Archie
COMICS
NO.1
1994
APPROVED BY THE COMICS CODE AUTHORITY
US $2.00
CAN $2.50
Betty and Veronica
SUMMER FUN
GIANT 48 PAGES Plus Free pull out poster!
Dan Parent
HENRY SCARPELLI
TM & © 1994 Archie Comic Publications, Inc.

GOTTA GET TO THE SALE BEFORE THE STORE CLOSES!
HUH ?! HEY!
OOOOOOF!
BEEEEE EEEEP!
WHAP!
WATCH IT, GRANDMA!
Betty IN..
"FOR ONE BRIEF MOMENT" PART I
SKREEEEEEEEEEEEEEEE
YOU OKAY, BETTY?
O-OKAY?
BUS

REGGIE... YOU CAME OUT OF NOWHERE! YOU... YOU SAVED MY LIFE!
HEY, FORGET IT! I WAS JUST ACROSS THE STREET!
BESIDES, IT WAS NOTHING ANY OTHER INCREDIBLY HANDSOME STAR ATHLETE COULDN'T HAVE DONE!

MAYBE... BUT YOU WERE THE ONLY INCREDIBLY HANDSOME STAR ATHLETE AROUND WHEN I NEEDED ONE!

ONE WEEK LATER...
BIG BOX! WHAT'S IN IT?
A LIST OF ANDREWS' FAULTS?
JUST OPEN IT!

GEE, BETTY... IT'S BEAUTIFUL! THANKS!
I KNITTED IT FOR YOU TO REPLACE THE ONE YOU RUINED KEEPING ME ALIVE!

SOMETHING THIS NICE DESERVES TO BE SEEN! WANT TO GO TO THE MOVIES WITH ME TONIGHT AND WATCH PEOPLE ADMIRE YOUR HANDIWORK?
SURE! WHY NOT? I HAVEN'T BEEN ESCORTED TO THE THEATER BY A HERO IN AGES!
2

AND LATER...
OH, REGGIE! THAT WAS SUCH A BEAUTIFUL MOVIE ...AND HERE I THOUGHT WE'D END UP SEEING THE HORROR FILM!
THEATRE 1
"FOR ONE BRIEF MOMENT"
NO WAY! A SWEATER THIS CLASSY NEEDED TO BE SEEN BY AN UPSCALE CROWD!
2 "NO FRE
LUNCH"
BLOOD POOL IV
HMMMM! REGGIE'S BEING SO NICE! I WISH ARCHIE COULD BE THIS CONSIDERATE ONCE IN A WHILE!!
...THANKS AGAIN FOR EVERYTHING, REGGIE!
OH, THAT WASN'T EVERYTHING! HERE!
COOPER
REGGIE! IT'S SO BEAUTIFUL! BUT I COULDN'T POSSIBLY ACCEPT IT!
HEY! YOU WENT AND MADE ME A SWEATER! ALL I DID WAS BUY THIS ONE SO WE'D BE EVEN!
BUT YOU TOOK ME TO THE MOVIES, TOO!
THE ONLY WAY WE COULD EVEN THINGS UP IS IF I TOOK YOU TO THE MOVIES TOMORROW!
OKAY, DEAL!
SEE YA TOMORROW!
AND...
3

26
FROM...

THOSE...

SMALL...

BEGINNINGS...

SURE HAS BEEN QUIET WITH BETTY AND REGGIE DATING ALL THE TIME...
DOESN'T THAT GIVE YOU VERONICA... ALL TO YOURSELF.... JUST LIKE YOU ALWAYS WANTED?
UH...WELL, SORTA, I GUESS!
Special

TROUBLE IN PARADISE, AMIGO?

I DON'T KNOW, JUG! I MEAN, AT FIRST I THOUGHT IT WAS JUST THAT I MISSED BETTY'S HELP WITH MY CAR...
UMMMM... THE OL' GIRL COULD STAND A LOOK-AT!
ARCH 1

AND DATING RONNIE FULL-TIME IS EXPENSIVE!
TRUE! TRUE!
SO I THOUGHT MAYBE I WAS JUST MISSING BETTY'S PRACTICALITY!

THEN I THOUGHT IT WAS HELP WITH MY STUDYING...
WHICH YOU SORELY NEED!

BUT LATELY I'VE BEEN THINKING... I JUST PLAIN MISS BETTY!

VERONICA LODGE! YOU MISS REGGIE MANTLE?
I KNOW IT SOUNDS DEMENTED, BUT THE BOY DOES HAVE THAT WICKED LITTLE MEAN STREAK THAT CAN BE SOOOO MUCH FUN!
BUT WHAT ABOUT ARCHIE?
5

OH MY PRECIOUS LITTLE ARCHIEKINS! I CAN'T HAVE HIM TAKING ME FOR GRANTED!
MY GOING OUT WITH REGGIE TONIGHT WILL TAKE CARE OF THAT!
HELLO, MRS. MANTLE! IS REGGIE HOME?
WELL, IF YOU MISS HER, CALL HER!
YOU'RE RIGHT, JUG!
IN FACT, I'M NOT JUST GOING TO CALL HER, I'M GOING TO ASK HER OUT FOR TONIGHT!
SUPER DOOPER TRIPLE SCOOPER
AND...
GOSH, ARCH... WHAT'D SHE SAY?
I CAN'T BELIEVE IT...
HE
SHE
SAID NO!
CONTINUED 6

"FOR ONE BRIEF MOMENT" PART II
I JUST TURNED DOWN A DATE WITH...
VERONICA FOR BETTY?!!
ARCHIE FOR REGGIE?!!
WAIT A MINUTE! WHAT'S GOING ON HERE...?

I CAN'T HAVE THIS! NO BOY TURNS DOWN A DATE WITH VERONICA LODGE!
BUT, RONNIE...
NO BOY!

JUG.. BETTY! OUR BETTY! DEAR, SWEET BETTY!
BLONDE GIRL, CUTE SMILE, ABOUT SO HIGH... DATES SOME GUY NAMED MANTLE, RIGHT?
BURGERS
HOT DOGS
TUNA
HAM & EGG
CHICKEN
B.L.T.

WELL,...NOT FOR LONG!
GONNA GET HER UNCLUTCHED, EH?
YOU'LL SEE! I'LL FIGURE OUT THE BEST, MOST IRRESISTIBLE DATE IN TOWN!

I'M GOING TO FIGURE OUT HOW TO BREAK THOSE TWO UP, ONCE AND FOR ALL!
7

THIS IS GETTING SERIOUS!
WE HAVE BEEN SPENDING A LOT OF TIME TOGETHER, LATELY!
I MEAN, I LIKE BETTY AND ALL, BUT I'D BETTER THINK ABOUT THIS!
"I'VE BEEN CHANGING ... I HAD A PERFECT CHANCE TO STICK IT TO OL' NEEDLENOSE THE OTHER DAY! I LET IT GO BY BECAUSE I WAS WITH BETTY..."
IT'S LIKE I'M STARTING TO TURN INTO SOME KIND OF NERD...
YIIIIII!
THAT'S NOT FAIR!
BETTY'S SO NICE, SO CARING ...AND SHE DOES MAKE A GUY FEEL SPECIAL!
YOU WANT TO LOSE ALL THAT?
8

OH, KITTY ... I DON'T KNOW WHAT TO DO!
SURE, I'VE HAD A LOT OF FUN WITH REGGIE, BUT HE'S JUST NOT MY TYPE!
IS HE?

I KNOW DEEP DOWN HE'S DYING TO PLAY PRANKS ON JUGGIE AND MOOSE, AND TO FLIRT WITH MIDGE...

HE'S BEEN SO SWEET ABOUT IT... PRETENDING TO BE NICE...
BUT WHAT IF HE'S NOT PRETENDING?

MAYBE YOU'RE NOT HEARING ANY BELLS BECAUSE YOU'RE SO HUNG UP ON ARCHIE YOU'RE NOT GIVING REGGIE A CHANCE!
HE HAS BEEN MAKING A BIG EFFORT TO CHANGE IN FRONT OF YOU...

DOESN'T THAT COUNT FOR ANYTHING?
DO YOU WANT TO LOSE SOMEONE WHO MIGHT REALLY CARE ABOUT YOU?

THAT NIGHT AT THE LIBRARY...
ER... WELL ... READY TO STUDY?
YEAH, AH... I GUESS!
9

BETTY, I'M SORRY! I JUST CANT THINK ABOUT HOMEWORK! I'VE BEEN THINKING ABOUT US ALL DAY!
I KNOW... ME, TOO!
I'M NOT SURE WHAT'S HAPPENING...
IT'S BEEN DRIVING ME CRAZY!
AND I REALLY LIKE YOU!
IT'S LIKE WE SEE SO MUCH OF EACH OTHER...
AND I REALLY LIKE YOU!
AND WE'VE BEEN GETTING SO SERIOUS!
AND WE'VE NEVER EVEN KISSED!
I KNOW!
I KNOW!

I MEAN...
I...

OHHHHHHHHHHH...
RONNIE...
ARCHIE...

10

HA HA HA HAW HAW HAH
HOOO HOO!
HEH HEH!
HAR HOO
HAW
HA!
HA
HAR

AH, VERONICA!
OH, ARCHIE!

COOPER, YOU'RE THE BEST!
YOU'RE PRETTY OKAY, TOO, MANTLE!

PLEASE RETURN BOOKS HERE
Thank you

BETTY!
YES, ARCHIE?
I'M NOT GOING TO STAND FOR ANY MORE OF THIS! I'VE GOT RESERVATIONS FOR DINNER AT EL SWANK'S TOMORROW...

... AND TICKETS TO THE HOTTEST SHOW IN TOWN FOR RIGHT AFTERWARD! NOW...
ARE YOU GOING WITH ME OR NOT?!

SURE!
IF YOU INSIST!
WHY NOT?
11

THE NEXT NIGHT...
OH...
OH...
OH...
OH...

HEY! LET'S NOT JUST STARE AT EACH OTHER...
RIGHT! THERE MUST BE SOME-THING WE COULD TALK ABOUT!
Intermission
NO
SMOKI

WELL, I MUST ADMIT, BETTY, I'D REALLY LIKE TO KNOW... WHERE DID YOU YOU GET THAT DARLING SWEATER?
WHY, THIS...
...N.Y. REVIEW
...L.A. CRITICS
...PITTSBURG
...BUFFALO

YEAH, MANTLE, I'LL ADMIT, YOU'RE LOOK-ING PRETTY OKAY TONIGHT, TOO! ...WHERE'D YOU GET YOURS?
MY SWEATER? WHY...
3 WEEKS ONLY
"BIRD BATH"
STARRI

I GOT IT FROM A REALLY GOOD FRIEND!
ME, TOO! A REALLY GOOD ONE!
THEY'RE DIMMING THE LIGHTS, EVERYONE!
USHER

INTERMISSION'S OVER!
USHER
CENTER AISLE
ROWS 1-65
rmission
NO
OKING
BUT THE PLAY NEVER ENDS!
END

## Attitudes

### *Betty & Veronica* #113, 1997

**by Kathleen Webb, Dan DeCarlo, Jimmy DeCarlo, Barry Grossman and Bill Yoshida**

**&**

## The "Voice" of Choice

### *Veronica* #69, 1997

**by Barbara Slate, Jeff Schultz, Rich Koslowski, Barry Grossman and Bill Yoshida**

The heart, compassion and humor that characterize the stories created by the Archie brand are a potent combination. Riverdale is a community where the inhabitants genuinely care about one another. Real world issues find their way into the storylines... always thoughtful and nonjudgmental. Readers and creators alike experience respite and discover a refuge in the "Archieverse."

**Janice Chiang**
*Comic book letterer*

## Downtime

### *Jughead* #110, 1998

**By Craig Boldman and Rex Lindsey**

I'm so appreciative to have grown up with Archie Comics, as so many have before me, and thankful that these characters have played such a significant role in not only my creative endeavors but my view of the world. That there is always light in an increasingly cynical society and that you'll always have friends you can rely on, even if they only live in the panels of a comic book.

**Joey Esposito**
*Writer of* ***Pawn Shop, Footprints, Captain Ultimate***

# Betty and Veronica in ATTITUDES

ARCHIE IS LATE!
HE'S ABOUT AS DEPENDABLE AS A TWO-DOLLAR WATCH! START THE MOVIE WITHOUT HIM!

Script: Kathleen Webb / Pencils: Dan DeCarlo / Inks: Jimmy DeCarlo / Letters: Bill Yoshida / Colors: Barry Grossman

WHAT'S IT ABOUT?
RHONDA ROZZ PLAYS A FAMOUS CAREER WOMAN BACK IN THE FIFTIES!
RHONDA
SOUNDS BOR-RING... DO WE HAVE TO WATCH?
YES, IF YOU WANT A SLICE OF MY BANANA CREAM PIE!
1

HER ABILITY TO GATHER NEWS WAS RECOGNIZED EVEN IN HIGH SCHOOL!
YUCK! YUCK! YOU MEAN SHE WAS A BIG GOSSIP!
EDITOR

WHY IS IT WHEN A FEMALE PASSES ON NEWS SHE'S A GOSSIP?

... BUT WHEN A MALE DOES IT, HE'S WELL-INFORMED!
TRUE!!

LOOK AT THE BOYS GATHER AROUND HER AT THE PROM!
WHAT A FLIRT!

THAT'S ANOTHER EXAMPLE OF YOUR SEXIST VOCABULARY!

WHEN A GIRL KNOWS A LOT OF BOYS SHE'S A FLIRT!
... AND WHEN IT'S THE REVERSE, EVERYONE SAYS THE BOY IS VERY POPULAR!
SLURP!
2

MOTHER, THEY JUST MADE ME MANAGER OF MY DEPARTMENT!
CAN YOU BELIEVE THIS CHARACTER? SHE'S SO BOSSY!
MR. OBNOXIOUS IS AT IT AGAIN!

WHEN A FEMALE GETS AHEAD, PEOPLE SAY SHE'S BOSSY!
BUT WHEN IT'S A MALE THEY SAY HE HAS LEADERSHIP ABILITY!

I'M SURPRISED AT YOU, REG!
RONNIE IS RIGHT, YOU'RE A REAL CHAUVINIST!

HEY, LADIES! I'VE HAD ENOUGH OF YOUR PUT-DOWNS FOR ONE NIGHT!

ADIOS, AND GOOD-BYE!
3

I JUST SAW REGGIE STORM OUT OF HERE!
WHAT'S EATING HIM?

WE HAD A LITTLE SPAT ABOUT HIS SEXIST VIEWS!
YEAH! HE'S GOT A VERY DATED ATTITUDE ON THAT SUBJECT!

THIS IS 2014! TIMES HAVE CHANGED!
YOU'VE GOT TO GIVE FEMALES ALL THE RESPECT THEY DESERVE!

AND I THINK ARCHIE DESERVES TWO PIECES OF MY PIE!

IF YOU HAVE SOME SPARE TIME I'D LIKE YOU BOTH TO HELP ME DELIVER THESE LEAFLETS!
MELISSA BAXTER
CLASS PRESIDENT

DON'T TELL ME YOU'RE VOTING FOR MELISSA!?
BUT SHE'S SO MUCH BETTER THAN HER OPPONENT WALTER ROGERS!
4

I THINK MELISSA HAS LEADERSHIP ABILITY! SHE'S WELL-INFORMED AND SHE'S POPULAR!
HA!

IN MY OPINION SHE'S BOSSY, LOVES TO GOSSIP... AND SHE'S A FLIRT!

BETTY, ARE YOU THINKING WHAT I'M THINKING?
YES!

INSTEAD OF JUST TWO PIECES, I THINK ARCHIE DESERVES THE WHOLE PIE!
I AGREE!
GREAT!!

END

Veronica in THE "VOICE" OF CHOICE
VERONICA! DID YOU JUST BUY OUT THE WIZARD?
NO, DADDY! IT'S JUST SOME STUFF FOR MY NEW SOUND STUDIO!
1

AND THIS IS EDDIE!
YO, MR. "L"!
YO?

HE'S THE BEST SOUND MAN IN ALL RIVERDALE!

WITH EDDIE AND ALL THIS EQUIPMENT, I CAN RELEASE MY VERY OWN COUNTRY AND WESTERN CD!

AND I CAN RELEASE A BIG, FAT CHECK!

SOON...
I WAS BORN AND RAISED ON A COUNTRY FARM...

THE BARN WAS RED AND THE COW GOT FED...
LODGE
2

HOURS LATER...
WELL, EDDIE, WHAT DID YOU THINK OF MY NEW SONG?
IT WAS MUSIC TO MY EARS!

FORTUNATELY, I'M LISTENING TO THE "SMASHIN' TURNIPS" WHILE I RECORD!

WHEN DO I GET THE CD?
I'LL JUST PUT THIS THROUGH THE MIX!

AND I SHOULD HAVE IT FOR YOU BY TOMORROW!
THAT'S FANTASTIC!

THEN I CAN DISTRIBUTE IT AND REBA WHAT'S-HER-NAME WATCH OUT...

HERE COMES VERONICA "THE VOICE" LODGE! THE NEXT COUNTRY AND WESTERN SENSATION!
♪ I WAS BORN AND RAISED... ♫
OUCH!
3

A WEEK LATER...
I HAD A DOG HIS NAME WAS ROVER...
NEWS

I SAID TO HIM COME OVER ROV...
RING

HELLO?
IS THIS VERONICA "THE VOICE"?

IT IS!
CONGRATULATIONS! OUR RADIO STATION W.H.C.M. IN CINCINNATI, HAS BEEN PLAYING YOUR CD ALL WEEK!

OUR FANS LOVE YOU, LITTLE LADY! YOU ARE NOMINATED FOR "BEST COUNTRY VOCALIST"!
WHCM

WOW! THANK YOU! THIS IS A GREAT HONOR!
4

CAN YOU FLY DOWN HERE, PRETTY LADY, AND ACCEPT THIS PRESTIGIOUS AWARD?
OF COURSE! I WOULDN'T MISS IT FOR THE WORLD!

THE NEXT WEEK...
IT WAS SO NICE OF YOUR FATHER TO FLY US ALL HERE, VERONICA!
OF COURSE!
TONITE
W.H.C.M
AWARDS!

JUST BECAUSE I'M A STAR, IT DOESN'T MEAN I'D FORGET ALL THE LITTLE PEOPLE BACK HOME!

CONGRATULATIONS!
I FEEL ANOTHER SONG COMING ON!

JUST BECAUSE I'M A STAR...

DOESN'T MEAN I'D GO AFAR...
AND NOW FOR THE BEST COUNTRY VOCALIST...
5

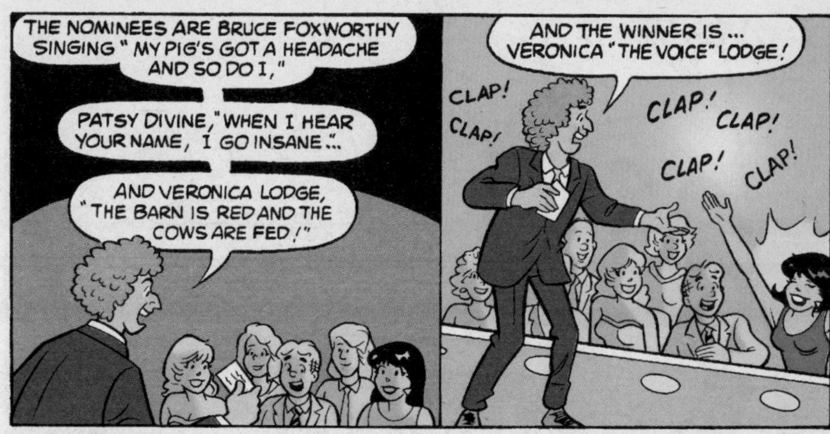
THE NOMINEES ARE BRUCE FOXWORTHY SINGING " MY PIG'S GOT A HEADACHE AND SO DO I,"
PATSY DIVINE, "WHEN I HEAR YOUR NAME, I GO INSANE..."
AND VERONICA LODGE, " THE BARN IS RED AND THE COWS ARE FED!"
AND THE WINNER IS ... VERONICA "THE VOICE" LODGE!
CLAP!
CLAP!
CLAP!
CLAP!
CLAP!
CLAP!

CONGRATULATIONS!
WHAT'S *THIS*?

IT'S OUR *W.H.C.M.* *WE HATE COUNTRY MUSIC* AWARD!
IT'S FOR THE *WORST* COUNTRY AND WESTERN SOUND, AND TO *US* THAT'S THE *BEST*!

W.H.C.M. IS *ONLY* ROCK AND ROLL AND WE LIKE IT!
ER... THANK YOU, I THINK!

DON'T FEEL BAD THAT YOU'RE NOT A *BIG* STAR, RONNIE!
YOU STILL GOT US, THE *LITTLE* PEOPLE!
END

JUGHEAD PRESENTS

# POP TATE DOWNTIME

THE OLD PLACE SURE GOES DEAD ONCE SCHOOL IS BACK IN SESSION!
MURDER MOST MESSY
HARD TO BELIEVE THAT JUST LAST WEEK THE SHOP WAS FILLED WITH LAUGHTER... DANCING...
THAT CEILING FAN SOUNDS A LITTLE OFF-BALANCE! I SHOULD LOOK INTO THAT!
HUM UM HUM UM
I HEAR A SODA SPIGOT DRIPPING! THAT'LL BE TOMORROW'S PROJECT!
FSSST!
ONLY TEN-THIRTY! WON'T SCHOOL EVER LET OUT?
TIK TOK TIK
TIK TOK FSSST!
WHY IS SUCH A QUIET PLACE SO NOISY?
HUM HUM UM
2

SIGH
KA-CHANK!
WHRRRR
SUGAR... AH, HONEY HONEY
TAP! TAP!
YOU ARE MY CANDY GIRL!
YOU'VE GOT ME WANT...
OW!
CAN'T BELIEVE I WARARRRRR*
BAM!
3

QUIET AGAIN! *TOO* QUIET!

SCRITCH
SCRATCH
SCRITCH
THUMP!

HMM? THAT'S NOT A *FAN!* OR A *CLOCK!*
SCRATCH
CHUNKLUNK!
SCRITCH!

CLAWING! DIGGING! FROM THE BACK ROOM!
SCRATCH
SCRITCH
SKREEE...
EMPLOYEES ONLY

SCRATCH
SCRITCH
BUMP...
EMPLOYEES ONLY
4

ALL RIGHT! I'M READY FOR YOU, WHOEVER...
EXIT
SCRATCH SCRITCH!
WELL!
YOU'LL HAVE TO SETTLE FOR BURGERS TODAY! TOMORROW I'LL STOCK SOME SIRLOIN!
COMING TO POPS?
LATER! POOR OLD HOT DOG! I BET HE GETS LONELY WHEN I START SCHOOL!
HERE I AM, HOT DOG!
UH...HOT DOG?
UH, MISS ME?
OH, SURE...
HOW LONG 'TIL YOU LEAVE FOR SCHOOL AGAIN?
THE END

## Clowning Around

***Sabrina* #16, 1998**

**by Bill Golliher, Dan DeCarlo Jr., Jon D'Agostino, Barry Grossman and Bill Yoshida**

**&**

## Double Play

***Betty & Veronica* #140, 1999**

**by Angelo DeCesare, Dan DeCarlo, Henry Scarpelli, Barry Grossman and Bill Yoshida**

My parents were big on reading and not-so-big on candy, so I always had access to Archie Comics. I suspect it was less of a threat to family peace to sit me somewhere with a Double Digest than to risk the tantrums of a youngest daughter in the throes of a Dubble Bubble sugar high. And Archie Comics were so unabashedly nice; what other collection of stories of high school students would you happily hand to a seven-year-old without fear or anxiety?

**Brenna Clarke Gray**
*Writer & educator*

## Ski Bummed

***Jughead* #120, 1999**

**&**

## Inflation Problem

***Jughead* #122, 1999**

**by Craig Boldman and Rex Lindsey**

The world of Archie and the gang was my first exposure to stories about real people. Real to me, at least. As much as I love superheroes, it's the stories about the regular folk that are truly appealing to me, and I believe that I have Archie and the gang to thank for that.

**Joey Esposito**
*Writer of **Pawn Shop, Footprints, Captain Ultimate***

# Sabrina in "CLOWNING AROUND"

HOW ABOUT A BALLOON ANIMAL FOR THE LITTLE LADY?

ATCHOO

BALLOON ANIMALS $1.00

SORRY ABOUT THAT! I ALWAYS WAS A LITTLE ALLERGIC TO GIRAFFES!
THAT'S OKAY!

HOW RUDE!
OH, HARVEY! HE DIDN'T KNOW HE WAS GOING TO SNEEZE!
1

COME ON! THERE'S THE WHIPLASH! LET'S GIVE IT A TRY!
JUST A SECOND... I'VE GOT TO...
THE WHIPLASH

ATCHOO!!
THAT CLOWN MUST HAVE GIVEN YOU SOMETHING!

I THINK YOU'RE RIGHT!
?

I'D BETTER GET HOME!
BUT SABRINA, WAIT! THE WHIPLASH!
THE WHIPLASH
?

HERE WE GO AGAIN! AH... AH...
AT-CHOO!

MOMMY! YOU LOOK FUNNY!
?
I'D BETTER HURRY!
2

SABRINA, WHAT'S WRONG? YOU DON'T LOOK WELL!
SOME CLOWN GAVE ME A COLD! NOW EVERY TIME I SNEEZE...
AT-CHOO!

SOMEONE TURNS INTO A CLOWN!
OH, YEAH! REAL FUNNY!

IT'S OBVIOUSLY SOME SORT OF WITCHCRAFT MALADY!
WE'LL TAKE YOU TO OUR FAMILY DOCTOR IN THE OTHER REALM!

A WITCH DOCTOR?!
PLEASE! HE PREFERS TO BE CALLED A WITCH SPECIALIST!

ATCHOO!!
THAT'S DEFINITELY YOUR COLOR!
OH, SHUT UP!

SOON...
DO EITHER OF YOU CLOWNS HAVE AN APPOINTMENT?!
POOF!
3

I'M AFRAID NOT! BUT SHE'S GOT AN EMERGENCY!
ATCHOO!

I SEE! C'MON! I'LL GET YOU RIGHT IN!

HILDA? ZELDA? YOU LOOK DIFFERENT!
DOCTOR, IT'S OUR NIECE, SABRINA! SHE'S CAUGHT SOME-THING!
AT-CHOO!

THANKS! I HAVEN'T LOOKED THIS GOOD IN YEARS!
HOW'D THIS START?

A CLOWN SNEEZED ON ME AT THE CARNIVAL!
AH-HA! WITCHES CAN BE VERY SENSITIVE TO CLOWNS! LAUGHTER IS INFECTIOUS, YOU KNOW!

NOT ONLY DID YOU PICK UP COLD GERMS, BUT CLOWN GERMS, TOO! AND NOW YOU'RE SPREADING THEM AROUND!
THAT'S RIDICULOUS!
AT-CHOO!
4

HEY!
QUIT CLOWNING AROUND! TELL US WHAT TO DO!

SIMPLE! I JUST HAVE TO MAKE A CLOWN OUT OF SABRINA FOR THE NEXT FEW DAYS!
ONCE THE GERMS ARE SATISFIED THAT YOU'RE A CLOWN THEY'LL STAY WITH YOU UNTIL THEY LOSE THEIR STRENGTH!
ZAP!

THIS IS RIDICULOUS! HOW AM I SUPPOSED TO WALK AROUND TOWN LIKE THIS?
WITH THESE REALLY BIG SHOES, OF COURSE!
ZAP

I'M SURE WE'LL THINK OF SOMETHING TO OCCUPY YOUR TIME!
POOF!
AH!

AND SO!
PEDIATRICS WARD
I'LL TAKE A DOGGIE!
MAKE ME A GIRAFFE!
ON SECOND THOUGHT I CAN'T THINK OF ANYTHING MORE FUN THAN BEING A CLOWN!
UNLESS, OF COURSE, IT'S BEING A WITCH!
END

# Betty and Veronica in "DOUBLE PLAY"

KEEP LOOKING, BETTY! YOU'LL SEE THE REASON WE CAME TO THIS FITNESS CAMP!

ALL I SEE IS A BUNCH OF PEOPLE DOING YOGA! I DON'T SEE ANYONE THAT I...

SCRIPT: ANGELO DECESARE PENCILS: DAN DECARLO INKING: HENRY SCARPELLI LETTERING: BILL YOSHIDA COLORING: BARRY GROSSMAN

WHAT ARE WE WAITING FOR? LET'S INTRODUCE OURSELVES!
HOLD ON, GIRL! THIS IS A VERY EXCLUSIVE AND PRIVATE CAMP!

YOU CAN'T CHARGE DOWN THE HILL LIKE YOU'RE TRYING TO CATCH THE LAST BUS TO SCHOOL! THEY'LL THROW US OUT OF CAMP!

IF WE'RE GOING TO MEET THEM, WE'VE GOT TO BE TOTALLY COOL ABOUT IT! NOW FOLLOW ME!
LET YOUR BODY AND YOUR SPIRIT RELAX!

WE'RE IN LUCK! EVERYONE HAS THEIR EYES CLOSED!
LET'S WORK OUR WAY OVER TO THE TWINS!

YOU ARE AT PEACE WITH NATURE!!
BZZZzzz
HUH?
2

A BEE! A BEE!
I'LL SWAT IT WITH MY HAT, RONNIE!
OW!!
WHAP!

LATER:
THAT WAS SO EMBARRASSING, BETTY!
TRUE, BUT AT LEAST THE TWINS NOTICED US!
SUN ISLAND RESORT

YEAH, THEY ASKED, "WHO ARE LAVERNE AND SHIRLEY"?! NOW LET'S TRY TO MEET THEM IN THE WORKOUT ROOM!

YOU TAKE THE TREADMILL ON THE RIGHT, AND I'LL TAKE THE ONE ON THE LEFT!
AND THIS TIME, BE COOL!
3

20 MINUTES LATER...
I'M GETTING TIRED! AND I DON'T THINK THE TWINS EVEN KNOW WE'RE HERE!
THEY'RE LEAVING! HOW DO YOU TURN THIS THING OFF?!
WHOOPS! THAT WASN'T THE WAY!
HELP!
I'M COMING, RONNIE!
I FOUND THE "OFF" BUTTON!
NO, RONNIE!
BOOP!
OOF!
ZOOM
4

KA-
BLAM!

NICE BOWLING, RONNIE... WE PICKED UP THE SPARE!

SOON...
MY BACK IS SO SORE!
WE'D BETTER STAY AWAY FROM THOSE TWINS FOR A WHILE!

BETTY! THEY'RE COMING INTO THE POOL! THEY'RE WITH A SECURITY GUARD!

DUCK!
ANY SIGN OF THOSE WACKY GIRLS?
NO! I THINK IT'S SAFE TO GO IN!
SPLASH!
SPLASH!
5

YOU CAN RELAX, SIRS! I'LL KEEP EVERYONE OUT OF THE POOL TILL YOU LEAVE!
THANKS!

MMMM!
YOU KNOW, THOSE TWO GIRLS WERE PESTS, BUT THEY WERE KINDA CUTE!

DO YOU REALLY THINK SO?
AAHHHHH!

NEXT DAY...
WE MAY AS WELL FACE IT, BETTY!

...THIS IS AS CLOSE AS WE'LL EVER AGAIN GET TO THE TWINS!
CHEW BOPPERPOP GUM
BUS STOP
END

Jughead
SKI BUMMED
KLIP! KLAP!
KLIP! KLIP!
KLAP!
KLIP! KLAP!
THE SOUND! IT'S GETTING LOUDER!! LOUDER! CLOSER! CLOSER!!
AAR-CHIEE!
KLIP! KLAP! KLIP! KLAP!
EEP!
HEY, HOW'S IT GOIN'?
JUGHEAD!
KLIP! KLAP!
KLIP! KLAP
KLAK!

YOU ALMOST CREEPED ME OUT OF A YEAR'S GROWTH!
SORRY! I DIDN'T KNOW YOU WERE SCARED OF SKIS!
YEAH, WHAT'S WITH THOSE?
IT'S MY LATEST BRAINSTORM!
YOU KNOW HOW I HAVE TROUBLE ON THE SKI SLOPES EACH WINTER?
"TROUBLE"? DON'T BE SO MODEST!
"LAST TIME, YOU ENDED UP SIPPING YOUR COCOA FROM A TRACTION BED!"
EXACTLY! I NEVER COULD GET THE HANG OF THOSE SKIS!
SO I FIGURED...
WHY NOT WEAR 'EM NOW, IN THE NICE WEATHER, AND GET REAL COMFORTABLE WITH 'EM!
WHY NOT! LET ME COUNT THE REASONS!
2

BY THE TIME WINTER COMES, THEY'LL BE LIKE PART OF MY BODY!
YEAH, YOUR HEAD! IT'S WOOD, TOO!
KLIP KLOP!
KLIP KLAP!

ISN'T IT DIFFICULT TO GET AROUND?
IT WAS AT FIRST!

BUT NOW I'M QUITE ADEPT!
QUITE A DOPE, YOU MEAN!

SCOFF IF YOU WILL! ONCE I'M USED TO THEM, DOWNHILL SKIING WILL BE CHILD'S PLAY!
KLIP! KLAK!

YOU'RE GOING IN THE HOUSE WITH 'EM?
THAT'S THE WHOLE IDEA! TO THINK OF THEM AS EVERYDAY FOOTWEAR!

LOOK AT THE CLOWN IN THE SHOES!
HARDEE-HAR! CLOWNS ARE SILLY AND BUMBLING!
3

I'M DOWNRIGHT GRACEFUL! CHECK OUT THE FANCY FOOTWORK!
TAP! TAPPY TAP!
TAP! TAP!
TAP!
TAP!
TA-DAAA!
YOOPS!
EEEK!
TRIP!
YOU MENACE TO SOCIETY!
I DIDN'T TRIP! HE DID!
JUGHEAD! DON'T TURN AROUND!
HUH?
WHY NOT, ARCH?
WAP!
4

SMASH!
WHO PUTS AN EXPENSIVE VASE ON A PEDESTAL?
WHAT'S GOING ON?
KLONK!
YEE-OWW!
VERONICA, YOU KNOW NOT TO LET YOUR FRIENDS RUN IN THE HOUSE WITH THEIR SKIS ON!
WHAT AM I SAYING?!
I'LL GET HIM! I'LL JUST FOLLOW THE TRAIL OF DESTRUCTION!
SAVE THE RANT, DADDY! THE CULPRIT'S GONE ALREADY!
KLIP! KLAP!
KLOP!
5

I'D BETTER SKI-DADDLE WHILE THE SKEDADDLING'S GOOD!
KLIP KLAK!
WOAH! WHAT'S THIS, NOW?!
MOMMY!!!
KRUMP!!
IT'S THE DOWNHILL PART THAT STILL GIVES ME TROUBLE!
SOMEHOW I FEEL WE'RE ALL SAFER THIS WAY!
The End

# Jughead® in the Inflation Problem

WHY THE *WORKOUT MAT?* DON'T TELL ME YOU'RE ACTUALLY PLANNING TO *EXERT* YOURSELF!

AU CONTRAIRE, MON AMI!

IT'S AN AIR MATTRESS!
OH, THAT MAKES A LOT MORE SENSE!
BOING!
SPROING!
I CAN CAT NAP IN PURE COMFORT!
YOU CAN'T TAKE NAPS IN SCHOOL!
SSSSSSSSS
YOU KIDDING? I'M BARELY CONSCIOUS AT THE BEST OF TIMES!
BUT ISN'T THIS A BIT FLAGRANT?
I'LL JUST CATCH A WINK HERE, A WINK THERE! SEE? THIS ELECTRIC PUMP INFLATES IT IN SECONDS!
SSSSSSSSS
YEAH, BUT YOU CAN'T JUST...
ZZZZZ!
MAYBE HE CAN!
ZZZZZZZ!
2

GATHER 'ROUND AND YOU SHALL HEAR OF THE FEEDING HABITS OF THE POISONOUS GILA MONSTER!

BLA BLA YACK YACK!
LOOKS LIKE HE'LL BE GOING ON AT LENGTH!

THE LIZARD IS KNOWN FOR ITS...
GOOD HEAVENS!
SSSSSS SSSSS

NOBODY MOVE! NO-BO-DY MOVE A M.U.S.C.L.E.!
SSSSS SSSSS

I'LL SAVE US ALL!
WHERE IS THAT SLIMY BEAST?
EEK!
SWISH!
CRASH!

YAWN! SOMEBODY CALL ME?
JUGHEAD?! IS THAT YOU HISSING?!
SSSSS
3

MY MATTRESS, ACTUALLY! IT INFLATES!
IT MADE A HISSING NOISE EXACTLY LIKE A POISONOUS HELODERMA HORRIDUM!
I'LL THANK YOU TO TRY TO STAY AWAKE DURING MY LECTURES!
RATS! I DO MY BEST SLEEP IN HIS CLASS!
YOU BLEW THAT THING UP FAST!
IT HAS A HAIR TRIGGER FOR QUICK INFLATION!
GYM
HERE'S A LIKELY SPOT!
ZZZZZ
THANK YOU!
HEH-HEH!
EVERYBODY INTO THE POOL! MOVE IT!
POOL AREA
4

SKREEEE!
SCREECH!
10 FT

ZZZZZZ
SPLISH!
SPLAT!
KER-PLUNK!

HE WRECKED MY WHOLE SWIM TEAM!
I'LL HANDLE HIM!

JUST GO BACK TO CLASS AND TRY TO BEHAVE! I'LL KEEP YOUR LATEST TORTURE DEVICE!

CAREFUL! IT'S VERY TOUCHY!
I THINK I CAN HANDLE IT!
PRINCIPAL'S OFFICE
5

I DON'T GET PAID NEARLY ENOUGH!
SSSSSSSSSSS
?
SSSSSS
BLAM!
BUMP!
WHAT A YOB! HE BAN MAKE BIG MESS AND TAKE NAP! SOME OF US GOT TO WORK! BY YIMINY!
SSSSS
THE END

# THE BEST OF Archie COMICS BOOK FOUR

# The 2000s

## Fight for the Privileged

***Betty & Veronica Spectacular* #44, 2000**

**by Dan Parent**

**&**

## Garbage In, Garbage Out

***Jughead* #125, 2000**

**by Craig Boldman, Rex Lindsey, Rich Koslowski, Barry Grossman and Bill Yoshida**

As a kid I moved around the country quite a bit, and one of the things I carried with me to keep me company were familiar comic characters, none of them more familiar than Archie Andrews and his pals. Even by the time I was a young comic book reader, there were decades of Archie comics to discover, and I could always depend on losing a few hours in an Archie digest brought home from the grocery store by my mother. I'd comb through dog-eared collections and snag yellowed copies of *Pep Comics* or *Archie's Madhouse*, and even after dumping so much of my collection over the past few years, I still cling to those books, as a reminder of what sucked me into comics in the first place. Of course, at this point I can look back on Archie titles over the decades and see contemporary pop culture reflected through the lens of talented cartoonists and writers, and it's fascinating to observe.

**B. Clay Moore**

*Writer of* ***Hawaiian Dick, Adventures of Superman, Vampire Diaries***

# Archie & Friends in "FIGHT FOR THE PRIVILEGED"

HOW ABOUT THAT OL' ARCH, EH ? TALK ABOUT LUCKY ! HE GETS TO GO TO THAT CRAZY ERIC CONCERT NEXT MONTH !

WISH *I'D* WON THAT CONTEST ! THAT'S GOING TO BE THE BIGGEST EVENT OF THE YEAR !

I'D SAY HE ONLY HAS ONE SMALL PROBLEM WITH WINNING THOSE TICKETS !
UH-HUH !

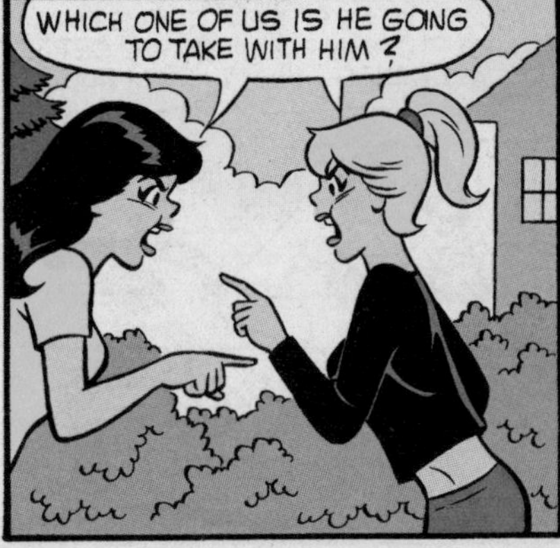

WHICH ONE OF US IS HE GOING TO TAKE WITH HIM ?

I GUESS YOU KNOW WHAT THIS MEANS, GOOD BUDDY!
UH-HUH, BOSOM CHUM!
THIS MEANS WAR!
HOSTILITY HAS JUST BROKEN OUT BETWEEN US!
IT'S EVERY GIRL FOR HERSELF!
I WANT TO GO TO THAT CONCERT, WITH ARCHIE!
HAH! I WILL GO TO THAT CONCERT WITH ARCHIE!
YOU KNOW HE'S LIKE PUTTY IN MY HANDS!
THAT'S ONLY IF YOU GET TO HIM FIRST!
NOT SO FAST, BLONDIE!
GOOD IDEA! I THINK I'LL RUN FASTER!
2

AND I'M WEARING RUNNING SHOES!
SO? I CAN STILL OUTRUN YOU IN HIGH HEELS!

UH-OH! TROUBLE AHEAD!
IT'S CHERYL! SHE'S HEADED TOWARDS ARCHIE'S PLACE!

TIME TO DECLARE A TRUCE!
AT LEAST UNTIL WE RID OURSELVES OF THE OPPOSITION!

NOT A CHANCE, CHERYL!
YOU'LL HAVE TO GO THROUGH US FIRST!

WHAT ON EARTH ARE YOU TALKING ABOUT?
ARCHIE! HE WON TWO TICKETS TO CRAZY ERIC'S CONCERT NEXT MONTH!

THAT'S NICE! I GET TO GO BACK-STAGE FOR AN INTERVIEW FOR MY 'ZINE, PLUS I HAVE A DATE WITH CRAZY ERIC HIMSELF!
3

THINK SHE'S TELLING THE TRUTH?
SHE **MUST** BE! IT'S THE ONLY WAY SHE'D TURN DOWN A DATE WITH ARCHIE!

THAT MEANS HE'S FREE AND FAIR GAME AGAIN!
WRONG! HE'S ALL MINE!

LISTEN, VERONICA, YOU GET HIM TO PAY THROUGH THE NOSE TO TAKE YOU TO ALL SORTS OF GREAT PLACES AND EVENTS!
AS IT SHOULD BE!

BY THE TIME HE GETS AROUND TO ME, HE'S BROKE! HE CAN BARELY AFFORD TO BUY ME A SODA!
SO? DON'T YOU LIKE SIMPLE PLEASURES?

WELL, THIS TIME IT'S **MY** TURN TO GO SOME-PLACE SPECIAL WITH ARCHIE... ESPECIALLY SINCE HE GOT THE TICKETS FOR FREE!
OH, YEAH?

WELL, SINCE HE GOT THEM FOR FREE, HE'LL HAVE ENOUGH MONEY TO TAKE ME TO A FANCY RESTAURANT AFTER THE CONCERT!
GREEDY!
4

OF COURSE! WHY DO YOU THINK I'M RICH? I WANT IT ALL!
WELL, THIS TIME YOU CAN'T HAVE IT!

ARCHIE! PICK ME! PICK ME!
NO, ME! YOU *KNOW* YOU WANT TO TAKE ME!

TAKE YOU? WHERE?
TO CRAZY ERIC'S CONCERT NEXT MONTH!

DIDN'T YOU WIN A CONTEST FOR SOME TICKETS?
NOPE! *I* DID!

I WON THE TICKETS, SO I ASKED ARCH TO GO!
SORRY, GIRLS! MAYBE NEXT TIME!

AND MAYBE NOT!
HEH, HEH! IT SURE MAKES A GUY FEEL GREAT TO HAVE GIRLS FIGHTING OVER HIM!
YOU CAN HAVE IT, THEN!
5

WAIT, JUGGIE, I'LL BUY YOU TONS OF HAMBURGERS, PIZZA AND HOT DOGS IF YOU'LL LET ARCHIE TAKE ME TO THE CONCERT INSTEAD OF YOU!
WHY, THAT...!! TWO CAN PLAY THAT GAME!
I'LL BAKE YOU TRUCKLOADS OF CHOCOLATE CHIP COOKIES IF YOU LET ARCHIE GO WITH ME!
A GRAND BUFFET AT MY COUNTRY CLUB!
ALL YOU CAN EAT AT JOE'S DINER!
AND I THOUGHT I WOULDN'T LIKE TO HAVE FEMALES FIGHT OVER ME!
DROOL! YOU BOTH WIN! WE'LL ALL GO TO THE CONCERT TOGETHER!
HUH? HOW?
JUG WON FOUR TICKETS, NOT JUST TWO!
AND SO... THE NIGHT OF THE CONCERT...
OH, ARCHIE♪ YOU WILL BUY ME A SODA AFTER THE CONCERT, WON'T YOU?
GET LOST, BLONDEBRAIN! HE'S BUYING ME ONE!
I NEVER THOUGHT I'D ADMIT IT COULD GET TIRING TO HAVE GIRLS FIGHT OVER ME!
OH, I DUNNO, ARCH.. IT HAS ITS UP SIDES! SLURP!
END

SCRIPT: CRAIG BOLDMAN PENCILLING: REX LINDSEY INKING: RICH KOSLOWSKI LETTERING: BILL YOSHIDA COLORING: BARRY GROSSMAN

NOT YET, BUT I WILL!
SIGH! I KNOW THAT TONE OF VOICE!

HEY, WHERE YOU GOING?
YOU SAY YOU WILL, BUT YOU'LL FORGET! I'M GOING TO MAKE SURE IT GETS DONE!
SALTOS

DAD, CHILL! I'LL DO IT RIGHT AFTER THIS MOVIE! I KID YOU NOT!
HUH, WELL, OKAY!

LATER...
ZZZ... MAN, THAT WAS A LONG FILM!
THE END

ZZZ... HOPE I CAN HAUL MYSELF TO BED!
2

MORNING...
CLATTER! KLUNK!
MAN! WHO'S BANGING GARBAGE CANS AROUND AT THIS HOUR?
GARBAGE CANS?
UH-OH!
THEY'RE AT THE GILMORE'S HOUSE!
MAYBE I CAN STILL MAKE IT!
⁝ GROAN ⁝ THERE THEY GO!
BRUMMM
I'M IN FOR A BIG "I TOLD YOU SO" FROM DAD!
3

THERE HE GOES TO WORK!
I'D BETTER STASH THESE WHERE HE WON'T FIND THEM!
LATE AGAIN! ALARM CLOCK SLOW?
NO, GARBAGE MEN, FAST!
I DON'T GET THAT, AND I DON'T THINK I WANT TO!
EXCELLENT CHOICE!
LATER...
LEAVING SO SOON? YOU'VE ONLY HAD TWELVE SODAS!
BETTER GO! I HAVEN'T EVEN BEEN BACK HOME YET, TODAY!
WOW, I AM LATE! DAD'S HOME ALREADY!
4

GROWLF!
YEESH!

BOY, THAT'S A MOOD! WHAT'S WITH DAD?
DON'T ASK!

UH-OH! I WONDER IF HE FOUND THE GARBAGE? MAYBE THAT'S WHAT SET HIM OFF!

NO, IT'S STILL HERE! BUT THIS IS RISKY! HE COULD SEE IT!

I'LL HIDE THE EVIDENCE IN PLAIN VIEW!

JUGHEAD, NOT ONLY ARE YOU A GENIUS... YOU'RE AN ARTIST, TOO!
5

NEXT MORN...
BZZZT!... QUITE A CHANGE FROM YESTERDAY'S COLD WAVE!
'MORNING!
OOOOOO
GRUMBLE, GRUMBLE!
WHOA! STILL IN A MOOD!
FORGET THE WINTER COAT! TAKE AN UMBRELLA!
UMBRELLA?
THE SNOW TURNED TO RAIN OVERNIGHT! WASHED AWAY MOST OF THE ACCUMULATION WE HAD!
WELL, I'M OFF!
UH-OH!
CONTINUED- 6

Jughead in
Garbage In Garbage Out
PART II
BEEP! BEEP!
ARCH IS HERE! I'M GONE, 'BYE!
ZOOM!
WAS THAT OUR SON?
I'VE NEVER SEEN HIM MOVE THAT FAST!
WHAT'S THIS?!
WET SACKS OF GARBAGE! DRIVE!
NO WAY, MAN! I DON'T KNOW WHAT IT'S ABOUT, BUT FRIENDSHIP ONLY GOES SO FAR!
S'OKAY, ARCH!
DAD'S LEFT! I'LL JUST DEPOSIT THESE IN MY NEXT-DOOR NEIGHBOR'S TRASH CANS!
I DIDN'T KNOW GOOGIE'S FAMILY HAD TRASH CANS! I THOUGHT THEY COMPOSTED EVERYTHING!
EVEN HEALTH FOOD NUTS MAKE MESSES!
7

YOU HAVE YOUR NERVE!
GOOGIE GILMORE!
EXIT

I SAW MY CAT, CLEO, AS I WAS LEAVING FOR SCHOOL! SHE HAD GOTTEN INTO THE TRASH!
UH-OH!

OUR HEALTHY TRASH HAD BEEN CONTAMINATED WITH FAST FOOD CONTAINERS, CANDY BAR WRAPPERS AND WHO-KNOWS-WHAT!
UH-OH!

THERE'S NO MISTAKING YOUR TRASH! I RETURNED IT TO YOUR YARD!
GAK!

"HEALTHY" GARBAGE! SHEESH!

SOME DAYS YOU JUST CAN'T GET RID OF TRASH BAGS!
BEAT IT, TROUBLE-MAKER!
MEOW!
8

ONLY ONE THING TO DO... I'LL HIDE IT IN MY ROOM 'TIL NEXT TRASH DAY!
NOW BACK TO SCHOOL!
HEARD OF SOAP, MR. JONES?
YOU SEEM AGITATED!
ARCH, MY LIFE IS FILLED WITH TRIALS AND TRIBULATIONS!
'EVENING!
GRUMBLE MUMBLE!
RIVERDALE REC
WUFF! THIS WASN'T SUCH A GOOD IDEA! PEE-YEW!
I GOTTA GET THIS OUT OF THE HOUSE, COME WHAT MAY!
9

NO WAY CAN I SNEAK PAST DAD! IN HIS FOUL MOOD HE'S LIABLE TO BEHEAD ME!
I'LL LOWER IT OUT THE WINDOW, THEN SNEAK OUT AND BURY IT OR SOMETHING!
STOP PACING, DEAR! YOU'RE WEARING OUT THE CARPET!
I CAN'T HELP IT!
OKAY, I'LL TAKE MY PACING OUTSIDE!
OOPS, THE BAG'S RIPPING!
SPLIT!
KRIP!
WUGH!
DAD?
SPLATT!
10

SO THIS IS HOW I SPENT THE LAST DAY OF MY LIFE!
JUGHEAD, I COULD KISS YOU!
URK! I'LL PASS, DAD!
LOOK, DEAR, IT'S MY PAYCHECK! THE GARBAGE MEN DIDN'T TAKE IT AWAY!
PAYCHECK?
SO JELLYBEAN DID ACCIDENTALLY PUT IT INTO THE TRASH!
AHA! SO THAT'S WHY DAD WAS SO GROUCHY!
WOO-HOO! YIPEE!
I'M GLAD I DON'T EAT JUNK FOOD! IT MAKES YOU CRAZY!
THE END

## See You in the Funny Papers

***Betty & Veronica* #149, 2000**

**by Kathleen Webb, Dan DeCarlo, Henry Scarpelli, Barry Grossman and Vickie Williams**

**&**

## Mission Nutrition

***Jughead* #127, 2000**

**by Craig Boldman, Rex Lindsey, Rich Koslowski, Bill Yoshida and Barry Grossman**

Thank God for Archie. Back before eBay, the explosion of Comic-Cons or TV shows like *Pawn Stars*, comic collectors were an isolated bunch, and there weren't many places to resell back issues. Every other junkyard we visited had some kid's carefully bundled stash for sale—TEN FOR A DOLLAR! the signs would read. My grubby little fingers pawed more first issues and ultra-rare finds than I could ever hope to afford today. To my parents' great relief, one stack of comics could keep me entertained for an entire weekend. Soon Archie, Betty, Jughead and Veronica were my constant traveling companions, and over the course of a decade, I consumed the entire Archie universe.

**Hugh Ryan**

*Journalist, **The New York Times, The Daily Beast***

# Betty and Veronica

BETTY! WHAT DO YOU THINK ABOUT THE BREAK-UP BETWEEN MISSY AND GREG?

SCRIPT: KATHLEEN WEBB | PENCILS: DAN DECARLO | INKING: HENRY SCARPELLI | LETTERING: VICKIE WILLIAMS | COLORING: BARRY GROSSMAN

WHAT ON EARTH IS THAT SUPPOSED TO MEAN?

I'M SPEECHLESS! COULDN'T YOU TELL BY MY EMPTY WORD BALLOON?

WORD BALLOON? WHAT ARE YOU TALKING ABOUT?
OH, COME ON, RON! YOU KNOW!

THE LITTLE BALLOONS THAT FOLLOW US AROUND EVERY TIME WE HAVE SOMETHING TO SAY!

YOU TALK LIKE WE'RE NOTHING MORE THAN MERE COMIC BOOK CHARACTERS!
PAPER DOLLS ON A PAPER PAGE!

WHY... IF WE WERE NOTHING MORE THAN CARTOONS, OUR WHOLE LIVES WOULD BE DIFFERENT!

FOR INSTANCE, EVERY TIME YOU SAW ARCHIE, LITTLE HEARTS WOULD FLOAT ALL AROUND YOUR HEAD!

AND EVERY TIME I CAUGHT YOU FLIRTING WITH HIM, FLAMES WOULD APPEAR AROUND MY HEAD!
2

TO BE FOLLOWED, OF COURSE, BY A LIGHT BULB, INDICATING MY FORMULATING AN IDEA TO GET HIM BACK!

AND THEN, IF I MOVED QUICKLY, I'D CREATE SPEED LINES!
ZOOM!

AND EACH MOVEMENT I MADE WOULD SHOW LITTLE LINES AROUND ME!

AND AS ARCHIE'S HEAD SPUN AROUND, THERE'D BE LITTLE SWIVEL LINES TO SHOW IT!

THEN HE'D PRODUCE DOZENS OF LITTLE HEARTS...

...AND YOU'D CHURN OUT CLOUDS OF SMOKE FROM YOUR EARS!
3

BUT THAT IS WHAT'S HAPPENING! CAN'T YOU SEE IT ?
OF COURSE NOT !

WE LIVE IN THE REAL WORLD, GIRL! NOT COMIC BOOKS !

WE CAN GO ANYWHERE WE WANT! WE'RE NOT LIMITED TO PANELS ON A PAGE !
OH, YEAH ?

YOU! TRY WALKING OFF THE EDGE OF THIS PAGE !
HAH! NO PROBLEM!

SEE ?
YOU JUST DEMONSTRATED THE WRAP-AROUND EFFECT, THAT'S ALL !

COMPUTERS DO IT ALL THE TIME WHENEVER YOU TYPE IN TEXT!
THAT'S ANOTHER THING !
4

WE CAN SAY OR DO WHATEVER WE LIKE!
IF WE WERE COMIC BOOK CHARACTERS...

...THERE'D BE WRITERS AND ARTISTS AND EDITORS DIRECTING OUR ACTIONS AND WORDS!
THAT REMINDS ME!

I'VE BEEN MEANING TO ASK THE EDITOR IF HE WOULD GET THE ARTISTS TO DRAW ME IN A MORE STYLISH OUTFIT NEXT TIME!
NICE TRY!

YOU CAN'T BLAME YOUR LOUSY SENSE OF FASHION TASTE ON SOME MYTHICAL ARTIST!
THANKS!

BESIDES, IF WE WERE ONLY COMIC BOOK CHARACTERS, THIS STORY WOULD BE COMING TO AN END SOON!
IT HAS TO! WE'VE RUN FIVE PAGES ALREADY!

YOU REALLY BELIEVE ALL THIS, DON'T YOU?
AND YOU DON'T?
5

OF COURSE NOT! I AM VERONICA LODGE! NO ONE CAN TELL ME WHAT I CAN AND CANNOT DO!
EXCEPT DEAR DADDY-KINS!

NO RIDICULOUS AMOUNT OF VISUAL SYMBOLS FOLLOW ME AROUND, HIGHLIGHTING MY EVERY MOVE!

WHAT'S WITH HER HIGHNESS? WHY IS SHE UPSET?
I'M NOT UPSET!

LOOK AT ME!
I'M THE PICTURE OF CALM PERFECTION!

OH? YOU'D NEVER KNOW IT BY ALL THE SWEAT BEADS, FLAMES OF FIRE AND PUFFS OF SMOKE DANCING AROUND YOUR HEAD!

HALP, SOMEBODY! ISN'T IT ABOUT TIME TO FINISH THIS STORY ?!?
DON'T WORRY, JUG... THIS IS REALLY...
...THE END

SCRIPT: CRAIG BOLDMAN PENCILS: REX LINDSEY INKING: RICH KOSLOWSKI LETTERING: BILL YOSHIDA COLORING: BARRY GROSSMAN

AND I DIDN'T WANT TO HEAR ANOTHER BORING LECTURE ABOUT MY EATING HABITS FROM GOOGIE GILMORE!
CRUNCH!
CHOC-O CHEW
WELL, I SUPPOSE STUFFING THEM IN YOUR EARS IS HEALTHIER THAN EATING THEM!
AT LEAST THIS WAY YOU DON'T POISON YOUR SYSTEM WITH ALL THOSE GRAMS OF FAT!
LALALA!
CHOC-O CHEW
KRUNCH!
CARAMEL CRUNCH
WHY DO YOU PERSIST? YOU WON'T CHANGE MY WAYS!
MY EATING HABITS ARE HARD WIRED INSIDE ME!
THOSE ARE PROBABLY HARDENED ARTERIES!
2

JUNK FOOD AND I ARE SYNONYMOUS! JUNK FOOD... JUGHEAD... JUGHEAD... JUNK FOOD!
POP!

JUNK EQUALS JUG! JUG EQUALS JUNK!
WELL, HE'S LEARNED HIS PLACE!

SO JUST DROP THE CAMPAIGN!
CHEW! CHOMP!
WHAT... YOU THINK I JUST TALK THIS WAY TO YOU?

I'M A CRUSADER FOR HEALTHY FOOD! I TALK IT UP TO EVERYBODY!

YOU WON'T CHANGE ANYBODY'S MIND!
YOU THINK NOT?
LOOK AND LISTEN!
EXIT
3

I'VE BEEN EATING MORE VEGGIES SINCE I LEARNED THEY'RE LOADED WITH PHYTO CHEMICALS!

GOOD FOR YOUR HEART!

RIVERDA

I'M PETITIONING FOR MS. BEAZLY TO ADD SOME SEITAN DISHES TO THE MENU!

GREAT! WE NEED ALL THE MEAT ALTERNATIVES WE CAN GET!

WHAT LANGUAGE WERE THEY TALKING?

A FOREIGN ONE TO YOU, OBVIOUSLY! HEALTH!

THE UNSAVORY CHATTER DOES SEEM TO BE WIDESPREAD!
SEE?

I'VE MADE AN IMPACT! MY CAMPAIGNING HAS PAID OFF!

GOOD GRIEF! I'VE BEEN ASLEEP AT THE SWITCH! IN MY OWN LITTLE DREAM WORLD!

MEANWHILE, THIS HEALTH STUFF IS RUNNING RAMPANT!
JUG!

HAVE SOME RAW BROCCOLI IN TOFU SAUCE! IT'S GOOD FOR YOU!
ARCH! NOT YOU TOO!

I DON'T EVEN KNOW YOU PEOPLE ANYMORE! IT'S LIKE A HORROR MOVIE! YOU'VE TURNED INTO PEA POD PEOPLE!
5

JOIN US!
JOIN US!
NO... NO...
HEY, JUGHEAD! SNAP OUT OF IT! YOU ZONED OUT THERE A MOMENT!
...UH? OH!
...PROBABLY FROM A LACK OF ZINC!
I WAS SAYING THAT MY HEALTH FOOD CAMPAIGN HAS PAID OFF!
?
WHERE ARE YOU OFF TO?
TO POP'S CHOCKLIT SHOPPE!
I'VE GOT A CAMPAIGN OF MY OWN TO ORGANIZE!
EXIT
PUSH
CONTINUED-6

MISSION: NUTRITION!
PART II
TUESDAY:
JUG, THAT ICE CREAM AND THOSE COOKIES ARE GOING TO RUIN YOUR LUNCH!
THAT IS HIS LUNCH!
NUTS
CREAM
MILK

IT'S HIS NEW DIET! NOTHING BUT FUN FOOD FOR BREAKFAST, LUNCH AND DINNER!
AND BETWEEN MEAL SNACKS!

I'M DRAWING A LINE IN THE SAND! I'M NOW A PRO-JUNK FOOD ACTIVIST!
UP WITH CAKE! DOWN WITH CARROTS!
NUTS

CHOCOLATE SHAKES GET A BAD SHAKE! DONUTS GET DISSED UNDESERVEDLY!

YOU'RE JUST MAKING JUNK FOOD LOOK UNAPPEALING! IT'S NOT WORKING!
REVOLUTIONS DON'T HAPPEN OVERNIGHT!
URP!
7

LOOK AROUND! IT'S LIKE SOME FREAKY FAIRY TALE WHERE A TWISTED CHARACTER HAS EVERYONE UNDER HER SPELL!
EVERYONE'S SO HUNG UP ON HEALTH FOOD, NO ONE'S HAVING ANY FUN!
MINERAL WATER
HE MAY HAVE A POINT!
BUT I LOST MY APPETITE JUST WATCHING HIM!
WEDNESDAY:
GO ON THE (SNACK) ATTACK!
PUFFO
CHEESE PUFFS ARE THE RIGHT STUFF!
VEGGIES DON'T HAVE CREME FILLING!
THURSDAY:
YOU NEED THE FOUR FOOD GROUPS EVERY DAY! COOKIES, SODA, CHIPS AND CANDY BARS!
50%
FRIDAY:
URP E-EAT... MORE... PEANUT... BRITTLE...
JUG, YOU'RE NOT LOOKING SO GOOD!
JUNK FOOD RULES
JUMP FOR JELLY BEAN
I'M ASTOUNDED HE'S LASTED THIS LONG!
8

CAN I BRING YOU SOMETHING?
SODA?
CANDY BAR?
BROCCOLI!
WHAT?
BROCCOLI!!
AND NOT CHOCOLATE DIPPED! STEAMED!!
WOW! LOOK AT HIM WOLF DOWN THAT SALAD! LIKE A SUPER RABBIT!
I GUESS HIS CELLS WERE SCREAMING FOR VEGGIES!
CRUNCH! SLURP! CRUNCH!
YOUR CAMPAIGN WAS DOOMED TO FAILURE! YOU CAN'T LIVE ON PURE JUNK FOOD!
I KNOW... SHE JUST GOT MY HACKLES UP!
LISTEN... YOU MAY NOT BELIEVE IT, BUT I EAT HEALTHY FOOD, TOO!
9

I ENJOY JUNK FOOD, BUT I MAKE SURE I EAT A BALANCED DIET!
WELL...

I'M GLAD TO HEAR IT! MODERATION IS THE KEY!
OH, I MODERATE BY THE TON!

HOW ABOUT YOU? DO YOU MODERATE?
ME?

WHEN'S THE LAST TIME YOU HAD A POTATO CHIP OR AN ICE CREAM CONE?
WELL, I HATE TO BE FANATICAL...
SHAKE!
KISSES

IN THE INTEREST OF MODERATION, I'LL TRY ONE OF THOSE CHOCOLATE CANDIES!
10

MMM! NOT BAD!
WOW! DID YOU SEE THAT?
OOOH!
IF GOOGIE CAN EAT CHOCOLATE, I GUESS I CAN TOO, ONCE IN A WHILE!
YEAH, WHY NOT?
AH! THEY'VE LOST THAT ZOMBIE-LIKE HEALTHY PALOR! I'M SEEING SOME LIFE IN THOSE EYES!
I THINK THE FEVER HAS BROKEN!
PIZZA
PIZZA
PORK RINDS
SO...
I GUESS THINGS ARE A LITTLE CLOSER TO NORMAL AGAIN!
SURE! AS IN THE BEST FAIRY TALES...
EXIT
COLA
I BROKE THE SPELL WITH A KISS!
THE END

## Pick Me Up

*Betty & Veronica* #151, 2000

by Kathleen Webb, Dan DeCarlo and Henry Scarpelli

&

## Summer Help

*Veronica* #128, 2002

by Dan Parent, Jim Amash, Bill Yoshida and Barry Grossman

Betty and Veronica shouldn't need an introduction. They've been around for so long that they're practically family to a lot of us, young and old. These two girls have stood the test of time, and for good reasons. They were designed to be love interests for Archie, and they served that purpose well (very well) but they had such dynamic personalities, readers wanted to see more. And more they got!

They were the original frenemies, and it's this intriguing relationship that keeps us following their adventures. Oh, and such adventures! Their stories are funny, fast-paced, full of heart, and NEVER boring. And it doesn't hurt that the art really makes their stories shine.

If you're discovering Betty and Veronica for the first time, all I can say is that you're holding in your hands some of the most fun stories ever written. If you've been away from Betty and Veronica, and want to rekindle your old friendship, this is the perfect place to start. You'll relive some of their greatest moments, and be reminded how these girls taught you the importance of friendship and how to earn it.

Now go read, the girls are waiting!

**Gisele**

*Archie Comics penciller*

# Betty and Veronica in "PICK ME UP"

TWO HOT DOGS AND A COUPLE OF ROOT BEERS, PLEASE!

HEY, GORGEOUS! CAN I ASK YOU A QUESTION?

HOT DOGS TACOS

YEAH, WELL, YOU WEREN'T ALL THAT CUTE ANYWAY!!
I GOTTA GET ANOTHER DIET ROOT BEER... MINE SLIPPED OUT OF MY HAND!

YOU EVER NOTICE HOW GUYS ARE COMING UP WITH DUMBER PICK-UP LINES THESE DAYS?
AND THEY EXPECT US TO FALL FOR THEM!

HI, BABES! HOW YA DOIN'?
DO WE KNOW YOU?

NOT YET, BUT I CAN TELL YOU'D REALLY LIKE TO!

HEY! I'M REALLY A NICE GUY ONCE YOU GET TO KNOW ME!
Y'KNOW, IF THEY JUST SHOWED SOME HONEST INTEREST IN US PERSONALLY...
LITTER

...THEY MIGHT GET A MORE POSITIVE REACTION!
BE REASONABLE, BETTY!
2

MOST OF THEM ARE TOO BUSY TELLING YOU HOW GREAT THEY ARE!
HEY, DARLIN'!

YOU TALKING TO ME?
OF COURSE! I NEVER PASS UP THE OPPORTUNITY TO SAY HELLO TO A BEAUTIFUL WOMAN!

OH, HE'S GOOD! DON'T YOU THINK SO, BETTY?
YEAH, HE'S NOT TOO BAD WITH A PICK-UP LINE!

I'M NOT PICKING HER UP... I'M PICKING HER OUT!
OOO! THINK YOU SHOULD BE HONORED AT THE PRIVILEGE, RON?

LIKE I SAID... I'M PICKING *HER* OUT!
I JUST HAD TO TALK TO YOU, BABE! SWEETNESS IS MY WEAKNESS!

YOU MAKE ME MELT LIKE AN ICE CUBE ON A HOT SIDEWALK!
REALLY?
3

THEN WHY DON'T YOU EVAPORATE AND BLOW AWAY?
AS I WAS SAYING... YOU ARE THE REAL REASON MEN FALL IN LOVE!
PUSH!
AND YOU ARE THE REASON WOMEN FALL OUT OF IT!
NOT TOO BAD AN APPROACH, JUNIOR...!
LET'S SEE HOW YOUR DEPARTURE IS! READY, BETTY?
YOU'RE ON, RON!
PUSH!!
YIKES!
HONESTLY! IF I HEAR ONE MORE PICK-UP LINE TODAY, I THINK I'LL SCREAM!
ME TOO!!
I DON'T THINK GUYS REALIZE JUST HOW INSULTING THEY ARE TO OUR INTELLIGENCE!
AMEN!
4

I'VE GOT AN IDEA! LET'S TRY A PICK-UP LINE ON THE NEXT GUY WE MEET, SO THEY CAN HEAR HOW OBNOXIOUS IT SOUNDS!
OKAY!

HERE'S A GOOD SPECIMEN, REGGIE!
"SPECIMEN" IS RIGHT!
HI, BABES!

OH, REGGIE... YOU MAKE ME MELT LIKE HOT FUDGE ON A SUNDAE!
BUT OF COURSE! AM I NOT MANTLE THE MAGNIFICENT?

C'MON, BETTY! WRONG TEST SUBJECT!

COME BACK! WE HAVEN'T FINISHED TALKING ABOUT HOW GREAT I AM!
THERE'S A COUPLE OF LIKELY PROSPECTS!
CUTE, TOO!

ARE YOU GUYS, LIKE SINGLE?
CAN WE, LIKE FLIRT WITH YOU?
?
5

YOU BET!
FIRE AWAY, BABES!

IS IT JUST ME, OR ARE GIRLS GETTING HARDER TO UNDERSTAND THE OLDER I GET?
LITTER

THAT'S IT! A POX ON ALL PICK-UP LINES! I DON'T CARE HOW ORIGINAL, CLEVER OR SINCERE THEY ARE!

I'VE HAD ENOUGH! I REFUSE TO RESPOND TO ANOTHER ONE!
HI, GIRLS!

GOING MY WAY, PERHAPS?
!
WINK!

UNLESS IT COMES FROM ARCHIE, RIGHT?
WE-ELL... YOU COULD HARDLY CALL THAT ORIGINAL, CLEVER OR SINCERE!
BUT IT'S ONE OF MY BEST PICKUP LINES!
END

# Veronica in Summer HELP

PART ONE

AH, THIS IS THE LIFE! I LOVE SUMMERTIME!
I CAN CATCH UP ON MY LOUNGING AND SOAP OPERA WATCHING!
Teen TIME

Script & Pencils: Dan Parent / Inks: Jim Amash / Letters: Bill Yoshida / Colors: Barry Grossman

MI-MI, I WANT A SODA POP, AND *I* WANT IT ***NOW!!***

OH, DEAR!

THAT'S MY ...ER... RAMBUNCTIOUS VERONICA!

PLEASE EXCUSE ME FOR A MINUTE...

VERONICA! WHY ARE YOU BEING SO RUDE?!

MI-MI DARED TO TELL ME SHE WAS ***TOO BUSY*** TO BRING ME A SODA!

WELL, SHE ***IS BUSY!*** SHE'S HELPING ME WITH MY LADIES' CHARITY CLUB MEETING!

OH!

I THINK YOU OWE BOTH OF US AN APOLOGY!
I'M SORRY!

THAT'S BETTER!
CAN YOU BRING ME MY SODA NOW?
2

THAT'S IT! YOU HAVE NOTHING TO DO BUT LOUNGE! GET IT YOURSELF!

WHEN I WAS YOUR AGE, DO YOU THINK I HAD PEOPLE WAITING ON ME HAND AND FOOT?
THAT'S WHAT YOU GET FOR NOT GROWING UP RICH!

I'M ESTABLISHING A NEW RULE FOR THE SUMMER! YOU ARE TO GET ALL YOUR OWN SNACKS, AS WELL AS CLEAN YOUR OWN ROOM!

WHAT?!!
AND THAT INCLUDES DOING ALL YOUR OWN LAUNDRY TOO!

WHAT? I DON'T KNOW HOW!
LEARN! BETTY CAN TEACH YOU! SHE'S ALWAYS HELPING OUT HER FAMILY!

BETTY THIS! BETTY THAT! I'LL SHOW YOU THAT I CAN DO ALL OF THIS STUFF!
3

A FEW DAYS LATER...
PREPARING MY OWN SNACKS IS NO BIG DEAL!
THESE LITTLE MICROWAVE ENTRÉES LOOK TASTY!

HMM! TWENTY MINUTES SHOULD BE GOOD!
I'LL DO SOME CLEANING UNTIL IT'S READY!

I SUPPOSE I SHOULD DO MY FIRST LOAD OF LAUNDRY!
I HAVE ONE PROBLEM...

WHERE'S OUR LAUNDRY ROOM?
I DON'T THINK I'VE EVER BEEN THERE!

I'LL LOOK IT UP ON OUR HOUSE MAP!
OH, IT'S IN WING D!
LODGE MANSION DIRECTORY

SO...
OKAY, THE CLOTHES ARE IN! NOW, WHERE'S THE SOAP?
THIS MUST BE IT!
4

I WANT TO MAKE SURE THEY'RE CLEAN!
I'LL DUMP IN A COUPLE OF BOXES!
POW!

LA DE DA! THIS HOUSEHOLD STUFF IS A PIECE OF CAKE!

SNIFF! SNIFF! I SMELL SMOKE!

IT'S COMING FROM THE KITCHEN!
MISS LODGE! WAS THIS YOURS?!

YES!
YOU OVERCOOKED IT! IT'S ONLY SUPPOSED TO GO IN FOR THREE MINUTES!

HOW WAS I SUPPOSED TO KNOW THAT?
HAVE YOU TRIED READING THE BOX?
5

OH, HERE ARE THE DIRECTIONS! HOW CONVENIENT!!
SMITHERS!! WE HAVE A PROBLEM!
Lean MEAL
WHAT?
FOLLOW ME!!
WE'RE BEING ATTACKED BY SUDS!
WHERE'S ALL THIS FOAM COMING FROM?
FOLLOW ME TO THE LAUNDRY ROOM!
OH, DEAR!
MISS LODGE! IS THIS YOUR DOING?
I'M AFRAID SO!
BUT LOOK AT THE BRIGHT SIDE!
MY CLOTHES ARE SPARKLING CLEAN...
CONTINUED-
6

# Veronica in Summer HELP Part Two

DO YOU THINK WE SHOULD STOP VERONICA'S DOMESTIC DUTIES BEFORE SHE DESTROYS OUR HOME?

ABSOLUTELY NOT! SHE'LL GET THE HANG OF IT EVENTUALLY!!

A WEEK LATER...
MY DIRTY CLOTHES ARE PILING UP!
MY HAMPERS ARE FULL!

I'VE ALSO STUFFED MY DIRTY LAUNDRY UNDER MY BED!
MY ROOM'S LOOKING PRETTY MESSY!
7

OH WELL, I'LL JUST SHUT THE DOOR AND LEAVE MY TROUBLES BEHIND!
KNOCK! KNOCK!

VERONICA, I'M HERE TO CHECK OUT YOUR ROOM!
UH-OH! CAN YOU GIVE ME JUST ONE MORE MINUTE...

OKAY, JUST ONE MIN...
SLAM!

WHAT TO DO? WHAT TO DO?
I'LL DUMP ALL MY LAUNDRY OUT THE WINDOW FOR NOW!

OKAY! LET'S SEE IT!!
NOT BAD, VERONICA! NOT BAD!

YOUR ROOM LOOKS QUITE TIDY!
I TRY, MUMSY!
8

KEEP IT UP, VERONICA!!
NOW, I'D BETTER CHECK ON MY STUFF OUTSIDE!
YIKES! ALL MY CLOTHES ARE ALL OVER THE POOL CABANA!!

OH, UM...NOTHING! JUST ENJOYING THE VIEW FROM UP HERE!
WELL, GET DOWN BEFORE YOU GET HURT!
A COUPLE OF DAYS LATER...
I'M GONNA HATE IT WHEN THIS SUMMER IS OVER...
BLAB! BLAB! BLAB!

WHAT'S ALL THE COMMOTION OUTSIDE, SMITHERS?
YOUR FATHER'S HAVING A POOL PARTY FOR HIS BUSINESS ASSOCIATES!

OH, THAT'S NICE...
WHAT?!! OH NO! THE CABANA!!

EVERYTHING LOOKS PEACEFUL SO FAR!!
THE CABANA DOOR IS LOCKED!
THANK GOODNESS I LOCKED THE DOOR!
I HAVE A KEY...
BUT WHAT'S THAT CREAKING NOISE?...
CR-REAK
10

DADDY! DON'T OPEN THAT DOOR!
LOOK OUT! IT'S GONNA BLOW!!
CREAK!
KA-BLAM!
CLOTHES EVERYWHERE!
AND FROM THE SMELL, I'D SAY THEY'RE NOT CLEAN!
VERONICA!
EEP!
SOON THEREAFTER...
THIS IS MY THIRD LOAD! CAN I TAKE A BREAK?!
AT THIS RATE, I WON'T FINISH UNTIL SCHOOL BEGINS AGAIN!!
THAT'S THE PLAN!
End

## The Legend of the Lost Lagoon
## *Free Comic Book Day*, 2007
## by Bob Bolling, Jim Amash, Barry Grossman and Teresa Davidson

Bob Bolling! Fifty years after his first *Little Archie* tales, his work still shines! A new reader would need no introduction to the characters; it's all there. The story begins with Mr. Weatherbee spinning a story around the campfire, the story then sends the campers out into the tale. Great pacing, beautiful artwork that benefits from Bolling's love of nature. My only disappointment is that it takes us 11 pages to get to the Lost Lagoon and we only get to see it for a page and a half... a sequel, perhaps? Maybe we need a teen Archie tale, where after years of trying he finally finds it again! How about it, Bob?

**Jack Copley**
*Archie Comics historian*

Over the course of my life, I've basically grown up with Archie. When I was a kid, I was first introduced to the brand through Little Archie, and as I got older, I moved on to teenage Archie's misadventures. Then, as an adult, I got to experience a grown-up version through the various "Archie Marries..." and *Life with Archie* titles. Looking back, one thing which I find keeps Archie enjoyable to this day is how reliving his classic stories not only allows me to look back on earlier points in my own life, but America's as well. Archie has been getting into trouble since 1941, and witnessing his evolution is like witnessing an evolution of America from the early 20th century to today, so it's pretty cool how he's able to basically transcend time and generations in such a way, and I look forward to seeing how he chronicles the future as well.

**David Oxford**
***The Mega Man Robot Master Field Guide, Nintendo Force Magazine, Nyteworks*** *blog network*

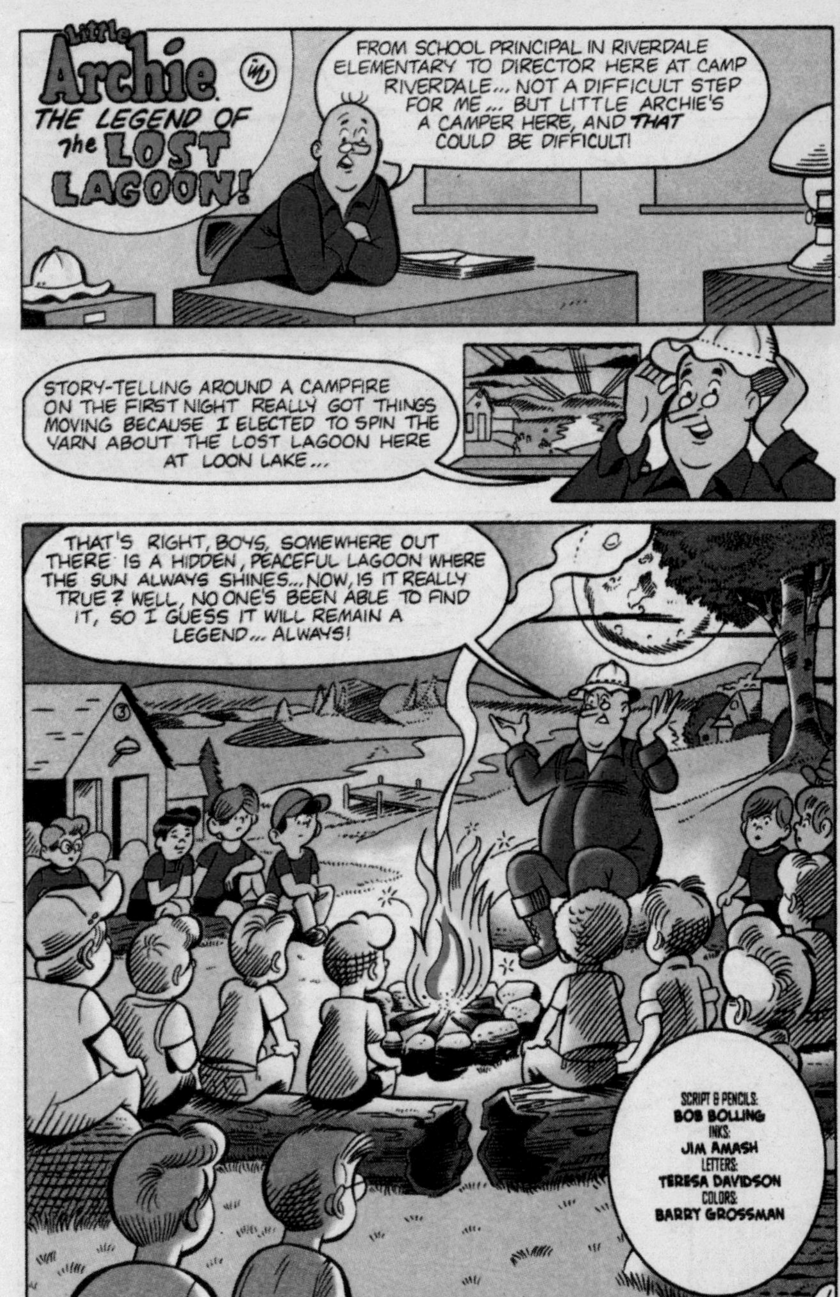
Little Archie
THE LEGEND OF the LOST LAGOON!
FROM SCHOOL PRINCIPAL IN RIVERDALE ELEMENTARY TO DIRECTOR HERE AT CAMP RIVERDALE... NOT A DIFFICULT STEP FOR ME... BUT LITTLE ARCHIE'S A CAMPER HERE, AND THAT COULD BE DIFFICULT!
STORY-TELLING AROUND A CAMPFIRE ON THE FIRST NIGHT REALLY GOT THINGS MOVING BECAUSE I ELECTED TO SPIN THE YARN ABOUT THE LOST LAGOON HERE AT LOON LAKE...
THAT'S RIGHT, BOYS, SOMEWHERE OUT THERE IS A HIDDEN, PEACEFUL LAGOON WHERE THE SUN ALWAYS SHINES... NOW, IS IT REALLY TRUE? WELL, NO ONE'S BEEN ABLE TO FIND IT, SO I GUESS IT WILL REMAIN A LEGEND... ALWAYS!
SCRIPT & PENCILS: BOB BOLLING
INKS: JIM AMASH
LETTERS: TERESA DAVIDSON
COLORS: BARRY GROSSMAN
1

--AND IT IS ALSO BELIEVED THAT, IF YOU'RE IN TROUBLE ON LOON LAKE, A **GOLDEN OWL** SHALL LEAD YOU TO THE SAFETY OF THE LOST LAGOON!

"THE NEXT MORNING, I GAVE BETTY COOPER'S BIG BROTHER, CHIC, A COUNSELOR HERE, PERMISSION TO TAKE THREE CAMPERS FROM THE CLEANEST CABIN FISHING..!"

SO! BETWEEN LITTLE ARCHIE, CHUCK CLAYTON AND BILLY WONG, I EXPECT TO SEE LOTS OF FISH!
I'M SURE GONNA TRY!
I **ALWAYS** CATCH SOMETHING BIG!
A SMALL FISH IS BETTER THAN NONE!
OKAY, CREW, TIE ON THOSE LIFE JACKETS!
RRRRRRRRRRR

ARE WE GOIN' OUT PAST THE FLAGS THAT MARK SAFE WATERS FOR SWIMMERS?
FOR SURE! I'M GOING TO HAVE YOU ALL TROLL AROUND THAT WOODED EAST SHORE!
WOW! THAT'S **GOTTA** BE GOOD!
2

WHEN THE WIND IS RIGHT, YOU CAN HEAR THE GIRLS SINGING!

YEAH, I CAN HEAR 'EM NOW... ♪OLD MACDONALD HAD A FARM...♫

Hmmm... THAT WIND IS PICKING UP A LITTLE TOO MUCH... WE'LL TROLL ON THE LEE SHORE OVER THERE!

MEANWHILE, COUNSELOR KIMBERLY CLARK IS PREPARING TO TAKE BETTY, NANCY AND VERONICA ON A NATURE TOUR...

CAMP PINEY ACRES

SHORTLY...
THAT'S A BLUE HERON WADING OVER THERE!
WHAT'S HE WADING FOR?
BREAKFAST!

BLOOP!
HE'S A GREAT MINNOW CATCHER!

LOOK!

AN OWL!

I HEARD ABOUT A GOLDEN OWL THAT CAN LEAD YOU OUT OF DANGER HERE!
SUPERSTITION, RON... JUST A MADE UP TALE.
4

MEANWHILE...
GOT ONE!
LOOKS LIKE A NICE PICKEREL! PLAY HIM, LITTLE ARCHIE... DON'T REEL IN TOO HARD!

SHORTLY...
NICE PICKEREL... TWO POUNDS I'D GUESS!
THEY GET BIGGER I HEARD!
I'M GONNA LET HIM GO!

GOOD FOR YOU, LITTLE ARCHIE... CATCH AND RELEASE IS THE BEST WAY!
I'LL CATCH HIM AGAIN NEXT YEAR!

MEANWHILE...
LOOK! MAMA DUCK AND HER DUCKLINGS ARE WALKING INTO THE LAKE!
WADDLE HAPPEN NEXT?

MAMA DUCK USUALLY TEACHES HER DUCKLINGS TO SWIM IN FORMATION...
5

I'LL CUT THE MOTOR AND WE'LL LOWER THE ANCHOR REAL EASY AND WATCH MAMA DUCK IN ACTION!
RRRRRRR
SPUT!

SEE HOW THE DUCKLINGS CHANGE FORMATION AT HER COMMANDS?
WAK! WAK!
WAK!

THEIR SAFETY DEPENDS ON OBEYING HER COMMANDS... YOUR LIFE JACKET'S UNTIED, NANCY!
OOPS!

NOW MAMA'S ORDERING HER BABIES OUT OF THE WATER!
I THINK I KNOW WHY...
WAK! WAK!
WAK!

THERE'S A MEAN SQUALL HEADED THIS WAY! LIFT ANCHOR AND I'LL START THE MOTOR AND HEAD BACK TO CAMP... PRONTO!
6

!
RRRRRR
SPUTE
RRRRR

OF ALL THE TIMES FOR THE KICKER TO CONK OUT!

I COULD TRY ROWING, BUT IT WON'T GET US BACK AHEAD OF THIS SQUALL!

WE'RE RIGHT IN THE PATH OF IT!

MEANWHILE...
CHIC! THERE'S A DANGEROUS LOOKIN' SQUALL HEADED TOWARD US!
RIGHT! AND IT SURE CAME UP FAST! LET'S CUT OUT!
7

WE CAN'T MAKE IT BACK TO CAMP BEFORE THAT STORM HITS US!
WE'LL RIDE IT OUT ON THE LEE SIDE OF CATFISH COVE!
RRRRRR

MEANWHILE...
I'LL ROW US TO THE NEAREST LEE SHORE... WE'LL FIND SOME SHELTER THERE!
LOOK! ANOTHER BOAT!

IT'S FROM CAMP RIVERDALE... ACROSS THE LAKE!
LET'S WAVE! MAYBE THEY'LL TAKE US IN TOW!

THEY SEE US!
IT'S MY BIG BROTHER, CHIC, AND LITTLE ARCHIE, CHUCK CLAYTON AND BILLY WONG!

WE CAN'T GO ON MEETING THIS WAY! WHAT'S UP?
WE'RE FIT TO BE TOWED!
8

SOON...
CATFISH COVE... KINDA SPOOKY!
WE'LL BE A LOT SAFER HERE!
I HOPE!

STORMS COMIN' IN STRONG AND THERE'S NO GOOD PLACE TO TIE UP IN HERE!
LOOK!

AN OWL!
THE GOLDEN OWL! IT--IT IS REAL!
9

HE'S CIRCLING OVER US...
NOW HE'S DIVING!
RIGHT FOR FOSSIL FALLS!

HE FLEW BEHIND THE FALLS!
Hmm...LET'S TIE UP OVER THERE!

"IN TIME OF DANGER, A GOLDEN OWL WILL APPEAR AND SHALL LEAD THE WAY TO SAFETY!"

?
10

SOME MEAN SQUALL COMING IN!
Hmm... LET'S STEP INSIDE!

WE'RE IN A--A TUNNEL!
AND THERE'S A LIGHT AT THE END OF IT!
THE GOLDEN OWL JUST FLEW INTO THAT LIGHT!

STAY BEHIND US, KIDS!
11

GASP!
THE LOST LAGOON!

IT'S NOT RAINING!

12

THE GOLDEN OWL IS LEAVING!
LET'S GO SEE IF THE SQUALL HAS PASSED!

C'MON, RON! WHA--? THE GOLDEN OWL IS BACK... ARE WE IN DANGER?
ONE LAST LOOK... IT'S JUST SO BEAUTIFUL...

RON! LOOK OUT!
RUMBLE!

CRASH!
13

YOU OKAY, RON?
WOW! YEAH... TH-THANKS, LITTLE ARCHIE!

THE ENTRANCE TO LOST LAGOON IS BLOCKED BY THAT HUGE BOULDER!
WE FOUND IT AND LOST IT!
LET'S GO BEFORE SOMETHIN' ELSE HAPPENS!

SEEMS LIKE THE GOLDEN OWL WANTS US TO FOLLOW!

THIS TUNNEL'S NOT SO CREEPY NOW!
Y'KNOW, LITTLE ARCHIE, THIS KINDA MAKES ME THINK OF WHAT BIG KIDS TALK ABOUT...
Huh?

...THE TUNNEL OF LOVE!
MY NAME IS CHARLES... AND YOU CAN CALL ME CHIC!
MY NAME IS KIMBERLY AND YOU CAN CALL ME ANY TIME!
14

THE SQUALL'S PASSED, CHIC!
GREAT, KIMBERLY! NOW I CAN GET YOU BACK TO CAMP PINEY ACRES!

WHEN WE GET THERE, I'M AFRAID I WON'T BE ABLE TO KEEP YOU IN PROTECTIVE CUSTODY!
?

RRRRRRRRRR

LOOKS LIKE QUITE A RECEPTION AWAITING YOU, KIMBERLY!
IT'S THE OTHER COUNSELORS... PROBABLY WORRIED ABOUT US!
15

MY! LOOK WHAT KIMBERLY'S CAUGHT!
THE CATCH OF THE DAY!
PRESENTING CHIC COOPER, COUNSELOR AT CAMP RIVERDALE, AND HIS THREE STALWART CAMPERS!

I'M SURE YOU ALL HAVE DUTIES... DON'T LET US KEEP YOU!
NO BOTHER!
NONE AT ALL!

DO YOU THINK WE'LL ACT THAT SILLY WHEN WE GROW UP?
I DUNNO... SOMETIMES I THINK I DON'T WANNA GROW UP!
MAYBE WE SHOULD GO! CAMP RIVERDALE LOOKS SO FAR AWAY!

YOU'D BETTER HURRY 'CAUSE IT'S GONNA RAIN AGAIN!
HOW DO YOU KNOW SO MUCH ABOUT WEATHER?
A TINY ELF TOLD ME!
HA HA! ELVES AREN'T REAL!
THEY'RE ONLY IN STORY BOOKS!
16

THEY ARE SO REAL! C'MON, I'LL SHOW YOU!
YEAH!
THIS HAS GOTTA BE GOOD!

BACK AT THE DOCK...
WHILE THE KIDS ARE OCCUPIED, WHY DON'T WE HAVE SOME COFFEE IN THE MESS HALL?
Er-- WHY, SURE!
...AND FIND OUT WHY WE CALL IT THE MESS HALL!

OUCH!

IT'S OKAY... JUST A SPLINTER!
FIRST AID!
MEDIC!

JUST SIT DOWN!
BREATHE DEEPLY, LIKE ME!
MY FIRST AID KIT'S IN THE BOAT!
Ummm... FEVERISH!
FIRST AID APPROACHIN'!

BUT IT'S ONLY A SPLINTER!
HE'S DELIRIOUS!
HE'LL HAVE TO STAY OVER-NIGHT!
MAYBE THE REST OF THE WEEK!
OR THE WHOLE SEASON!

LOTS OF BANDAGES!
HEY!
MORE BANDAGES!

NOT FAR AWAY...
Shh! LOOK UNDER THAT TOADSTOOL... YOU'LL SEE A TINY ELF!

WHENEVER HE SITS UNDER IT, RAIN COMES!
HARD TO SEE... BUT IT KINDA DOES LOOK LIKE AN ELF!
WALL STREET JOURNAL
18

WELL, IF THERE'S GOLDEN OWLS, THERE'S GOTTA BE ELVES!
AND JUST IN CASE HE DOES KNOW A STORM IS COMIN', WE'D BETTER HEAD BACK!

ALL THE COUNSELORS ARE STILL ON THE DOCK!
WHERE'S CHIC?

WHAT'S GOIN' ON?
FIRST AID...
AND YOUR COUNSELOR'S GOING TO BE JUST FINE!
WE JUST ATTENDED TO HIS--

--SPLINTER!
MMMFFF!
19

BA-BOOM!
ANOTHER STORM!
Er... GOT TO GET MY LITTLE CAMPERS BACK IN A HURRY!
I'LL ALWAYS REMEMBER MUMMY!
I THOUGHT HE WAS TOO WRAPPED UP IN HIMSELF!
SHORTLY...
I WONDER JUST HOW MANY YEARS WILL HAVE TO GO BY BEFORE THE BOATING MUMMY BECOMES ANOTHER LEGEND HERE AT CAMP RIVERDALE?!
END

# THE BEST OF Archie® COMICS BOOK FOUR

# The 2010s

## Disinterested Parties
## *Betty & Veronica* #254, 2011
## by Craig Boldman, Jeff Shultz, Jim Amash and Jack Morelli

I always wanted to be Archie. He had the best jalopy around. He had the best friends. The best enemies. He was occasionally a superhero. He had Betty. And Veronica. He had Betty AND Veronica! As a young boy, I couldn't WAIT for the days when girls started fighting over me, which I assumed was the natural order of things. In my youth... in those days when I had hair, it was red, a big billowing blossom of red not unlike a blazing red mushroom that had perched atop my head. This meant that Archie and I had a kinship. We were like brothers. I would fit right into Riverdale, perhaps as a visiting cousin that the girls would fawn over, that a jealous Reggie would try to discredit, and they would all find out... in the end... that I was actually some rock star or world-renowned athlete in disguise. I would give them all tickets to the big game, or the big concert. I wouldn't give any tickets to Reggie of course. He could listen to the cheers from outside the stadium.

I always wanted to be Archie. It's never faded. He's still youthful, while I no longer have my big mop of red hair. Despite that, we're still brothers. Despite how I now know how expensive it is to maintain a jalopy, and that relationships are a bit more complicated than Archie was leading me to believe, he remains a hero to me. Because he always solves the problem in the end. He always ends up with a lipstick kiss on either side of his cheeks. He always makes it out of detention in time for the next adventure.

I always wanted to be Archie.

Unless I was hungry.

Then... Jughead.

**Paul Tobin**
*Eisner Award-winning author of **Bandette** and **Colder***

IN

# The DISINTERESTED PARTIES!

IT'S THE MYSTERY OF THE AGES-- WHAT DOES VERONICA SEE IN ARCHIE?!

AFTER ALL, HE'S SO ORDINARY AND SHE'S SO ELITE!

VERY SIMPLE!
VERONICA IS COMPETITIVE BY NATURE! SHE SEES THAT HER BEST FRIEND BETTY COVETS ARCHIE...

...ERGO, VERONICA WANTS HIM TOO!
THAT MAKES SENSE.!
WHAT OTHER LOGICAL REASON COULD THERE BE?
SHE ONLY WANTS HIM BECAUSE I WANT HIM.!
WELL, DOESN'T THAT JUST BURN YOUR GRANDMOTHER'S MUFFINS?
BUT I JUST HAD A THOUGHT!
ARE YOU SAYING THAT IF I STOPPED LIKING ARCHIE, VERONICA WOULD DROP HIM LIKE LAST YEAR'S PRADA SHOES IN CLEARANCE?
I'D SAY THE LOGIC IN YOUR STATEMENT IS APPARENT!
I COULD LEARN TO LIKE LOGIC!
THANKS, DILLY!
SMAK
2

SO!
I WONDER WHAT ARCHIE'S UP TO TODAY!
FRANKLY, I COULDN'T CARE LESS!

SCREECH

MY HEARING AID MUST BE ON THE BLINK! I THOUGHT I HEARD YOU SAY YOU COULDN'T CARE LESS!

...ABOUT ARCHIE!
THUMP

WAIT A MINUTE! I DON'T WEAR A HEARING AID! SO EXPLAIN YOURSELF!
REALLY, VERONICA!

I AM SO OVER THAT BOY!
YOU ARE, huh? AND WHAT BROUGHT ON THIS RADICAL CHANGE OF PERSONALITY?

I'M A SIXTEEN-YEAR-OLD GIRL, LIKE YOU! IT'S WHAT WE DO! WE HAVE CRUSHES, WE GET PAST THEM, WE MOVE ON!

FACE IT, ARCHIE'S MOST NOTEWORTHY TRAIT IS HIS *UN*-NOTEWORTHINESS!
AVERAGE SMARTS, AVERAGE LOOKS, AVERAGE SKILLS, AVERAGE AVERAGE AVERAGE!!
YOU TALK A GOOD TALK! ON PAPER, IT EVEN MAKES SENSE!
SO, YOU'RE SAYING YOU DON'T MIND IF *I* CALL ARCHIE AND BOOK HIM FOR DATES *EVERY NIGHT* THIS WEEK?
I DON'T MIND!
*Nah!* WON'T DO IT! SOUNDS LIKE A *BORE*!
4

WHEW! SHE ALMOST CALLED MY BLUFF! BUT I THINK IT WORKED!

SOON...
HUH! VERONICA HASN'T BEEN AVAILABLE LATELY!
I'M AVAILABLE!

ACTUALLY, I'M GETTING THE FEELING THAT SHE'S JUST LOST INTEREST!
I'M INTERESTED!

I ALMOST THINK I'D BE BETTER OFF WITH YOU, BETTY!
I ALMOST LIKE THE WAY YOU THINK!

WELL, GREAT! I LIKE TO SPEND MY TIME WITH SOMEONE WHO APPRECIATES ME!

AND THAT'S THE WAY THAT WORKS!
5

BETTY AND ARCHIE HAVE BECOME QUITE THE ITEM! QUITE A SWITCH!

YEAH, AND IT'LL REMAIN THAT WAY!

AS LONG AS WORD DOESN'T GET BACK TO *VERONICA*!

SHE'S TAKEN STEPS TO ENSURE THAT DOESN'T HAPPEN!

SHE MAKES SURE SHE AND ARCHIE ONLY GO TO PLACES THAT RONNIE DOESN'T CARE FOR-- LIKE THE *THEME PARK*!

SPEAKING OF VERONICA...

OH, MIDGE! I'M SORRY I DIDN'T SEE YOU THERE!

Boutique ELITE

ARE YOU HURT?
IT'S MY ANKLE! AND I'VE GOT TO GET TO WORK!!

BETTY, I GOTTA TELL YOU, I MADE A GOOD CHOICE THROWING MY LOT IN WITH YOU!
I LIKE YOU A LOT TOO, ARCHIE!

EVERY TIME I RAN INTO VERONICA THIS WEEK, SHE'S LIKE, "I'M SO OVER YOU!"
TSK! TSK!

YOU DESERVE SOMEONE WHO'S EXCITED TO BE WITH YOU, ARCHIE!
RIGHT, BETTY! I DESERVE YOU!
WIN

YOU'RE ATTENTIVE, YOU'RE APPRECIATIVE, AND YOU'RE PROUD TO BE SEEN WITH ME!

ALL'S RIGHT WITH THE WORLD! I'M FINALLY JUST WHERE I WANT TO BE WITH ARCHIE!

IF ONLY I DIDN'T FEEL LIKE I HAD TO SNEAK AROUND TO BE THERE!
WHAT DO YOU WANT TO RIDE FIRST?
JUST A MINUTE, ARCHIE!
BEEPA DEEP
7

ER...HI, VERONICA! WHAT'S UP?
YOU'LL NEVER GUESS WHAT I'M DOING TODAY!

FILLING IN FOR MIDGE AT HER JOB AT THE THEME PARK!
EEEK!!

BETTY, YOU LOST YOUR PHONE!
HOT D

LAST I HEARD, MIDGE WAS PLAYING ONE OF THE PARK'S COSTUMED CHARACTERS! BUT WHICH ONE?

IF VERONICA SEES ME SHOWING INTEREST IN ARCHIE AGAIN, IT'LL JUST RE-LIGHT HER ENGINES!

BETTY, IS SOMETHING WRONG?
NO! WHY DO YOU ASK?
8

YOU SUDDENLY SEEM STRANGELY DISTANT!

HOW ABOUT A LITTLE KISS?

PLEASE, ARCHIE! NOT IN FRONT OF THE RACCOON!

HEY, THE MERRY-GO-ROUND! DOESN'T THAT SOUND LIKE FUN?
YEAH!
TICKETS

ER... SAY! WHERE'D YOU GO?
WHILE YOU'RE DOING THAT, I'LL BE RIDING THE TILTY SWIRL!
9

WHY DON'T YOU WANT TO RIDE TOGETHER ON THE SAME RIDE?
ER... WE COVER MORE GROUND THIS WAY!
WHY ARE YOU WALKING TWELVE FEET AWAY FROM ME?
GERMS, ARCHIE! DON'T WANT TO RISK GETTING A SUMMER COLD!
IF VERONICA SEES US TOGETHER, THE WHOLE HOUSE OF CARDS COLLAPSES!
SHE'S SURE TO BE LOOKING OUT THROUGH THE EYE HOLES OF ONE OF THESE CARTOON CHARACTERS!
BETTY?! WHERE'D YOU RUN OFF TO NOW?
PSST! QUICK, ARCHIE! BEHIND THIS FENCE!
TRASH
I DON'T UNDERSTAND YOU, BETTY! IT'S ALMOST LIKE YOU DON'T WANT TO BE AROUND ME!
10

THAT WAS TEASING! JUST MY FUNNY WAY OF FLIRTING!
DOWNRIGHT PECULIAR, IT WAS!

BUT THIS IS BETTER, DON'T YOU THINK?
SMOOCH

ER... ARE YOU TALKING TO ME, STRANGER?
WHAT?!

DON'T GET NEAR ME, ARCHIE! THE CARTOON CHARACTERS MIGHT BE WATCHING!!
?!

BETTY, I THINK YOU'RE TOO UPTIGHT TO BE IN A RELATIONSHIP!

GRRR!
IT'S DRIVING ME CRAZY! THIS ISN'T WHO I AM!
11

I AM INTERESTED IN ARCHIE.! AND I DON'T CARE IF PIG, SHARK, KOALA BEAR, BUNNY, GORILLA, CHICKEN OR WOODPECKER KNOWS IT.!!

THAT'S QUITE A DECLARATION.!
VERONICA!!
FUDGE CAKES

I THOUGHT YOU WERE IN ONE OF THOSE ANIMAL COSTUMES.!
Oh, NO-- MIDGE WAS PROMOTED TO FUDGE CAKE!

!
GOOD! THAT'S JUST WHAT I DESERVE! TAKE THAT, BETTY!
SMUSH
?!
CAKE

YOU'RE AN INTERESTING DATE, I'LL SAY THAT, BETTY!
SOME PEOPLE JUST WEREN'T CUT OUT TO BE SNEAKY!
CAKE
END

## A Really Hot Date
## *Archie* #646, 2013
### by Angelo DeCesare, Gisele, Rich Koslowski, Jack Morelli and Digikore Studios

As I grew into adulthood, it was Archie and his friends that showed me the person I would become, more than those spandex superheroes that I wanted to be. For every moral shown in a Batman comic there were three more in *Jughead*. For every secret of womankind I learned in *Wonder Woman*, there were a dozen more discovered in *Betty & Veronica*. The inhabitants of Riverdale weren't those of Gotham City, these were welcoming, warm and friendly. To sit down with an Archie comic was to revisit old friends and even now, all these years later, the accident-prone adventures of Archibald "Archie" Andrews will always return the smile to my face.

**Tony Lee**

***New York Times*** *bestselling author*

Archie Comics has pulled off the tricky feat of reaching through time to connect generations. My mother grew up reading the antics of Betty & Veronica in the 1950s and passed that love on to me. Every week meant a trip to the grocery store and a shiny new *Archie Double Digest* from the magazine rack at check-out. Now, decades later my daughter knows the bi-monthly trip to the comic store means a fat paperback of fashion and friendship. With anthologies, old favorite stories can trigger a cascade of childhood memories to be treasured and shared.

**Donna Dickens,**

*Entertainment Editor,* ***HitFix.com***

OVER SIXTY MILLION MILES FROM EARTH, A LONELY ROVER MOVES ACROSS THE VAST, BARREN LAND-SCAPE OF MARS.
MARS ROVER

SUDDENLY, IT COMES TO A STOP...
MARS ROVER

...AND BEGINS TRANSMITTING DATA BACK TO EARTH!

AT NASA, SCIENTISTS LOOKING AT THEIR SCREENS ARE MYSTIFIED...
NASA
?
?
?
?
?

WHAT IS THE STRANGE, METALLIC OBJECT THAT GLIMMERS ON THE MARTIAN SURFACE?
1

TO UNCOVER THE ANSWER TO THIS MYSTERY, WE MUST TRAVEL BACK THOUSANDS OF YEARS! WAY, WAY BACK TO A PERIOD THAT YOU CANNOT IMAGINE! BEFORE CELL PHONES WERE EVEN INVENTED!!
TO A MIGHTY CIVILIZATION KNOWN AS MARS!
A REALLY HOT DATE!
YES, MARS! WHERE THERE LIVED A RACE OF PEOPLE VASTLY SUPERIOR TO ANY FOUND ON OUR PLANET!
ANGELO DeCESARE STORY
GISELE PENCILS
RICH KOSLOWSKI INKS
JACK MORELLI LETTERS
DIGIKORE STUDIOS COLORS
VICTOR GORELICK CHIEF
MIKE PELLERITO PREZ!

UH... WITH A FEW EXCEPTIONS...
ARCHIE ANDROMEDA! GET UP RIGHT NOW OR YOU'LL BE LATE FOR SCHOOL AGAIN!
ZZZZZZ!!
BWEEP BWEEP BWEEP
WHA...?! HUH?! ALARM...NEED MORE SLEEP...
BWEEP
MUST PRESS... SNOOZE BUTTON...!
7:45
ONK
ROBOT
SNOOZE
DOOP! DOOP! DOOP! DOOP!
ZZZZZ!
DOOP! DOOP!
HEY?!
3

DOOP! DOOP!
BOING
AHHH!!

K-THUD!
I GOTTA FIGURE OUT HOW TO WORK THAT ALARM!
ZOINKS!
LOOK AT THE TIME! I'D BETTER GET A MOVE ON!
7:46

COMPUTER, TRANSPORT ME TO THE KITCHEN!
FRZOOP!
ARCHIE! YOU ALMOST LANDED IN MY BOWL OF HOT GLOPP!
I DON'T KNOW WHAT'S MORE ANNOYING-- YOU OR THIS MARTIAN HEAT!
4

SOON...

I'LL BET I'M THE ONLY KID IN SCHOOL WHO STILL DRIVES A ROTO-CAR!

CRATERDALE HIGH SCHOOL

P

5

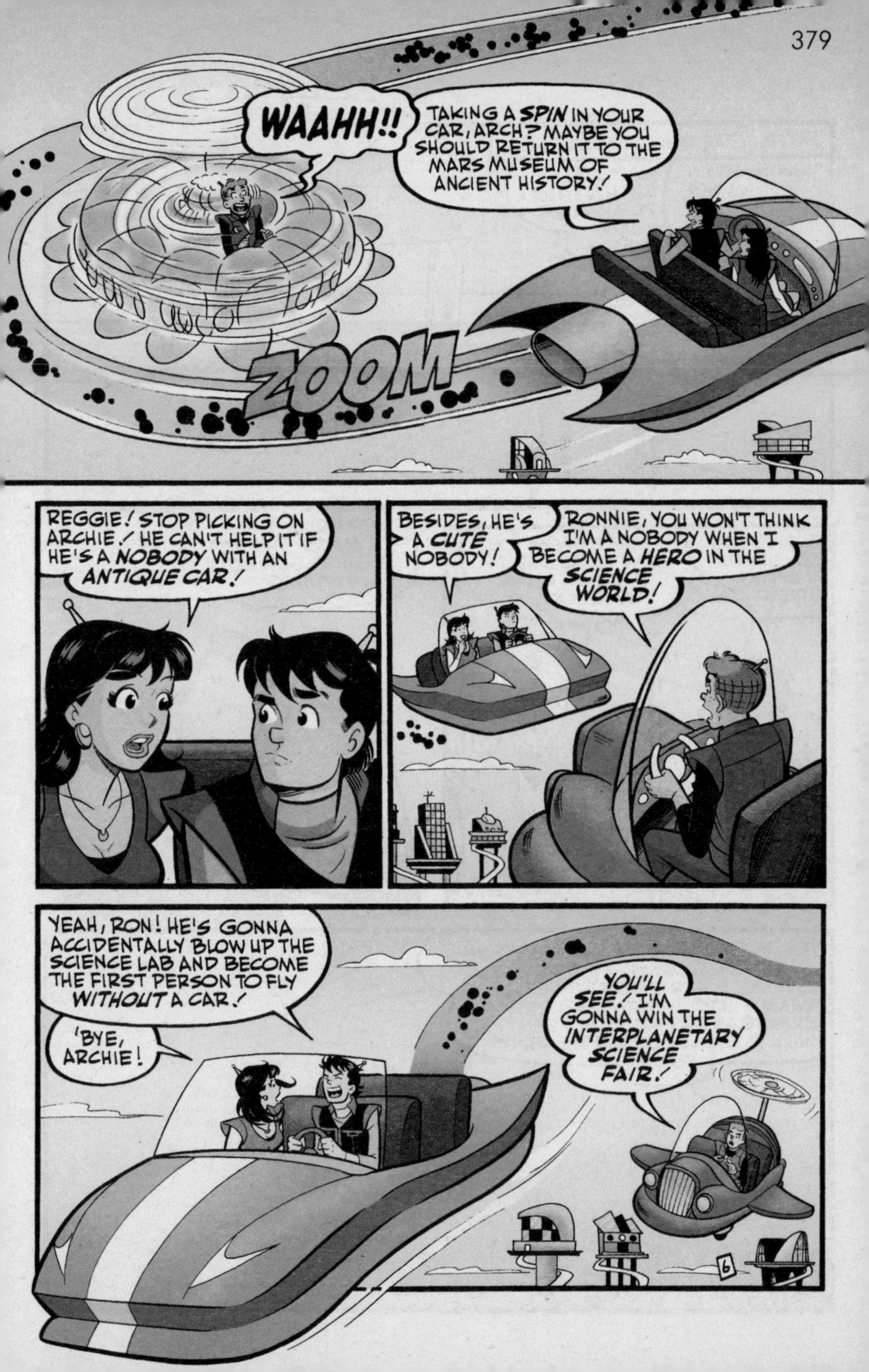

WAAHH!!
TAKING A SPIN IN YOUR CAR, ARCH? MAYBE YOU SHOULD RETURN IT TO THE MARS MUSEUM OF ANCIENT HISTORY!
ZOOM

REGGIE! STOP PICKING ON ARCHIE! HE CAN'T HELP IT IF HE'S A NOBODY WITH AN ANTIQUE CAR!

BESIDES, HE'S A CUTE NOBODY!
RONNIE, YOU WON'T THINK I'M A NOBODY WHEN I BECOME A HERO IN THE SCIENCE WORLD!

YEAH, RON! HE'S GONNA ACCIDENTALLY BLOW UP THE SCIENCE LAB AND BECOME THE FIRST PERSON TO FLY WITHOUT A CAR!
'BYE, ARCHIE!
YOU'LL SEE! I'M GONNA WIN THE INTERPLANETARY SCIENCE FAIR!

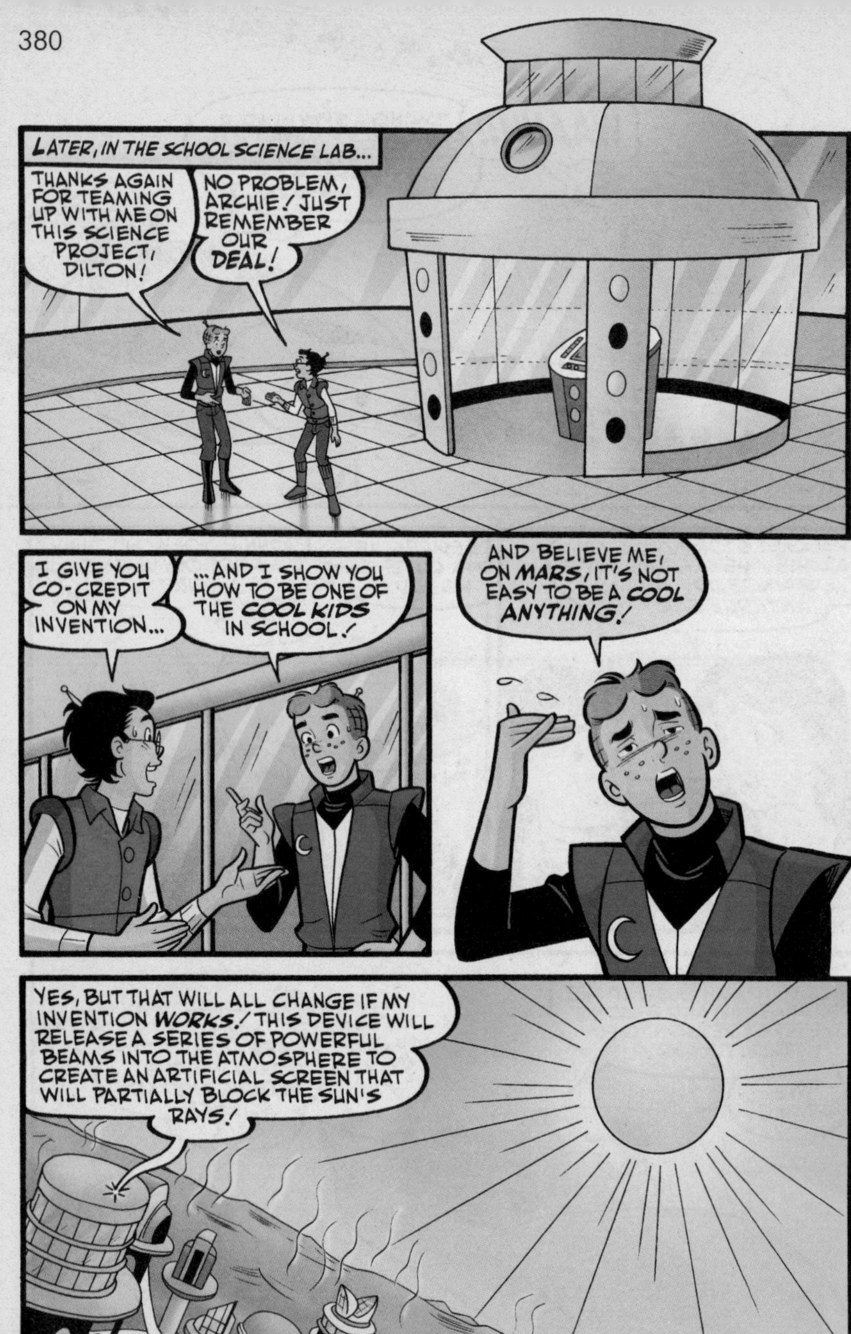
LATER, IN THE SCHOOL SCIENCE LAB...
THANKS AGAIN FOR TEAMING UP WITH ME ON THIS SCIENCE PROJECT, DILTON!
NO PROBLEM, ARCHIE! JUST REMEMBER OUR DEAL!
I GIVE YOU CO-CREDIT ON MY INVENTION...
...AND I SHOW YOU HOW TO BE ONE OF THE COOL KIDS IN SCHOOL!
AND BELIEVE ME, ON MARS, IT'S NOT EASY TO BE A COOL ANYTHING!
YES, BUT THAT WILL ALL CHANGE IF MY INVENTION WORKS! THIS DEVICE WILL RELEASE A SERIES OF POWERFUL BEAMS INTO THE ATMOSPHERE TO CREATE AN ARTIFICIAL SCREEN THAT WILL PARTIALLY BLOCK THE SUN'S RAYS!
7

DO YOU KNOW WHAT THAT MEANS, ARCHIE?
YEAH, IT MEANS RON WILL FORGET ALL ABOUT REGGIE AND BE MY GIRLFRIEND!

BY THE WAY, DILTON, SINCE YOU KNOW SO MUCH ABOUT SCIENCE, WHY DO WE MARTIANS HAVE THESE ANTENNAE ON OUR HEADS?

NO ONE KNOWS FOR SURE, ARCHIE, BUT WE BELIEVE THAT THEY'RE IMPORTANT. THEY MAY BE WHAT MAKES US INTELLIGENT!

NEXT QUESTION--WHERE CAN I GET A NEW ONE?

AFTER SCHOOL...
GOOD LUCK IN THE SCIENCE FAIR TO-MORROW, ARCHIE!
THANKS, BETTY! YOU'VE ALWAYS BEEN MY BIGGEST SUPPORTER AND MY BEST FRIEND ON MARS!
8

EXCEPT FOR MY PAL JUGHEAD, OF COURSE!
OF COURSE!
ARCH! ARCH! I HAVE SOME-THING VERY IMPORTANT TO TELL YOU!

BUT I'M SO WEAK FROM HUNGER... I CAN'T REMEMBER...

CAN YOU REMEMBER IF I BUY YOU A GLOPP BURGER?

NO, BUT I CAN REMEMBER IF YOU BUY ME FIVE GLOPP BURGERS AND A GLOPP PIZZA!
WHY IS ALL THE FOOD ON THIS PLANET MADE WITH GLOPP?

WHAT'S UP, JUG?
I JUST SAW REG SNOOPING AROUND THE SCIENCE LAB!

ZOINKS! THAT SPACE-SNEAK MIGHT SABOTAGE OUR INVENTION! I'VE GOTTA STOP HIM!
GLOPP SHOPPE
9

MOMENTS LATER...
THANKS FOR LETTING ME USE YOUR CAR, JUG!
ANYTHING FOR MY BEST BUD!
YOU NOW OWE ME TEN GLOPP BURGERS, FIVE GLOPP PIZZAS, AND A GLOPP SHAKE!

LOOK! THERE'S REGGIE LEAVING THE LAB!
AND HE'S GOT SOMETHING IN HIS HAND!
FROOOM

I'LL TRY TO CATCH HIM! LEND ME YOUR POWER PACK, JUG!

HERE I GO!
STOP, ARCH! THAT'S MY SCHOOL BACK PACK!
WHY DON'T THEY MAKE THESE THINGS LOOK DIFFERENT?! A GUY COULD GET HURT!
10

Whoa!
TOO FAST!
ZOOOM

I KNOW YOU TOOK SOMETHING FROM THE SCIENCE LAB, REGGIE! HAND IT OVER!

GO PLAY CATCH WITH A COMET, ELECTRON BRAIN!

WHAT'S GOING ON HERE, BOYS?!

RONNIE!

REGGIE HAS SOMETHING THAT BELONGS TO ME AND HE WON'T GIVE IT BACK!

IF YOU TWO DON'T STOP ACTING LIKE CHILDREN, I'M GOING TO THE PROM WITH A BOY FROM THE OMEGA GALAXY!

HE HAS TWO ANTENNAE!

FINE! TAKE IT! I WAS ONLY HAVING A LITTLE FUN!

ZOINKS! THIS IS A PART OF OUR SCIENCE PROJECT!

NEED A RIDE, ARCH?
YEAH, TAKE ME TO DILTON'S HOUSE, JUG!
I'VE GOT TO GIVE HIM THIS PART SO HE CAN PUT IT BACK-- WHOOPS!!
JUG, I--I DROPPED IT! AND I DON'T KNOW WHERE IT WENT!
IF DILTON FINDS OUT, HE'LL CANCEL OUR DEAL AND THERE GOES MY CHANCE WITH RONNIE!
WAIT! I HAVE AN IDEA! MY ANTENNA MUST REALLY BE WORKING!
SOON...
THERE'S A PART ON MY ROTO-CAR'S DASHBOARD THAT LOOKS JUST LIKE THE ONE I LOST!
13

THE NEXT DAY...

THAT'S RIGHT, LADIES AND GENTLEMEN--

--WE'VE CREATED A MACHINE THAT WILL ***LOWER TEMPERATURES*** EVERYWHERE ON MARS!

***REMARKABLE!***

IS IT ***POSSIBLE?***

THE DEVICE WILL SEND A SERIES OF POWERFUL BEAMS INTO THE MARTIAN ATMOSPHERE! THIS WILL CAUSE AN IMMEDIATE CHAIN REACTION...

...AND MAKE MARS A MUCH COOLER PLANET!
NOW SOMEONE WILL HAVE TO IN-VENT THERMAL UNDERWEAR!
IT DOES FEEL DIFFERENT!
YEAH... BUT IT FEELS... HOTTER!

I--I DON'T UNDERSTAND! THE SURFACE TEMPERATURE IS GOING UP!
YOU YOUNG FOOL! YOU'VE MADE OUR CLIMATE EVEN WORSE!
IT'S NOT DILTON'S FAULT!
IT'S MINE!
I LOST A PART OF THE DEVICE! I GUESS THE THING I REPLACED IT WITH ISN'T WORKING!
15

CAN THE PROCESS BE *REVERSED?!*
I HAVE *NO* IDEA!
MAYBE YOUR *ANTENNAE'S* NOT WORKING, DILTON!
THIS HEAT'S GOING TO BE *UNBEARABLE!* WE WON'T *SURVIVE* IF WE *STAY* HERE!

IT'S TIME TO IMPLEMENT THE GOVERNMENT'S SECRET PLAN AND SAY *GOODBYE* TO *MARS!*

AND SO, ON A FATEFUL DAY IN MARTIAN HISTORY...
WE'RE ALL RELOCATING TO ANOTHER GALAXY, BUT YOU *ANDROMEDAS* WON'T BE MAKING THE TRIP!

IT'S A *LONG JOURNEY*, AND WE'RE NOT TAKING ANY CHANCES BY BRINGING *ARCHIE* ALONG!
*SORRY*, DAD! I GUESS I *MESSED UP!*
YOU *THINK?!*
16

LIGHT YEARS AWAY...

HERE IT IS, OUR NEW HOME... *EARTH!*

IT SURE DOESN'T *LOOK* LIKE MARS! WHAT'S ALL THE *WHITE STUFF,* DAD?

I DON'T KNOW, SON, BUT AT LEAST IT'S...

...COLD.

SOON...
LET'S TRY AND FIND A PLACE WHERE WE CAN SET UP HOUSE!
SNAP!

WHAT WAS THAT?
IT'S SO COLD THAT MY ANTENNA JUST FROZE AND BROKE OFF!

YOU SEEM OKAY, ARCHIE!
WHAT A RELIEF! I THOUGHT I WOULD LOSE MY INTELLIGENCE!
...

WELL, I DON'T CARE HOW COLD IT IS! NOTHING CAN BE WORSE THAN THAT MARTIAN HEAT!

RRUMBLE
?
?!
??
18

HEAD FOR THAT CAVE!!

FWEET!

LATER...

THE GOOD NEWS IS WE BROUGHT ALONG PLENTY OF GLOPP TO EAT!

ARCHIE, IN SPITE OF EVERYTHING, I'M SORRY THAT YOU HAVE TO LIVE ON THIS STRANGE PLANET!

Oh, I DON'T KNOW, DAD...

HEY! WATCH WHERE YOU'RE GOING!
SCIENTISTS REMAIN PUZZLED BY THE METALLIC OBJECT SEEN ON MARS...
TELL RONNIE I'LL BE RIGHT THERE, MOM!
NASA

KRASH!
ARCHIE, I'M SO GLAD YOU'RE NOT IN CHARGE OF THE WORLD! THE EARTH WOULDN'T STAND A CHANCE!
DON'T BE RIDICULOUS, DAD...

AS IF ONE PERSON COULD DESTROY AN ENTIRE PLANET!
THE END

## The Clod of Thunder

### *Archie* #648, 2013

### by Tom DeFalco, Fernando Ruiz, Rich Koslowski, John Workman and Digikore Studios

I was an avid Archie collector as a child... It has so much cultural significance but also so much personal significance, and to get to play with these beloved characters is a wild creative opportunity.

**Lena Dunham**
*Creator/star of HBO's* ***Girls***
*(Excerpted from* ***The Guardian)***

Archie Comics has been inextricably linked to idyllic Americana for the better part of the last century. And rightfully so—friends of mine who (perhaps misguidedly!) consider themselves "non-comics readers" still have a soft spot for the appeal of the assuring backdrop of Riverdale. To them, the Archie universe represents a place that's filled with old friends and familiar faces to greet you and welcome you into their world. In recent years, the cast and storylines have progressively expanded to encompass marginalized groups of people—people much like those same non-comics-reading friends. For many of us, finally seeing under-represented stories and faces like ours in those pages tells us that we, too, can belong. By prioritizing diversity, Archie Comics is saying that there is a space in their accessible, ideal world for people from all walks of life.

**Alice Meichi Li**
*Artist and illustrator,*
***Mega Man, Elephantmen, CMYK Magazine***

BEYOND THE FARTHEST STAR, THERE IS A WORLD OF **MYTH AND LEGEND** CALLED **ALLGOOD!**

A NOBLE REALM FILLED WITH **IMMORTAL WARRIORS** AND **HEAVENLY GIRLS!**

UNFORTUNATELY, SOME OF THEM ARE RATHER **CLUMSY** AND THIS IS THE STORY OF...

# ARCHIE the clod of thunder

LET THE HERALDS SING AND THE HEAVENS REJOICE!!!

FOR I AM **ARCHIE**, THE MASTER OF THE STORM AND THE SON OF ANDREWS THE ALL-FATHER!

TOGETHER WITH MY WARRIORS TRIO, WE WILL GET THIS PARTY STARTED FOR FUN!

FOR **GIRLS!**

FOR **ALLGOOD!**

TURN THE PAGE FOR **AWESOME ACTION AND ABSOLUTE ABSURDITY!**

WRITER: TOM DEFALCO
PENCILS: FERNANDO RUIZ
INKS: RICH KOSLOWSKI
LETTERS: JOHN WORKMAN
COLORS: DIGIKORE STUDIOS
EDITOR-INCHIEF: VICTOR GORELICK
PRESIDENT: MIKE PELLERITO

JUGHEAD THE HUNGRY!

CHUCK THE CHARMING!

SAYID THE SMILING!

FOR COUNTLESS CENTURIES, ARCHIE AND HIS WARRIORS TRIO HAVE JOURNEYED FROM THE GATES OF GLEAMING ALLGOOD IN SEARCH OF HONOR, GLORY, AND GIRLS.
YE OLDE TOLL BRIDGE
WE TAKE EZ DASH
BUT THEY USUALLY END UP IN ALL-GOOD'S EATS.
SIGH
BEING AN IMMORTAL WARRIOR ISN'T ALL IT'S CRACKED UP TO BE!
YEAR AFTER YEAR, DAY AFTER DAY, WE END UP IN THE SAME PLACE, DATING THE SAME GIRLS...
...AND DOING THE SAME THINGS.

I AM SO BORED OF ALL GOOD!
NOTHING EVER CHANGES AROUND HERE.
MAYBE NOT, BUT I'M STILL TRYING TO BEAT YOU--
--ESPECIALLY WHEN IT COMES TO A CERTAIN BLONDE GODDESS!
ETERNAL LIFE DOES HAVE ITS ADVANTAGES, ARCH.
WE CAN EAT INTO INFINITY AND BEYOND!
NO WONDER THEY CALL YOU JUGHEAD THE HUNGRY!
WE'RE ALSO SURROUNDED BY THE MOST HEAVENLY WOMEN OF ALL!
=SIGH= LIKE I HAVEN'T HEARD THAT LINE A FEW MILLION TIMES...
...IN THE PAST TEN THOUSAND YEARS.
YOU DON'T UNDERSTAND.
I'M SUPPOSED TO BE A HERO--
--A WARRIOR-BORN!
3

I NEED A LITTLE EXCITEMENT AND ADVENTURE IN MY LIFE.
BE CAREFUL WHAT YOU WISH FOR, STORM STOOGE!
REGGIE THE WICKED HAS PLANS FOR YOU.
YOU MAY BE THE CLOD OF THUNDER--
--BUT I AM THE MASTER OF MISCHIEF!
REJOICE, NOBLE ARCHIE!
I HAVE THE SOLUTION TO YOUR BOREDOM.
I'VE GOT A LINE ON A HOT CUTIE THAT LIVES NEAR THE STORM GIANTS.
DON'T TRUST THIS TWISTED TRICKSTER, ARCH!
YEAH, YOUR FATHER TOLD US TO AVOID THOSE BIG BOZOS AND THEIR TURF.
4

RELAX, PAL! IT'S NOT LIKE YOU'RE GOING TO START A... WAR OR ANY-THING.
YOU JUST WANT A GIRL'S DIGITS.
BUT IT'S THE SACRED DUTY OF EVERY TRUE ALLGOODIAN TO OBEY ANDREWS THE ALL--BELLOWING!
SUIT YOUR-SELF!
YOU'RE MISSING QUITE A BEAUTY.
EXACTLY HOW PRETTY IS SHE?
ON A SCALE OF ONE TO TEN--
--AT LEAST A THOUSAND!
I'M IN.
SO BE IT!
5

MAGIC IS THE ONLY WAY TO TRAVEL.
IT'S MUCH FASTER THAN A HORSE AND VERY FUEL EFFICIENT.
QUIT BRAGGING AND SHOW ME THIS--
WOW!
WOULD YOU LIKE TO SEE MY MAGIC HAMMER?
IT DOES ALL SORTS OF AMAZING TRICKS.
CAN IT MAKE YOU DIS-APPEAR?
YOU'D BETTER KEEP YOUR DISTANCE.
MY BOYFRIEND IS VERY JEALOUS.
WHO DARES HIT ON MY GIRL-FRIEND?
DO YOU THINK THE SON OF ANDREWS THE ALL-AGGRAVATING IS AFRAID OF ANYONE...?
EEP
6

I WILL CRUSH YOU LIKE AN INSECT.
HEY, REGGIE! MAKE WITH THE MAGIC AND GET US OUT OF HERE BEFORE--
REGGIE?
REGGIE?
WHERE DID HE GO?!?
GREETINGS, NOBLE SIR!
YOUR MOST DUTIFUL SERVANT BEGS AN AUDIENCE WITH YOU WHO ARE THE WORD, THE WAY, AND THE EXREMELY WIDE.
ENOUGH WITH THE FALSE FLATTERY, WISE GUY.
WHAT'S ON YOUR MIND?
I BRING YOU BAD TIDINGS, MILORD.
DO YOU KNOW WHERE YOUR SON IS?

HELP ME STOMP THIS ANNOVING ALLGOODIAN, VICTOR.
MY PLEASURE, MOOSE.
HE'S ALREADY GIVING ME A HEADACHE.
BEWARE, GIANTS!
NONE MAY ATTACK A PRINCE OF THE GOLDEN REALM.
I AM ARCHIE, THE CLOD OF THUNDER AND LORD OF--
KRAKA KOOM!
--LIGHTNING !?!
TRICKY STUFF, THAT LIGHTNING.
8

ENOUGH!
I HAVE SEEN ENOUGH OF THIS FOOLISHNESS!
H-HEY, DAD!
WHAT'S NEW?
MY SON IS A GIRL-CRAZY GOOFBALL--
--WHO MUST BE PUNISHED FOR HIS ARROGANCE AND STUPIDITY!
NO LONGER SHALL YOU POSSESS THE POWER OF AN ALLGOODIAN-BORN!
NO MORE WILL YOUR MAGIC HAMMER SERVE YOU!
UNTIL FURTHER NOTICE, YOU ARE BANISHED TO PLANET EARTH--

"--AND THE LAND CALLED RIVERDALE!"
KER-RASH!
OUCH!
DISOBEYING ONE'S FATHER CAN BE VERY HAZARDOUS--
--ESPECIALLY WHEN HE'S--
--THE ALL-BLOATING BIG WHEEL OF ALL-GOOD!
I CAN'T BELIEVE HE WOULD DELIBERATELY STRAND ME ON THIS DULL, PRIMITIVE, BACKWARD--
HUBBA-HUBBA!

POOR ARCHIE!
EATS
STEAKS·HOT STEW·TURKEY LEGS·ICED TEA
LLGOOD'S
THERE MUST BE A WAY TO MAKE PEACE BETWEEN HIM AND ANDREWS THE ALL-FLATULENT.
I'M SURE HIS FATHER WILL EVENTUALLY FORGIVE HIM--
--ALTHOUGH IT MAY TAKE A FEW DOZEN CENTURIES.
THIS IS YOUR FAULT. YOU TRICKED MY ARCHIE.
WHAT PART OF MASTER OF MISCHIEF WAS TOO SUBTLE FOR HIM?
LET'S LOOK IN ON THE DEAR BOY... SHALL WE?
WHY, THAT FOUR-TIMING--!
THIS ISN'T WORKING QUITE THE WAY I PLANNED.

ARRGH!
WHAT FUN IS IT TO PULL A PRACTICAL JOKE ON SOMEONE--
--IF THEY ENJOY IT?!?

I'M GOING TO HAVE TO JOIN ARCHIE ON EARTH--

--AND MAKE HIS LIFE MISERABLE.
RIVERDA
HIGH SCHO

SORRY! I DIDN'T NOTICE YOU STANDING THERE!

APOLOGY NOT ACCEPTED.
?!?
KZAK!
12

IT'S BEEN AGES SINCE I VISITED EARTH--
--AND THE INHABITANTS ARE STILL FALLING FOR...
--THE SAME OLD GAGS.
IT'S TRUE! YOU'RE THE MOST HEAVENLY GIRL I'VE EVER SEEN!
÷SIGH÷ LIKE I HAVEN'T ALREADY HEARD THAT LINE...
...A FEW MILLION TIMES.
I SEE YOU'RE AS CLUMSY AS EVER WHEN IT COMES TO GIRLS.
REGGIE! WHAT ARE YOU DOING HERE?
RIVERDALE HIGH SCHOOL
RHS

I'VE COME TO ADD A LITTLE SPICE...
...INTO YOUR OTHERWISE DRAB AND DULL EXISTENCE.
A KICK ME SIGN ?!?
KICK ME!
IS THAT THE BEST YOU CAN DO?
KICK ME!
SPWAKK
HARDLY!
AFTER ALL, I AM THE PRINCE OF PRANKSTERS --!
HEY!
WHAT'S THE BIG IDEA?
YOU'RE PAYING FOR MY DRY-CLEANING, MISTER!
SPLATT!

SORRY FOR BARGING IN ON YOU, SIRE--
--BUT SOMETHING STINKS ON EARTH!
ARE YOU REFERRING TO MY SON, LADY BETTY?
HE SHOULD KNOW THAT CLEANLINESS IS NEXT TO GODLINESS!
I'M MORE CONCERNED WITH A CERTAIN JOKE-DEALING DELINQUENT.
YOU'RE RIGHT, BETTY.
REGGIE THE WICKED HAS FOLLOWED ARCHIE TO EARTH.
15

WHAT ARE WE GOING TO DO, SIRE?
BELIEVE IT OR NOT, I ALREADY ANTICIPATED THIS PARTICULAR PLOT DEVELOPMENT.
AFTER ALL, I AM ANDREWS, THE ALL-KNOWING, ALL-SEEING--
--AND ALL-HEARING!
ALL-FLATULENT, INDEED!
SORRY ABOUT THAT, SIRE!
WHAT ABOUT ARCHIE?
WATCH AND LEARN!
R
SCREEEECH!

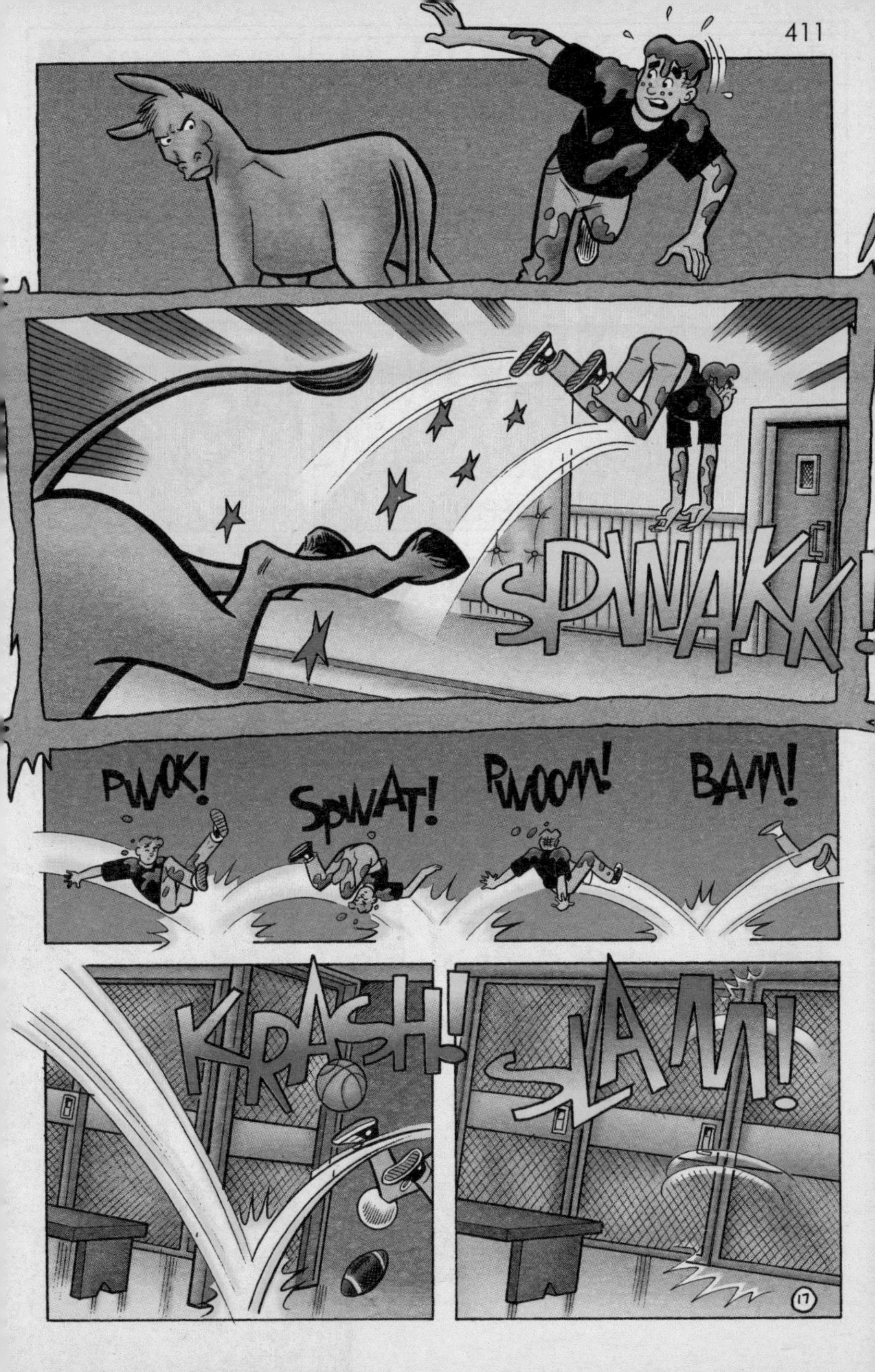
SPWAKK!
PWOK!
SPWAT!
PWOOM!
BAM!
KRASH!
SLAM!
17

IT'S HOPELESS. THE DOOR MUST HAVE LOCKED BEHIND ME.
I CAN'T BUDGE IT.

LOOKS LIKE REGGIE GETS THE LAST LAUGH AFTER ALL.
I'M TRAPPED WITHIN THIS EQUIP-MENT LOCKER.
TRAPPED!

MAYBE I CAN USE THAT BASEBALL BAT TO FORCE MY WAY FREE.

HERE GOES NOTHING--!

KRAKA
KOOM
WHA-- ?!?

GGIE COME EAN.
U CAN RETURN LGOOD, SON.
THANKS FOR THE OFFER, DAD.
RTH IS A RE FUN LLGOOD.
SOMETHING NEW IS ALWAYS HAPPENING DOWN HERE--
--AND THE GIRLS ARE VERY PRETTY!
FR
SHED 1941
RDALE
CHOOL
I'M GOING TO STICK AROUND JUST IN CASE THIS WORLD EVER NEEDS--
--ARCHIE --the clod of thunder!
THE END... FOR NO
SOMETHING'S HAPPENING! THE BASEBALL BAT IS CHANGING!
TRANS-FORMING!
AND SO AM I!
MY POWER IS RETURNED!
ONCE AGAIN, I AM ARCHIE --the clod of thunder!
ANDREWS THE ALL-FATHER MUST HAVE KNOWN I'D EVENTUALLY NEED MY MAGIC HAMMER--
--WHICH IS WHY I SHOULD REALLLLLLY STOP TRYING TO PULL ANYTHING BEHIND HIS BACK.

"THE TIME HAS COME FOR ME TO FIND REGGIE THE WICKED!"

I'M SERIOUS. YOU'RE THE MOST HEAVENLY GIRL I'VE EVER SEEN.

AM I BEING PUNKED? IS THAT WHY EVERYONE'S USING THAT STUPID LINE?

YOU'VE PULLED YOUR LAST PRANK, REGGIE.

YOU MUST RETURN TO ALLGOOD.

FORGET IT, BLUNDER BOY!

I LIKE IT HERE.

HAVE YOU FORGOTTEN THAT I AM A MASTER OF MAGIC AS WELL AS MISCHIEF?

I CAN SUMMON ARMIES OF STORM GIANTS--

--AND UNSTOPPABLE ENGINES OF PURE DESTRUCTION!

I'M ALSO SMARTER, RICHER, AND BETTER-LOOKING THAN YOU.

HOW CAN YOU EVEN HOPE TO COMPETE WITH ME?

OKAY, I CAN CONCEDE EVERY POINT--

--WHICH CAN IMMEDIATELY SEND YOU BACK TO ALLGOOD!